Knotty
NAUGHTY
BITS

VOLUME 1

by Aviva Vaughn

Table of Contents

Legal Stuff

AvivaVaughn.com

This is a work of fiction. Names, characters, businesses, places, events and incidents are either the products of the author's imagination or used in a fictitious manner. Any resemblance to actual persons, living or dead, or actual events is purely coincidental.

ISBN: 1-947420-17-8
ISBN13: 978-1-947420-17-5

About the Author

Aviva Vaughn (ah-VEE-vah) loves to bring diverse, inspiring, sex positive characters to life. She believes consent is a must, condoms are sexy, food is culture, and travel is mind-expanding. Avocado toast, coconut lattes, and Korean spas are her favorite indulgences, and she is a die-hard Angeleno. For a list of her favorite books, visit AvivaVaugh.com/about

Other Titles from Aviva Vaughn

Novels
    BECKONED (join the conversation at **Aviva Vaughn's Jetsetters on Facebook)**
      -Part 1: From London with Love **AVAILABLE NOW (link)**
      -Part 2: From Bath with Love **AVAILABLE NOW (link)**
      -Part 3: From Los Angeles with Love **AVAILABLE NOW (link)**
      -Part 4: From Barcelona with Love **AVAILABLE NOW (link)**
      -Part 5: Adrift in Costa Rica **AVAILABLE NOW (link)**
      -Part 6: Adrift in New Zealand **AVAILABLE NOW (link)**
    BEYOND BECKONED
      -Roaring in Rio (about Nacho Sol from BECKONED) **LATE 2019**
      -Confused in California (about Erin Hung from BECKONED) **EARLY 2020**

Short Stories
    Pressure (included in Beckoned, Part 4)
    Knotty Naughty Bits Volume 1 **AVAILABLE NOW (link)**
    Knotty Naughty Bits Volume 2 **MID 2020**

Links

Subscribe to Aviva's list to be notified of new releases and special offers—and get her favorite **FOOD | BOOK | TRAVEL tips** by clicking **SmartURL.it/BECKONEDfan**

<u>Dedication</u>

July 2019

To anyone who has a dream and the *cojones* to follow it.

Actually, let's make that phrase more inclusive.

To anyone who has a dream and the vulva—or *cojones*—to follow it.

This is for you.

Wishing you love and romance,

About This Book

Knotty Naughty Bits Volume 1: a collection of tangled romantic shorts

Remember the first time you met someone you loved? There was *something* there; a stolen look, a held breath, a frisson of electricity. This book is a collection of those tense, awkward, exciting moments when you have no idea where your feelings are taking you, but you are dying to find out! Featuring a diverse array of characters at different stages in their romantic entanglements.

Fun, flirty, fervent, this is Aviva Vaughn at her lightest (and maybe steamiest?). New characters as well as characters from her BECKONED series make an appearance in this first volume of "Tangled Romantic Shorts".

From the craggy peaks of the Austrian Alps to the white sand beaches of Rio de Janeiro, from Madrid's kinetic Puerta del Sol to Portland's funky Pearl District, Aviva's seductive combination of food, travel, and (steamy) Austen-esque relationships will draw you in and leave you wanting more.

Note from the author: For readers of BECKONED, I've included a line at the beginning of each short story that includes a BECKONED character, placing it in relationship to the series in terms of "timeline." There is one character that you might not remember, so I'll point him out now: "Rolfe" in Havana Club is the MBA-school friend that Angela dances with in Soren's apartment in London.

Winter Wonderland

Gema looked up in the air, marveling at the swirls of soft snow falling around her. The sky was almost devoid of light, the silhouettes of tall fir trees black against the inky sky that was practically obscured by the spiraling descent of the tiny snowflakes. The clean smell of the forest permeated the air with the icy crispness of frozen pine needles. The luminous winter light seemed to come from below rather than above, as the moon's faint light reflected off the deeply blanketed ground.

"Do you like it?" Nicolas whispered into her ear, his voice subdued, mirroring the snow-dampened sounds of the forest, but with an urgency she'd come to recognize as his desire to please her.

Goosebumps prickled along her arms at the sound of his voice. She gazed around, at a loss for words. For someone from the sunny city of Phoenix, Arizona, the beauty of this winter wonderland was a lot to take in. "It's wondrous," she offered, weakly, shaking her head. "I'm a bit overwhelmed."

Nicolas smiled, his teeth brilliant against the featureless darkness of his face, but she didn't need light to know that the unruly curls of his light brown hair would be trying to escape from his woolen cap, or that his caramel brown eyes would be crinkled up at the corners in that perpetual smile he seemed to wear.

When they had first met at the German-language school she was attending in Salzburg, she'd imagined his smile to be mocking, but over the months, she'd come to learn that she amused him, in a good way; or perhaps bemused him was a better explanation. Of course, while he was her language instructor, their relationship had all been rather above board.

Although only two years older than her twenty-five, Nicolas had always showed up to her intensive language class wearing a button-down shirt, underneath a knit vest, topped by a light wool blazer, as suited a lecturer.

Even as the weather had changed from fall to winter, his clothing had remained the same. Whereas she had needed to add a layer with each passing month, she'd never seen him add so much as a hat, until they'd set out tonight, to go sledding in the dark forest surrounding his hometown of Hallein.

"You've done this before, right?" her voice full of uncertainty.

They'd been walking uphill for over twenty minutes on a mild incline. Her heavy winter boots—borrowed from a cousin of Nicolas along with the rest of the heavy snow gear—sunk about five inches into the new, soft snow with each step.

Nicolas laughed, his baritone chuckle punctuating the quiet air. "My whole life. This is our favorite hill to sled when the snow is deep enough. We're about halfway to the top."

"You walk this far to sled?" she asked, a little out of breath. The only time Gema had ever been sledding, had been on a twenty-foot embankment against the side of a road when she was ten. Her parents had driven her and her older sister three-hours to see snow for the first time, although even then, the snow hadn't been deep enough to cover the surrounding dirt.

"The longer the walk, the longer the ride," he answered, in his typically concise and confident manner.

It was this characteristic above all others that had attracted her to him, during the long hours of German verb conjugation and language labs. Nicolas exuded certainty; he didn't seem to have an ounce of doubt in his body. He did what he wanted, when he wanted, how he wanted.

It was exhilarating.

Gema's life—on the other hand—was full of doubt, which was how she had ended up in Austria in the first place.

She was planning to apply to Ph.D. programs in philosophy the following year, where a reading knowledge in French, German, Latin, or Greek was a prerequisite. Without any preference of her own, she applied for fellowships, winning one to Austria, the choice of language made for her.

She found it rather pathetic that she hadn't even *chosen* to study German; it had chosen her. Some days, she wasn't even sure why she was studying philosophy to begin with, but she didn't know what else to do besides continue her studies in the field that she'd already earned a bachelor's and master's in. Nothing else called to her.

She longed for the kind of certainty that Nicolas emanated from his pores.

However, Austria had proven to be a good fit. With her dark coloring, petite stature, and bright personality, the locals seemed to find her endearing, often referring to her as a "sweet little mouse." At first she'd thought they'd been making fun of her, however, Nicolas had assured her that being called a mouse was the highest form of praise as far as Austrian endearments went. After being called such by no fewer than a dozen people—all with warm, honest smiles—she'd come to believe him.

Nicolas hummed quietly as they continued walking, comfortable with the long silences that stretched between them, which were almost as big as the physical distance separating them, which had to measure at least two feet.

She snuck a glance at his tall, lanky profile; still surprised that they were actually here, hiking through the woods, together.

He had been all business most of the semester. If it hadn't been for the occasional slightly-longer-than-normal glances he gave her, she would never had suspected he had felt something more. It wasn't until that day, a couple of weeks ago, when she and her classmates had been walking out of class, that she'd had an inkling he might be interested in her.

They had all been putting on their winter clothing, to head to a local restaurant that had become their go-to place for dinner after their five-hour long classes, when Nicolas asked, "Mind if I join you?" in his lilting, Austrian-flavored German.

"Not at all," said Michael, an American businessman from Chicago, shrugging on his jacket. At forty-five, he was the eldest of the twelve students in Nicolas's class, and often liked to speak as though he was their leader.

Gema grabbed her coat, trying to ignore the tingling sensation in her neck that meant Nicolas was nearby; she was always hyperaware of his proximity.

As everyone began filing out the door, Nicolas sidled up to Gema.

"Walk with me?" he asked, although it sounded more like a statement than a question.

A shiver of anticipation shot up Gema's back. She nodded, turning her head as she pulled on her ivory beret, hoping he wouldn't see the flush of color that made her cheeks feel like they were on fire.

The class set out into the frigid night air; Gema lifting her bag higher on her shoulder, as though hugging the straps might give her some extra warmth.

"May I?" Nicolas asked, taking her bag and throwing it over his shoulder as though it weighed nothing.

How chivalrous, she thought. She'd never had a man ask to carry her bag before.

The contrast between her Bordeaux-colored tapestry backpack and his chiseled jawline, made him look even more masculine.

Gema had often wondered exactly how tall Nicolas was. She was certain he was almost a foot taller than her 5'-6". Probably 6'-3" or even 6'-4". She had often fantasized about what he looked like under all his clothes; she imagined him to be lean but cut, like a swimmer or a water polo player.

"Do you agree?" Nicolas asked, a smirk on his face.

Gema suddenly realized that she had missed a question while daydreaming about her German instructor naked. "I'm sorry. I think I missed your question."

Nicolas laughed, and it was loud enough that the other students turned back towards them, curious looks on their faces.

"I said that I think your German has progressed a lot these four months. Probably enough so that you can read your philosophy books now," his English clipped and formal, and somehow flatter than his native tongue.

She nodded, fussing with her beret to give her something to focus on as she stared at his caramel eyes, which twinkled in the reflected glow of the streetlights as they passed storefront after storefront.

She cleared her throat. "I think you're right. My scholarship will pay for another semester though, so I am planning on staying."

He seemed to brighten. "I'll make sure I'm not your instructor then."

A ping of disappointment thumped in her chest. Seeing Nicolas every day, Monday through Friday had been like a gift. "But why? You're such a good teacher," she said, hoping that her disappointment wasn't evident.

He frowned. "But if I'm your teacher..." he trailed off, gesturing between them with his hand. "Then this can never be more."

Gema was certain the very tips of her ears would catch fire if it hadn't been so cold. She managed to keep her voice even as she asked, "This?"

He stopped in his tracks, and she did the same, like magnets snapping into place.

He cleared his throat. "Our relationship as teacher and student...it is," he paused, but she wasn't sure if it was because he was hesitating or confused. Finally, he said, "That relationship is inversely proportional to the amount of time we have left in the semester."

A laugh burbled up in her chest and she felt a sudden lightness at the implication of his words.

He frowned, "Did I misuse these English words? Inversely proportional, is that incorrect?"

She smiled, and shook her head. "No, I think you used them correctly, if I understand your meaning. I'm just surprised, that's all. In a good way."

He exhaled and said her name forlornly, like a sigh, and it felt like his professorial mask fell, just a bit.

She wished she could have captured the sound in a bottle.

"There is much I want to say, but can't...yet," his tone, full of promise. "Gema, what are you doing the weekend after classes end?" he asked, his mask coming back up.

She shifted her feet in the snow, wondering if she had imagined the moment of intimacy. "I don't know. Nothing I guess."

"I'm from an old salt mining town about half-an-hour from here. There's something I'd like to show you…" he trailed off again.

She'd never seen him uncertain before, and there was something endearing about it.

"Great. I'd love to," she'd replied.

Which was how she'd come to be walking up a snowy incline in the dark of night, Christmas only days away. Either it was the most romantic thing she'd ever experienced, or it was the stuff of crime scenes.

Although she'd known Nicolas for many months, she didn't really *know* him. Maybe walking in the middle of nowhere with an almost stranger wasn't the best idea.

"How much further are we going?" she asked in what she hoped was a neutral tone.

He must have sensed her unease, because he gave her a confident smile that made her feel instantly better. "Not much further and it will be worth it. I promise you are going to love it."

Although his words were soothing, she still wondered if she had misread his intentions. She'd seemed certain that he was interested in her romantically, and yet he hadn't made a single move to touch her in the two hours they'd been in each other's company. It was all a bit confusing.

After another ten minutes of walking, he came to a sudden stop. "We're here," he said, bending down as he turned the long, wooden sled he'd been pulling behind them so that it pointed downhill.

Gema looked around, confused. "Why here?" It looked exactly like the fifty feet in front of them and the fifty feet behind them.

Nicolas held out his hands as though it was perfectly obvious. "If we go higher, the incline becomes a bit steeper and you'll go too fast. This is the perfect place. The longest ride at a manageable speed. Trust me."

Again, with his concise confidence. If it didn't turn her on so much she'd be annoyed out of her mind.

He looked down at the wood sled—its long rails curling up at the front like elf shoes—before straddling it, by planting his feet firmly in the snow, sitting down, and scooting to the rear. "Come here," he said, patting to the space in front of him.

A thrill of heat zipped up her spine. *Finally some body contact.* Even though she had on six layers of clothing—bra, undershirt, long-sleeve base layer, thin turtleneck, thick cardigan, heavy coat—she was still excited to be between his legs.

"Put your legs inside mine, like that," Nicolas said breathily into her ear as he folded himself around her.

Gema's body tingled all over as Nicolas's chest pressed against her back, their arms and legs lined up as if she was putting him on like a suit. It was divine.

"Ready?" he whispered, his cheek abrading hers, leaving a sexy, scratchy burn in its wake.

"Yes," she said, her voice shaky, as she looked down at the thick ribbon of white that she'd be sledding down any second. The path looked like it went on for hundreds of feet; had they really walked that far?

To their right was the side of the mountain, jutting up in steep verticals as the Alps were prone to do. She swung her head to the left, but couldn't make it out, anything visible was below them. "What's over there?" she said, gesturing to the veiled darkness.

"Just the side of the hill sloping down. Like this," he said, gesturing to their right, "Except downhill."

She gulped. She was on a twelve-foot wide path sandwiched between a ravine and a wall. She'd never felt claustrophobic before, but she suddenly felt a weight on her chest.

"Don't worry," he purred into her ear, squeezing her arm reassuringly. "I've done this hundreds of times. Are you ready?"

She swallowed hard and nodded, the solid strength of his chin against her head, calming her.

"Just follow my lead. Lean with me." He gathered the sled's ropes in his gloved hands, encased her between his arms, lifted his feet off the ground and then suddenly they were gliding down the hill.

It felt like flying, the sugary crunch of snow beneath the wooden rails the only proof that they were moving.

There were no words to describe the beauty as they sailed quietly down the hill, the *shushing* of the dry snow the only sound. Nicolas was right; the mild incline provided just the right amount of speed. It wasn't the exhilarating rush of a roller coaster, but more like the serene weightlessness of a bike on a smoothly paved street.

Nicolas leaned back onto the sled—pulling Gema with him—stars peeking out between the puffs of clouds overhead. She closed her eyes as the wind whipped her face, basking in the feeling of having Nicolas envelop her so completely. Her heart was beating slow but hard, a strange combination of comfort and joy.

When they slid to a stop at the bottom of the hill, they sat in silence for a few moments.

"Did you like it?" Nicolas whispered, not wanting to break the quiet of the night, his arms and legs still touching hers.

"That was the most amazing sensation I've ever felt."

About an hour later, they pulled up to a two-story wooden house. In the dark of night, the wood looked gray, and the house had a haphazard feel to it, as though someone had built it without any blueprints.

"Where are we?" Gema asked, getting out of Nicolas' compact car, whose flaking paint job attested to the many harsh Austrian winters it had endured.

"It's a cabin that's been in my family for generations." He held out his hand, squeezing hers when she gave it to him.

She smiled, whatever uncertainty she had felt earlier in the night, was finally gone.

Noticing no lights on in the house, she asked, "Is anyone here?"

Nicolas shook his head. "Not tonight. It's my parents' turn for the cabin this weekend. We have a calendar with all my cousins so that everyone gets a chance to use it." He inserted a large brass key into what was surely the oldest door Gema had ever seen and opened it with some effort.

He pushed through the door, pulling her along, feeling along the side of the wall for lights. "It's always colder in here than outside. I'll get a fire going, stay close."

He built a fire in an ancient fireplace-cum-stove covered in green tiles reminiscent of dragon scales, with a built-in stovetop where a copper kettle sat expectantly.

It's not a romantic open hearth, but it looks like it will get the job done, Gema thought as she hugged herself, the cold, stagnant air chilling her from the inside out.

Even Nicolas seemed to feel the cold as he blew on the kindling, a shiver undulating down his back.

Gema shivered too, but not because of the cold.

"It will take a couple of hours to heat the whole house. We should stay in front of the fire until it does. I'll get the kettle going so we can have something warm to drink," he said quickly, as though reading it off a card.

Clearly, he's said these things before. Gema wondered if he said it to all the women he brought here. The thought made her frown.

He returned with the kettle, opened the stove's brass door, and added another log, before sitting beside her on a well-worn gray loveseat a few feet from the stove.

The compactness of the couch made it impossible for him not to touch her, and she was grateful for the contact. She'd missed how connected she'd felt to him on the sled.

"Still cold?" he asked.

She nodded.

He grabbed a heavy blanket from an adjacent armchair. "Here, take your coat off. You'll warm up faster without it."

He took her black puffer coat and threw the blanket over her torso and lap, quickly shrugging off his coat, putting his arm around her shoulders, and pulling the blanket up to his neck.

Gema warmed up immediately, although she wasn't sure if it was because of his strong, protective grip or her surprise at said grip.

"Better?" he asked, concerned.

She nodded but her chattering teeth gave her away.

"That won't do. Take off your boots and snow pants, now," he said, leaving no room for argument.

Gema hesitated. She was wearing leggings and silk hose under her snow pants, but still...

"Now!" he said sternly. "We have to warm you up." He had already taken off his boots and was working on his belt, the clanking of the metal causing Gema to warm a few more degrees. When he slid down his snow pants, he revealed thick thighs clad in a layer of merino wool, a noticeable bulge between his legs.

Gema stared, longing to run her hands over the curves of his quads and—

"Well at least your teeth aren't rattling anymore."

Gema looked up and saw him smirking, clearly catching her stare.

She quickly kicked off her boots and slid her cold snow pants off modestly under the blanket.

"I don't get to stare too?" His voice playful and demanding at the same time.

Gema swallowed hard. There was no mistaking his intentions now, and after four months of pining for him, she couldn't wait to see how far this night would go. If it was as far as she wanted, there would be no sleeping tonight.

He leaned towards her and she closed her eyes feeling his hands tuck the blanket around her, waiting for the feel of his lips on hers but then...

She heard him walk away from her and opened her eyes to see why.

He walked to the kettle, grabbed its wooden handle, and poured some dark liquid into two waiting mugs.

Was it possible for women to get blue balls? she thought, watching his sculpted ass move, his back muscles ripple, with the sheen of the firelight only serving to highlight the definition.

He walked back towards her, two steaming mugs in his hand, and handed her one, before nestling beside her under the blanket.

She tried to ignore the tingling fire erupting through her body as his hard legs and torso pressed against her right side, focusing instead on the hot mug in her hands. She took a sip, a tangy, clove and orange scent tickling her nose and spreading through her mouth, heating her from the inside out as it traveled down her throat.

The mulled wine hit the spot, warming and relaxing her perfectly.

She drained the mug quickly, enjoying the way it made her head and body soften.

Handing Nicolas the mug, she pulled her legs onto the loveseat and leaned into his chest, folding herself into the warmth of his chest.

He pulled her closer to him with his free arm, as he drained his own mug, setting it down beside hers on the floor.

"Better?" he asked.

"Mmmm..." she hummed lazily, her lips feeling warm and cozy. "You knew exactly what to do. You must have brought hundreds of women here."

He lifted her chin and she opened her eyes, gasping at the longing in their golden depths.

His eyes crinkled up as he smirked. "Hundreds?" he asked, challenging.

She pursed her lips and smiled, nodding her head slowly. "At least dozens..."

He arched a brow and tutted. "Not even that."

His eyes flicked down to her lips and her heart skipped a beat. "How many?"

He frowned, caressing the side of her face with his finger as he licked his lips. "I've only brought one woman here."

Her mouth felt dry. "One woman before me?" she croaked weakly.

He leaned towards her and whispered. "No, Gema, just you," he said, before laying his full, warm lips gently on hers, his mouth tasting of cinnamon and wine. He groaned as he kissed her. "Finally," he said between licks and sucks.

Gema's lips curled up into a smile as he continued to explore her mouth. He'd wanted her as long as she'd wanted him. The knowledge was fuel to her desire and she pulled him tighter to her, moaning as his lips kissed a trail of fire along her jaw to her ear and neck as the roughness of his stubble abraded her skin. "Ohhh," she moaned into his ear.

Her sounds seemed to affect him directly as he immediately increased the pressure on her neck, licking and biting her, as a pool of want puddled in her nethers; her hands running over the peaks and valleys of his back.

His tongue snaked along her jawline and down her throat.

Oh, God, this feels good.

The cool air of the room created a tingling sensation as he licked his way down her chest, tugging at the neckline of her shirt as he went.

But it wasn't enough. The taut fabric kept his tongue from doing the things she wanted him to do.

"Take my shirt off," she said.

If his weight hadn't been bearing down on her, she would have done it herself.

He made a satisfied sound as he shifted his weight, unbuttoning and removing her cardigan and then lifting up the edge of her turtleneck carefully so as not to jostle the blanket.

She could tell he was concerned about her staying warm, but he didn't need to worry, her skin was on fire.

"How many layers do you have on?" he asked, teasingly.

"Only four or five more, but only the last one has a lock on it."

He growled playfully. "I hope you'll give me the key."

"Keep doing what you're doing and you won't need a key…"

He nuzzled her neck as he lifted up her whisper-thin base layer and undershirt at the same time, skimming the tips of his fingers along her side.

She laughed, twisting at the tickling sensation.

"Ticklish, I see," he said, his voice full of playful glee as he trailed his fingers up and down her side, her laughter subsiding as his large hand cupped the underside of her breast, his caramel eyes focused on hers. "You're beautiful, Gema," he said with an exhale. "I'm amazed I was able to teach this past semester. I was so distracted by you."

She smiled, raising her hand to sweep a curl out of his face, surprised at how soft his hair was. "You did a good job hiding it."

He shook his head. "I did not. The only reason you didn't notice was because you were equally distracted."

Her mouth dropped open in protest.

"Don't pretend that you weren't. Every time I looked up at you, you had a dreamy, far-away look in your eyes."

"I'm so embarrassed." She blushed furiously, grateful for the darkness.

He tsked. "Don't be. I was glad for it. It helped me get through the semester. I've been fantasizing about bringing you here for the last four months, and now that I have you here, I want everything to be perfect. I want to please you in every way possible."

Her flush of embarrassment was replaced with one of pleasure. She was looking forward to being "pleased."

"May I?" he asked, running a finger along the edge of her satiny bra.

"Yes, yes," her voice, ragged.

He pulled down the filmy fabric. "Rosebuds," he said quietly, bringing his mouth down on her puckered nipples, the soft heat of his tongue and lips sending bolts of sensation straight to her clit.

She moaned as she wrapped a leg around his, pulling him tighter against her, the pressure of his growing erection delicious against her mons.

He arched away from her, a swirl of cool air hitting her stomach. The combination of hot and cold was surprisingly pleasurable, making her awareness of him that much higher since every point of warmth indicated a place where he was touching her: his mouth on her breasts, his hands on her waist, his erection against her thigh.

They kissed and caressed each other for a long while, until the warmth of the room matched the warmth of their bodies, and the sounds of rustling blankets no longer competed with the murmurs and moans of their voices.

After what seemed like hours, Gema's brain was a muddled stew of longing. All she wanted to do was strip off all of her clothes, climb on top of Nicolas and release all of the pent-up anticipation that had been building for the last many months in an explosive grinding of limbs.

"I *want* you," she moaned.

He murmured his agreement.

"Please tell me you brought condoms."

"Just in case," he said quietly.

Thank god, she thought. Gema thought of condoms as the perfect triumvirate: disease prevention, pregnancy protection, and she didn't have to deal with the messy side of sex. She never had sex without one.

She reached down and stroked him through the fine merino, which allowed a wonderfully sensual slip to her ministrations.

Nicolas groaned. "You are going to ruin me."

She nibbled his ear. Keeping her voice low, she asked, "Have you been tested since your last partner?"

He nodded. "I haven't been with anyone in over a year, but I was tested. All clean. You?"

"Tested six months ago, all good."

He smiled as he closed his mouth over hers and clothing began disappearing. There were momentary flashes of cool air hitting her newly unsheathed skin, and then suddenly she was flaming hot, as his naked body pressed against hers, his erection tight against her belly, the slight scratchiness of his chest hair tickling her skin.

She breathed him in, a combination of the mulled wine and musk, it was heady.

He licked his way down her torso, kissing and nibbling at her inner thighs, inhaling deeply at her vee. He growled threateningly. "You smell so good." He nudged her thighs apart, licking her outer lips in delicious torture.

"Oh god," she gasped, praying for his mouth on her clit.

With long lapping strokes he licked his way closer and closer—each delightfully light pass pulling gasps from her—before diving in with the flat of his tongue, licking her from bottom to top like a dessert he couldn't get enough of.

He grabbed her hips, massaging her pelvis with talented thumbs, her torso gyrating as he brought her closer to the edge.

He removed one hand and gently rubbed his thumb at her entrance, seeking permission as it slid against her slickness.

"Yes," she whispered. "Please," arching her back towards his waiting finger, he pushed into her, his tongue continuing to lash her clit.

She opened her legs wider, pressing against his hand, weaving her fingers through his curls, as he penetrated her slowly at first and then faster, the speed of his tongue in perfect accord with his hand.

Her hips swiveled in time with his finger, pleasure pinging off her insides as his talented digit stroked her inner walls. "That's it," she said, pushing and pulling on his curls as her orgasm began to coil up within her.

He clamped down with his lips on her clit, sucking continually as he sped up his finger, pumping faster and harder.

"Yesssss..." she hissed as she rocked her ass upwards, riding his palm, meeting his finger as her climax rippled over her from the small of her back up her neck and then crashing down the front of her torso.

He continued to pump her, slowing his speed as his tongue lapped her thick, throbbing lips; riding the waves of her climax with her like a benevolent passenger.

He squeezed her hips as she convulsed, biting his way back up to her torso, sucking and kissing her tight nipples.

She trailed her fingertips along his back, aching to have him inside her.

He wiped his mouth and gave her a gleeful smile before kissing her deeply.

She pulled him to her, meeting his kiss with equal intensity. "Grab the condom," she whispered as she broke their kiss.

He nodded, rummaging through the clothes on the floor and pulling one out.

"Turn over," she commanded.

He wrapped his arms around her and flipped them both over as if she weighed nothing.

She took the condom from his hands, squeezing the little rubber disc to the side, before ripping the edge with her teeth.

He sucked in his breath, running a hand down the edge of his thick erection.

She took out the ring, pinched the air out of the tip, and grabbed the base of his veiny cock as she gently sheathed him with her other hand.

"You make it look so sexy," he whispered.

She smiled, squeezing the base of his erection as she moved to straddle him, placing his tip at her swollen opening.

He waited calmly like a perfect gentleman—no impatient thrusts, no trying to pull her lower, no rushing—as she bobbed on his tip, stretching and teasing so that when she finally took him his sizable length would slide in easily.

Leaning forward she kissed him gently, all the while rubbing his thick head against her wet folds, the dull pressure against her most private parts, intoxicating.

He smoothed one of her dark curls out of her face, winding it gently behind her ear. "Beautiful mouse..." he murmured.

She placed her hands against his chest and rose up, closing her eyes while simultaneously lowering herself onto him in one fluid thrust.

Ecstasy.

He groaned loudly.

She swiveled her hips in a small circle, enjoying the sharp fullness inside her.

Slowly she leaned forward onto his chest, bobbing lightly a few times on his head and then thrusting down again.

He sucked in a breath.

Her eyes fluttered open and came to rest on the majestic peaks of the snow-capped Alps, framed through the living room window in front of her. The thought of climaxing with that view seemed so decadent, that she began to move her hips quicker, bracing herself against his pecs as she rode him the way she'd been fantasizing about for the last many months.

He moved his hips in time with hers, driving himself deeper inside her, her clit rubbing temptingly against his happy trail, winding her up until she was beyond conscious thought, the white mountains calling.

"Oh, hmmm," she panted, falling onto his chest as her climax ripped up her spine, her nipples puckering tightly, a chill of pleasure rippling out across her neck and torso.

He kissed her head gently, hugging her sweetly, as his hips continued to move slowly.

Her head was a swirling soup of satisfaction as she melted into him, barely noticing when he wrapped his arm around her waist and turned her over, the weight of his body pressing him into her further.

She gasped. She'd never felt this full before in her life.

He thrust expertly, small movements, changing direction, exploring and probing her insides as though he knew her already.

His breathing was deep but even; she could tell that he could go on like this for a while.

His movements seemed to elongate her climax, and ripples of pleasure continued to shudder through her as she lifted her hips, meeting his grinding thrusts for even deeper access.

He moaned his approval.

Leaning down he claimed her mouth, swirling his tongue and hips in perfect harmony. He whispered in her ear, "You feel so good."

She smiled. "I love how deep you're fucking me."

He inhaled quickly, a sound of mock horror. Then he groaned. "I want to fuck you even deeper."

Was that even possible?

He wrapped his long arms over her shoulders, grabbed her ass and pulled her to the hilt of his rock-hard cock with a single thrust.

Oh fuck. It is possible.

With each intense push, he pulsed against her clit. Her third climax began coiling up within her pelvis. He was going to make her come so hard, although it some ways it felt like she hadn't even finished her second orgasm as low waves of pleasure continued to wash over her.

With mewling groans she unleashed a string of blasphemous babble, as she pulled him to her, her orgasm going off like an atom bomb.

Nicolas began thrusting faster as he lowered his mouth to Gema's neck, nipping and nibbling until his own release trembled through his body and he groaned into her jaw. "Oh, Gema."

They lay there together—their bodies continuing to shudder in pleasure—as they caught their breath.

Nicolas reached for the blanket with his long arms, bundled at the base of the couch and pulled it back over them, a sweaty, tangled heap of gelatinous limbs; the potent mix of post-coital bliss, warmth, and exhaustion making for a heady cuddle.

He wrapped his arms around her and kissed her nose. "I definitely cannot be your German teacher next semester."

Gema laughed. "I'd much rather have you as my lover anyway."

They kissed and she sighed, contented as she began to drift off in a luxurious cloud of satisfaction.

Another six months in Austria sounded like pure heaven.

If you'd like me to write more about Nicolas and Gema, cast your vote by visiting SmartURL.it/KNB1survey

Thanks!

Havana Club

Soundtrack: "Señorita" by Camila Cabello and Shawn Mendes
Start when you read the first "¡Ole!"

One year before BECKONED, Part 1: From London with Love

Stella's clothing was a reflection of her mood: drab. Her pants and shoes were the color of cold oatmeal, as though she'd poured a pot of it over her head and let it set. Her turtleneck sweater, pants, and even her canvas sneakers were all in the same ivory-gray color family, which she had topped with a thin black hooded slicker—small enough to ball up and stuff into her cross body bag—since the forecast had called for light rain.

"Come on. We're almost there," Nathan said, with barely a glance back as he walked a full five feet in front of her.

If he'd been looking at her, he would have noticed the roll of her eyes and frustrated line of her lips, pressed tightly together.

If she had been in a better mood, she would have been able to admire the beauty of the scene; walking through the lively streets of Madrid on a chilly autumn night. It was Friday and they were heading to the Plaza del Sol to meet up with a group of Nathan's friends from university.

"Can you believe all the people?" Nathan said, calling back, turning halfway towards her so she could hear him, and then immediately turning forward, like a spring-loaded Jack-in-the-box. His head sprung back again. "It's like this almost every night of the week. I love it here!" he exclaimed, although Stella wasn't sure if it was for her benefit or his own.

She jogged a bit, struggling to keep up with Nathan who was walking, and talking, unnaturally fast. Ever since she arrived earlier this evening, flying in from London where she was attending university, things had felt "off".

She watched his back as he continued walking in front of her—the distance never varied, as though he sped up when she did—and he occasionally looked back to make sure she was still there.

What the hell?

When they'd met a year ago in Chicago, at a conference designed to encourage students of color to attend graduate school, they'd hit it off immediately. But she'd been dating someone at the time, and kept Nathan at arm's length despite the zing of attraction she had felt when they'd met. They parted as friends, promising that if they both went to school in Europe as planned, they would visit each other there. Then she went back home to New Jersey and he returned to "the Rez"—as he called the tribal land he lived on—in Utah.

The email she'd received from him a few months ago, inviting her to visit him, had been sweet and flirty. "I hope you'll come stay with me in Madrid. I haven't been able to stop thinking about you."

She'd wrote to him accepting, echoing his sentiments now that she was unattached. However, ever since she arrived, Nathan had been emotionally, and physically, distant.

When he mentioned meeting up with friends for the evening, she hadn't bothered changing out of her travel clothes. She felt drab, so she might as well look it too. Now that they were approaching their destination, she realized it might be good to be around other people since Nathan was being such poor company.

They rounded a corner and spilled out into a large open space, the ambient noise level rising many decibels with the incoherent din of thousands of conversations.

"This is Puerta del Sol," Nathan called back.

Door of the Sun, she thought, and looked around. "Where's the door?"

Nathan shook his head. "When Madrid was a walled city, there was a gate here that faced east, hence Door of the Sun. But now it's just a public square located at the center of the city. All of Madrid's street addresses radiate out from here," he said, slowing for the first time and scanning the floor. "In fact, there's a plaque somewhere on the ground marking it as Kilometre Zero for all of Spain."

Nathan had almost come to a stop as he looked around, however, he must have sensed Stella's proximity because he looked up, his eyes widening, and then took off walking again.

Stella sighed, readjusted her cross body bag, and wondered why he was even bothering to play tour guide.

Fortunately, the people watching of Puerta del Sol was very diverting. Denim-clad hordes of people, from teenagers to thirty-somethings, filled the space, coalescing into large groups that would tear off and regroup like the cells that divided under her microscope back in London.

Back home in the States, no one wore head-to-toe denim, but the young people here seemed to love the look. The plaza was almost three-quarters full and was infused with a kinetic energy like a rock concert waiting to happen. The feeling was contagious, and her mood lifted, suddenly making her wish she were wearing something more festive than oatmeal.

"Is something happening?" she yelled toward Nathan.

He shook his head. "Nope. This is just a normal Friday night."

Stella raised her brows. There was nothing like this back home in New Jersey, where a gathering of young people this large would only happen at an event like a Springsteen or Bon Jovi concert. She turned her attention to the different groups, wondering what people were talking about. Although Spanish was the language she caught most in the wind, she also heard snippets of other languages including English, German, and Italian. Catching bits of English and Spanish conversations, it seemed like hanging out at the plaza was *the* plan, not just an in-between meeting place.

How fascinating.

"Stella? Stella!"

The sound of her name snapped her head forward to where Nathan was looking at her, his lips pressed tightly in consternation.

A flare of frustration shot through her, her good mood evaporating.

Why is he so being such a dick? They'd spent almost three days together at the conference last year, and he'd never acted like this.

"We're here," he said, pointing to a small club, and then walking towards the entrance, leaving her in his wake once more.

I wonder if it's too late to find a hotel. She pursed her lips, remembering the luggage she'd left back at Nathan's and glancing at her watch. It was already after ten, making a change of accommodation highly unlikely, not to mention expensive on her grad school budget.

She entered the club after him, surprised when no one asked her for ID.

Back home, muscular men in black shirts could always be counted on to ask anyone that looked younger than forty for their driver's license, proving they were over twenty-one. Most of the bouncers seemed to take their role as gatekeeper a little too seriously, and even though she was twenty-six, it still made her nervous when someone asked for ID. However, during her month in London, she'd learned that unless there was a cover charge, entering a club or bar was simply a matter of walking in, just like a restaurant.

She coughed, eyes stinging as she walked into the dark, low-ceilinged space, cigarette smoke hanging heavy in the air. Waving her hand in front of her nose, she bobbed her head, trying not to lose sight of Nathan as he receded into the crowd. People were standing around, drinks in hand, bodies bobbing lightly to the music. She thought he had been moving in the direction of the stage, where four men were playing old Motown hits, the crooning lead singer dressed in something resembling a Las-Vegas-years-Elvis outfit.

She stood on tiptoes to find Nathan, but couldn't distinguish his dark hair from a sea of dark hair, punctuated occasionally by blond.

She sighed. *Why did I come?*

She could have been back in London, compiling her research on DNA combination. Right now she would have preferred to be at her desk, analyzing the DNA sequences of same sex siblings.

She had always been curious about dominant and recessive traits, which she chalked up to how different she and her siblings looked. Her multicultural parents were such a smorgasbord of genetic options that she had been born with curly auburn hair, chocolate brown eyes, and was short.

Her older brother and younger sister, however, both had straight black hair, cleft chins, and were tall. It had always bothered her that while both of her siblings got the dominant cleft chin and recessive tall genes, she'd gotten the recessive regular chin and dominant short genes. However, in a way she was grateful for her boring chin and short stature since they had inspired her life's work researching the "why" between dominant and recessive gene expression.

Right now though, her siblings' tall genes would have come in handy finding Nathan.

She jumped up a few times—garnering a few strange stares—and spotted Nathan sitting at a small, round table near the stage, illuminated in the runoff of the stage-light. He was talking to a couple of women seated at the table next to his and shrugged, jerking his head back towards the entrance.

Her cheeks grew hot. *He's probably telling them he lost me in the crowd. What a waste of a hundred bucks* she thought, thinking about the cost of her plane ticket from London to Madrid. She had eaten more than her usual share of canned soup the last month in order to save up for this trip.

She laughed inwardly at the strange, and unexplained, turn of events. This whole week had been spent in excited anticipation of reconnecting with Nathan. Although the email he sent this week had not been as flirty as the original invitation, she was still staying at his apartment. Wasn't that essentially a booty call?

Her gut tightened, sad that the anticipated intimacy, both physical and emotional, was not going to happen. She had built up the imagined rapport with Nathan in the months they'd been apart, plus it would have been so nice to get her mind off school.

She sighed. Maybe I should just ask Nathan for his key and go back to his place to sleep. At least then she'd be doing something she enjoyed.

She decided to make one more effort and pushed her way through the crowd towards the table where Nathan was sitting. He was chatting animatedly with a handful of twenty-somethings all with the dominant gene expression of brown hair, and most with the recessive gene of tall height.

It was difficult for her to look at people and not catalog their dominant and recessive traits.

She approached Nathan and tapped his shoulder. He turned around and gave her a tight smile. "Oh, hi," he said, his tone, lackluster.

What the hell? She forced herself to speak, raising her voice to be heard over the din of *Proud Mary*, being belted out by the Elvis singer. "Who are your friends?"

Nathan turned to his left. "Stella, this is Gianni," he said, pointing to a medium height man with straight, chin length brown hair.

Recessive, dominant.

"Ciao. Nice to meet you," Gianni said, standing as he offered Stella two cheek kisses, his rich Italian accent seeming to hang in the air. He had kind, sparkling eyes and Stella liked him immediately, grateful that there would be someone to talk to besides Nathan.

Nathan continued introducing his friends. "This is Carlos, Susana, and Bernd," Stella greeted each of them, slowly going around the table before she turned to her right, and inhaled quickly.

Sitting in front of her was a man with eyes that twinkled with amusement, his mouth curled up in a naughty smirk, as though he knew that underneath her drab, oatmeal garb she was wearing a black lacy bra and thong set that she only wore on special occasions, and that he couldn't wait to see for himself.

She blushed furiously.

"I'm Ekaterina," said the tall, blonde woman sitting on Smirky Guy's lap, as she offered her hand to Stella, her lips pursed.

Smirky Guy has a woman sitting on his lap? Apparently, she'd been so dazzled by him, she hadn't noticed the passenger riding shotgun.

"Oh, hi. I'm Stella," she replied to Ekaterina, struggling to keep her gaze from drifting back towards Smirky Guy's twinkling eyes.

Ekaterina gave Stella a curt nod.

"And I'm Rolfe," said Smirky Guy.

He stood up, forcing Ekaterina out of his lap—a dark expression passing over her lovely face—and leaned forward, kissing Stella on both cheeks, lingering just a bit longer than necessary.

He smelled of peppermint soap and rum and his proximity made Stella's heart thrum like the wings of a hummingbird.

Maybe Madrid wouldn't be a total bust after all.

"Please, sit." Rolfe pulled out a chair for Stella, and then sat back down; Ekaterina deposited herself back in his lap, giving Stella a self-satisfied smile, like a cat who's just found the perfect sunbeam.

Stella frowned.

"Are you a studying here in Madrid?" Rolfe asked.

"No. I'm at school in London. I came to visit Nathan. We know each other from the States."

Rolfe arched a brow. "Mr. Nathan has no shortage of admirers, with his dark good looks."

A waiter had come around, and asked Stella if she wanted something. She eyed Rolfe's drink.

"It's a rum and Coke with Havana Club. Do you want to try it?" He held his drink up to her.

Stella felt Ekaterina's look of disapproval and took a sip, just to spite her.

"Yum. That's delicious." She turned to the waiter. "I'll have one of those, thanks."

"What are you studying?" Rolfe raised his drink to his lips.

A shiver ran up Stella's neck as the tip of his tongue pushed the straw aside, his lips wrapping themselves around the rim of his glass. Her nipples tightened and she swallowed tightly. "I'm a Ph.D. candidate in biosciences. I study gene expression."

His brow arched. "Smart and beautiful."

She was used to being called smart, but smart and beautiful...at the same time? *Damn he's good.*

His eyes were trained on Stella as if she was the only person in the world, which was strange considering a statuesque blonde was sitting on his lap. However, she noted he was not paying attention to said blonde. If Ekaterina had been a cat, she would have leapt off long ago and looked for a more accommodating lap.

Stella felt beads of sweat break out along her hairline.

She removed her slicker, pulled off her turtleneck, and unbuttoned the top of her blouse, suddenly wishing she'd worn something as pretty on top as she had underneath.

"*Tu bebida, señorita.*" The waiter put her drink down on the table, the tall glass sweating with condensation, gold letters spelling "Havana Club" glittering in the low light.

She took a long swallow, the cold drink soothing her ramped-up nerves while the fizzy bubbles tickled her throat. Although she'd studied animal pheromones, and knew that scientists believed their role in human attraction was negligible, she wondered if Rolfe might be an exception to the rule, because whatever he was emitting, she was feeling big time.

She fanned herself, glancing around to see if anyone else was feeling hot, but no one seemed to notice. Her fingers went to the next button on her blouse, but she hesitated, unsure if that might reveal the top of her bra.

Fuck it! She undid the button, grateful for the relief around her neck and throat.

Rolfe's eyes darted down and when they jumped back up to her eyes, they narrowed seductively.

She gulped.

Suddenly, the music stopped and the singer was saying something into the microphone, and then looked out at the crowd, his hand shading his eyes.

Stella was so disoriented by her body's response to Rolfe that all she heard was the "Wah wah wah wah wah," like an adult speaking in a *Peanuts* cartoon.

"Do you know that song?" Rolfe asked Stella. Clearly reading the confusion in her face, he said, "The singer asked if anyone knew the words to the American song *When the Saints Come Marching In*. Do you?"

Stella shrugged, wiping at her brow and wondering if she had a fever. "I suppose." Although she wasn't certain, a part of her felt like she must. "Why?"

Rolfe stuck two fingers in his mouth and whistled loud. "*¡Aqui! ¡Aqui!*" He yelled, pointing at Stella.

A spotlight illuminated her face, and she blinked. "What?" Her fingertips feeling suddenly cold.

"*Venga, señorita.*" The Elvis singer said into his microphone as he walked over to her, his arm outstretched.

Rolfe was clapping, urging her to stand. "Go sing!"

She hadn't sung since undergrad, a few years ago. Okay, well maybe a Christmas carol here or there, but that was it.

Elvis waggled his fingers at her. "*Venga. Come.*"

Rolfe stood, dumping Ekaterina off his lap for a second time, and pulled Stella up.

She grabbed her drink with her free hand and took a huge gulp. *Here goes nothing.*

Rolfe placed Stella's hand in Elvis', as though he was transferring custody, and Elvis pulled her up onto the stage as the club broke out in loud applause and whistles.

"You know the song?" Elvis whispered in her ear.

She nodded.

"Just sing loud and have fun," said Elvis, giving her a wink and a smiling as he conjured another microphone and handed it to her.

She tapped the end of it to make sure it was live, and took a deep breath.

The band began a bluesy rendition of the song, and Stella sang along quietly with Elvis through the first verse, her heartbeat audible in her ears. About halfway through the verse she panicked. *Are there more words?* However, she was quickly pacified when the singer started repeating the same lyrics over again. Her nerves relaxing, she sang a little louder, and the audience clapped in response.

The lights were too bright to see Rolfe, but she heard his loud wolf whistle once again, and her nerves seemed to dissipate with the sound.

Let's try some harmony, she thought, as she continued to sing, growing more animated and confident as she and Elvis guy continued to sing the same verse, over and over, the audience and band becoming more animated with each verse.

Stella laughed. *This is fun!* Who knew that her trip to Madrid would include an impromptu concert?

Elvis twirled his finger in the air, indicating that they would wrap up the song, and Stella took a deep breath, preparing to hold the last note until she ran out of breath. "How I'll want, to be in that number. When the saints go marching innnnnnnnnnn..." she sang, her head thrown back in the joy of the moment as she raised her arm up in the air, the drummer crashing down on a cymbal just as she finished.

The club erupted in loud applause and shouts as Elvis grabbed Stella's hand, raised it in the air, and then pulled her down in to a deep bow.

She stood back up, unsure if the lightheaded feeling she had was from the blood rushing back to her head or from the exhilaration of the crowd. She'd forgotten how much fun singing could be.

Elvis pulled her to him, depositing sweaty kisses on each cheek. "*Muchas gracias.*" Then he walked her back to her seat, where the people she'd just been sitting with were on their feet, clapping, looking at her with new eyes, as though she'd transformed into someone infinitely more interesting while on stage.

Even Ekaterina had a smile for her.

Rolfe held out his hand and helped her off the stage, pulling her to him in a hug. "You were magnificent," he whispered, his hot breath sending pulsing rivulets of energy up her neck and scalp.

Everyone nearby nodded and smiled at her, and when she turned to Nathan, he was giving her a sheepish smile. "Well done," he mouthed.

The rest of Stella's evening was spent holding court as stranger after stranger came to Stella's table to praise her singing and buy her drinks. When one of her admirers became a bit too bold, Rolfe put a hand to his chest and said, "You're done, my friend. She's with me."

Stella wasn't sure if she imagined it, but it appeared as though Ekaterina's face froze into a fake smile at the words.

Rolfe scooted his chair closer to hers, the outside edges of their thighs connecting.

Her face flushed again and she fanned herself.

Rolfe leaned in. "Do you need to stay here with Nathan, or can I give you the midnight tour of Madrid."

Stella could have cared less about Nathan at that point, but she still needed a way to get into his apartment. "One second," she said, standing up and moving a few chairs over to where Nathan was sitting, talking on his mobile phone. As Stella approached, he put the phone in his pocket.

He gave her a chagrined smile. "You did really good up on stage."

She waved his comment away. "I guess my old choir training kicked in," she said, feeling gracious.

He ran a hand through his hair, as though he had something difficult to say. "Look, Stella, I'm not sure how to say this, but, I'm seeing someone, and she's really unhappy about the idea of you staying at my place."

Stella's eyes widened. She was about to ask why he didn't tell her this earlier when he added, "So I'm going to stay at her place tonight, and you can have the keys to my apartment. I'm sorry I've been acting like such a weirdo tonight, but my girl was really pissed, and I was preoccupied. You understand, right?"

Understand? No. But hallelujah anyway! She tried to make her face look neutral, and said, "Sure, I understand. No problem."

He broke out into a huge smile, put his hand in his pocket, and pressed a few keys into her palm while kissing her on both cheeks. "Just lock up when you leave tomorrow and put the keys under the mat. I gotta run. Good seeing you," he said without a trace of irony, giving her a backwards wave.

Stella watched him retreat, recognizing the excitement of new lust in the way he was rushing away from her. She shook her head, and laughed inwardly at the turn of events, as she walked back to Rolfe.

"Where did Nathan go? Is something wrong?" His brows furrowed.

Stella shook her head. "Not at all. I guess he's been seeing someone and he had to go meet her."

Rolfe sighed. "I wondered why Adriana wasn't here. She's been throwing herself at Nathan for a while. I guess she finally prevailed." He paused, and gave her a smile. "Does that mean I have you all to myself?" He smiled bigger when Stella nodded. Standing up, he shrugged on a lightweight olive-green jacket and grabbed her hand. "Let's go."

A spark of electricity zoomed up her arm as he interlaced his fingers with hers.

Rolfe murmured quick goodbyes to everyone and then pulled her in the direction of the exit, Ekaterina shooting a baleful look in their direction.

Stella giggled as they burst out into the plaza, which was even fuller than it had been when she'd walked into the club a few hours ago.

She couldn't believe how light she felt, as though the carbonation in her beverage had worked its way into her bloodstream. She was positively fizzing with joy. She opened her arms skyward and yelled, "I love Madrid!"

Rolfe whistled in appreciation causing Stella to laugh again.

What a difference a few hours could make.

Rolfe took her hand back in his and led her deeper into the plaza.

Stella gasped as warm pulses of delight wound up her arm. Rolfe seemed to be her own personal heater, everything about him—his touch, his smile, his voice—caused her temperature to rise.

He squeezed her hand. "Your singing was terrific. Do you sing often?"

She shook her head. "Not anymore," she said loudly over the cacophony of the masses. "I sang in choirs growing up, and then in an a cappella group in college, but I didn't have an outlet the last couple of years, and I haven't looked for a group in London."

"What a pity," he said, his brown eyes suddenly serious. "You have a gift most people would kill for. You shouldn't squander it."

Her brows knit together. "Kill for? I don't know about that—"

"Have you seen yourself onstage?" When she shook her head, he continued, "Perhaps you spent too many years hiding behind the groups you sang with. I doubt anyone else in that club could have lit up the stage the way you did. You were," he looked up in the sky, as though the right word was swimming somewhere just in front of his eyes. Finally, his gaze landed back on her. "You were magnificent."

Stella's knees faltered. Was there anything hotter than a man you were attracted to calling you magnificent? She had the sudden urge to kiss him.

His eyes crinkled up with amusement. "Your mouth is hanging open."

She closed her mouth, her cheeks burning.

"I believe the polite thing to do is to say 'thank you'," he said, squeezing her hand.

"Thank you," she said, her voice raspy.

His brows arched. "Perhaps we should do a tour another night? I would love to get another glimpse of your black lace bra..." he narrowed his eyes wolfishly.

Was she that obvious? Apparently, her lusty feelings had been broadcast onto the peaks and valleys of her face. She struggled to find the right response.

As the seconds drew on, his lips twitched. "Why don't you nod if you want me to take you to my place right now, and shake your head if you want to wait until after the tour."

Stella was sure her eyes must have been like two full moons, but she nodded, almost without realizing it.

"Thank god. If we waited until after the tour, I might have exploded. Can I kiss you now?"

Stella nodded again, and Rolfe swept her into his arms, somehow making nothing of the vast height difference between them as his lips met hers.

His kisses were soft and seeking, full of the tantalizing promise of what was to come. The faint taste of rum lingered on his lips, and she ran her hand through his gentle curls, which were as soft as a baby's.

Despite his claims of pent up desire, he was fully in control, teasing and probing her mouth the same way he teased and probed her with his questions.

When they broke apart, he searched her face. "Magnificent."

Her heart leapt and they started walking again, smiling at each other as if they had a secret.

"Since I'm not giving you a proper tour," he said in his formal English, which felt a little bit old-fashioned, "I'll give you the mini version, okay?" He waved his long arm gracefully up to the statue of a man on horseback, the base metal invisible under a thick green patina. "This is King Carlos the third. He's remembered for doing a lot of building here in Madrid."

Stella glimpsed at the statue, but was more interested in the man in front of her. "Tell me about you. What are you studying?"

He waved his hand in the air as though that was the most boring topic in the world and pointed at a statue of a bear, but she pressed, "If we are going to exchange bodily fluids, I need to know more about you."

"Fair enough." He looked away for a moment before saying, "I'm not doing anything as interesting as genetics. I'm studying Spanish in preparation for going to business school in Barcelona next year. I'm just a boring capitalist.

"What else?" she asked. "Where are you from? What are your hobbies?" She felt certain that there was more to Rolfe than he was letting on.

He shrugged. "I'm from Vienna. Have you ever been? No, I didn't think so. You aren't missing much. I'm an only child and my parents are very upset that I've left the country. Oh, your parents feel similarly. Yes, I miss them, but I'm enjoying my time here. I love the nightlife, and…oh yes. I used to be a professional ballroom dancer."

Stella's eyebrows shot skyward. "A professional dancer?"

Rolfe gave her a playful frown. "Do you doubt me?" He asked, suddenly striking a dramatic pose, one arm over his head, his index curling upward in a flourish, the other hand grabbing the edge of his jacket like it was a bolero.

It reminded her of a poster she'd seen of a bullfighter earlier that day.

After holding her gaze for what seemed like minutes, he clapped his hands loudly, stamping his feet against the ground in time. A few people around them turned at the sound, one shouting, *"¡Ole!"* as Rolfe made a quick spin, clapping and stomping some more.

His movements were mesmerizing, full of masculine strength and bravado. He threw out his long, graceful arms to the side, thrusting and arching his chest and back like a cobra spreading its hood, his syncopated movements punctuated by the occasional "Ha!"

After a couple more minutes—during which the gathering crowd clapped in time—he lowered both hands to his thighs and began stomping his feet, faster and faster as he arced his arms simultaneously upwards. When his hands reached their apex, he clapped them together loudly over his head, his feet joining in perfect harmony, and then jumped with both feet, throwing his arms out towards Stella as he landed, his head whipping back with a snap, eyes fiery.

"¡Ole!" the audience shouted, clapping loudly as Rolfe's eyes stayed trained on Stella as though she was an audience of one.

His performance left her breathless. She'd never seen anything so beautiful, so graceful, so powerful. *Damn that was hot!*

She was certain that no boy from West Windsor-Plainsboro High School could have done anything like that. The fact that Rolfe had performed it on a public plaza, surrounded by strangers, somehow made it even sexier.

He stared at her with searching eyes, like he was waiting for something. His gaze flicked to her hand, and she placed it in his palm. He pulled her to him, kissing her hard, his face damp with perspiration. His lips tasted salty now, and this embrace was different from the first, less controlled, more passionate, as though the dancing had ignited something within him.

When they broke apart, the claps and whistling of their audience were now for the two of them.

Stella flushed.

"We have admirers," Rolfe said, his eyes twinkling without a trace of embarrassment.

Stella covered her face with her hand, but Rolfe pulled it away. "In Spain, you never need to apologize for being passionate. It's one of my favorite things about this place," he said. "Come on, my apartment in only ten minutes away."

He pulled her along, parting the crowd easily as he walked, wrapping an arm around her shoulder in the denser areas so as not to lose her in the mass of people. Eventually they veered off onto a side street leading them away from the plaza. The volume dropped off as they left the crowds behind them, although even the side streets were still full of people; singles, doubles, and groups passing them frequently.

"I've never seen anything like this. Where are people going?" Stella asked.

Rolfe shrugged. "Who knows. It could be dinner or dancing. Madrid never sleeps. Are you here this whole weekend?"

She shook her head. "My flight leaves tomorrow. There's a brunch for Ph.D. Candidates on Sunday that I need to get back for."

"What a pity. I should have liked to take you out for a proper date."

Warmth bloomed in her chest. "I would have liked that."

A dark shadow crossed his face and he rolled his shoulders as though an uncomfortable weight had been placed upon them.

"What's wrong?" she asked as they stopped at a corner, waiting to cross the street.

He shook his head. "Nothing. Let's cross."

She followed his lead, but felt as though a distance had grown between them. She tried to close it with conversation. "Why are you going to business school?"

He sighed. "Honestly? I'm not sure. When I stopped dancing, it seemed like a sensible degree, and I've always wanted to live in Spain and become fluent in the language. The Latin dances were always my favorite. So here I am. Maybe I'll work for a non-profit or manage a live theatre space. I'm not sure."

"Was that a Latin dance that you did back there?"

He nodded. "It was a type of modified flamenco. Something you might see in a Paso Doble, a ballroom dance inspired by bullfighting." He pulled her to a metal bench on the sidewalk, facing an old stone building, four stories high with storefronts on the street level and wrought iron balconies above.

"Bbrrr," she said, jumping up, the cold metal leaching through her thin knit pants.

Rolfe chuckled, patting his lap. "Come. Sit here."

He pulled her onto his legs and wound his arms around her torso, pulling her close.

She melted into his chest, surprised at how comfortable she felt.

Laying her head on his chest, she enjoyed the warmth he radiated that seemed to flow to the very tips of her fingers and toes. "Mmmmm, that's nice." She hummed. *No wonder Ekaterina had enjoyed sitting on him.*

As she thought of the tall blonde, she stiffened.

"What's wrong?" He asked, rubbing her back.

"I was just thinking that I'm not the only woman who's sat on your lap tonight..."

He pulled away, searching her eyes. "Are you jealous?" he asked, bemusement dancing on his face, which was illuminated by the dappled light of the streetlamps shining through a canopy of trees overhead.

She pursed her lips. "I might have a better understanding of the chemistry of the human body than most, but it doesn't mean I'm immune to my feelings."

He arched a brow. "Well said." He pulled her head back down to her chest. "Ekaterina is just a friend. She's actually interested in Gianni, the Italian man who was sitting with us, and for some reason she thinks sitting on my lap will help her efforts."

Stella harrumphed and a low, throaty chuckle rolled out of Rolfe.

He pulled her face towards his and kissed her possessively, moaning into her mouth, the sound melting her doubts away. Her thighs grew heated as his hand traced its way from her neck, down the curve of her torso, and along the perimeter of her legs. She could practically feel her heart aching to fuse with his as pleasure swam through her veins. *Damn oxytocin*, she thought, cognitively aware of the bonding hormone Rolfe was releasing in her with his fantastic kisses, and yet, still helpless to stop its effects.

She sighed when he released her. It was almost a relief to break apart, the intensity of their embraces, overwhelming. "No fair. I can't think clearly when you kiss me like that."

"Who said I was going to play fair?" He growled, pushing her hair back as he nuzzled at her neck, the gentle rasp of his stubble sending delicious frissons of want deep into her bones.

"Oh god," she moaned as she felt him hardening under her ass, her cries, spurring him on as he alternated between hard, erotic bites and gentle, sweet nips.

She wanted to melt into him.

"You taste so good," he growled in her ear. "Like honey and lavender."

She giggled, his tongue finding a ticklish spot on her ear lobe.

"I bet you taste good everywhere," he said.

Oh damn. Her body responded with a gush of heat at her core. For a second she considered straddling him right here, wanting to feel his erection against her clit. Her thin pants the perfect gauge for grinding against him. Then she remembered where they were and she stopped herself.

She opened her eyes, and pinked when she realized that she was moaning and aching on a public street.

While her eyes had been closed, she could almost pretend that it was just the two of them, protected from prying stares by a cocoon woven from want. The surprising thing was, no one was giving them a second look.

"I told you. You never have to apologize for being passionate in Spain. People practically have sex on the streets. As long as we keep our clothes on, no one will stop us," he said, leaning his mouth towards her throat.

Just then, a couple in their fifties, dressed in prim black, the man wearing a vest and racing cap and the woman a fringed shawl and thick heels, walked by chatting in rapid fire Spanish without even a glance in their direction.

"How amazing," Stella murmured. "But I would still prefer some privacy. How much farther to your apartment?"

He stopped nuzzling her neck and sighed. "It's very close, but I don't think we should go there."

She frowned. "Why?"

It was as though he turned up the intensity of his eyes; they darkened and seemed to look right into her. His voice lowered. "Because, if I get you alone, inside, there's no telling what will happen."

A shiver danced up her spine at his menacing tone, but she wasn't scared, she was thrilled.

He continued, "Stella, I want to undress you slowly, peel back every inch of your clothing to reveal that black lace I caught a glimpse of earlier. But I won't take that off, instead, I would pull and tug the lace aside as I lick, kiss, and nibble your luscious skin until you're writhing under me, begging me to make you come."

Her entire body ached dully, like she was a tuning fork that had been plucked.

He squeezed his eyes and lips tight—as though in pain—taking a few deep breaths, all the while, his erection advertising his desire with its incessant pressing against her ass.

Stella tried to swallow, but her throat was dry with longing. It had been so long since she'd experienced physical pleasure, she'd almost forgotten she could.

He pressed his eyes tighter until even his lashes weren't visible.

Stella was surprised at how distant she felt from him despite the fact that she was sitting on his lap. It was as though he had erected an invisible wall between them by closing his eyes. She shivered.

His lids lifted, and he pulled her close to him. "I'm sorry. Are you cold?"

She nodded as he tucked her head under his chin and rubbed her back.

"What happened? It was like you weren't here anymore," she said.

He sighed into her hair, his warm breath sending a blast of heat through her scalp. She shivered again, although this time it wasn't because she was cold.

He clutched her tighter, tsking, as though scolding himself. "We shouldn't stay out here, you'll catch a cold."

Stella didn't bother to correct him, happy for any excuse that would get her inside with him.

He pulled his head back lifting her chin to gaze directly into her face. 'I'll take you inside on one condition."

She nodded quickly. She would have given him just about anything to be alone with him...in a room...with a bed...and a condom.

He hesitated. "The condition is, I'm in control. You of course can always say no..."

Why would I ever say no? she thought, suddenly noticing how perfectly formed his lips were, their slightly swollen look even more enticing. If giving up control was the price she had to pay to have those lips on her body, it was a steal. "Okay," she said.

His faced brightened and he pulled her towards him, their lips meeting in a kiss that tasted of relief and desperation. When he broke the kiss, he took her hand and stood, pulling her to the building directly in front of them.

"This is your place?" She laughed.

He gave her a chagrined nod, working a brass key into its lock.

"Why have we been sitting outside all this time?" she asked, an ounce of doubt pouring into her veins.

Maybe he was only bringing her inside because he was concerned for her health.

Maybe there was part of him that doubted his attraction to her?

Suddenly self-conscious, she shifted in her plain oatmeal sneakers, brushing her hair with her fingers, wishing once again that she had taken a moment with her appearance.

Rolfe pulled her fingers out of her hair, and tugged her to him, his thick erection cutting a firm line against her hip. "Don't doubt yourself," he said, his voice raspy. "It doesn't become you."

She frowned, annoyed at how easily he read her most private thoughts. She lifted her chin, straightening her stance.

He nodded approvingly. "That's it. That's the Stella I saw on stage."

"But why have we been outside this whole time when your apartment was only a few feet away?" she asked, following him inside, the solid wood door closing behind her with a thunk.

For a moment they stood in the inky, dense black, and yet, she knew exactly were Rolfe was, she could practically see his outline with her mind's eye, radiating with desire.

He flicked a switched, bursting her night vision—and the moment—with the bright incandescent light.

"That's better," he said quietly, almost to himself.

He hung his jacket and keys on a hook by the door, and then reached for her slicker, hanging it as well. "Let me make you something warm to drink. I can get a fire going in the living room."

He pulled her into a small but beautifully appointed room just off the entry, A large picture window to her left looked out towards the street, across from it a large stone fireplace. "It's been converted to gas. Ordinarily I hate it, but right now, I appreciate that I can start it so quickly," he said, moving as he spoke; every gesture, graceful and efficient, as though he'd choreographed a dance for how to start a fire and was executing it for her now. "Please sit." He pointed to a couch facing the sofa, its worn, tapestry upholstery, soft and inviting.

Stella took of her shoes, pulling her knees to her chest.

Once the fire was started, Rolfe excused himself to the kitchen, and she surveyed the room from her perch. The apartment was somehow both warm and impersonal. Nothing in the space felt like Rolfe, the vases on the mantel were too staid, the ornate moldings too ostentatious. She imagined Rolfe in a space that was contemporary, with energetic but restrained artwork. When he came back with two steaming mugs, she took one, happy for the warmth.

"Is this a furnished rental?"

He nodded. "The language school helped me find it. I wanted to be close to the Puerta del Sol. I just love its energy."

"That explains it..."

He cocked a brow. "Explains what?"

"The decor. This doesn't feel like you."

His lips tugged upwards. "Oh? What would be more me?" He said, scooting closer to her on the couch.

She shook her head. Rolfe's proximity seemed to short-circuit her body's ability to think. *Those researchers have to be wrong about pheromones*. She laughed inwardly.

"What's so funny?" he asked, inching closer.

She took a deep breath and shook her head. "You know, scientists think that pheromones don't play a role in human attraction..."

His gaze flicked from her eyes to her lips. "But you disagree?" He snaked a hand along the back of the couch, pushing her hair away from her neck.

She tightened as his fingers approached her bare skin slowly.

He sucked in a breath. "I love how responsive you are to me. So passionate," he murmured. Then his face darkened and he pulled his hands back to his mug, concentrating on his tea as though he might foretell his future in its wispy tendrils of steam.

Stella wondered if the future told of her leaving with or without relief of the ache throbbing in her gut.

She started when he asked, "So tell me about your research."

Blech, she thought.

"Excuse me?"

"Did I say that out loud? Sorry, I was just thinking that my research is the last thing I want to talk about." When he frowned, she explained, "It's just that...my research consumes my life, and I was hoping for some..." *Action?* "I was hoping to get my mind off it this weekend. Especially since I'm feeling stuck. I was thinking if I could divert my mind, the solution might present itself on Monday."

"I thought I was the only person who did that," Rolfe said, his eyes suddenly bright. "I've always found that when I can't figure something out directly, it helps to approach it indirectly by not thinking about. I've never heard anyone else say that before."

"Oh yes, there's a term for it in psychology. It's called 'incubating a problem'. It means that your subconscious mind works on the problem in the background."

Rolfe's breath caught. "I didn't realize the brain could sound so sexy."

Stella almost spit out the tea in her mouth. "Now you're just making fun of me."

Rolfe shook his head. "No really, I'm not. If I had my way—" he stopped abruptly.

"You would?"

Rolfe's eyes settled on her mouth as he licked his lips.

Stella bobbled her tea, spilling a bit on her oatmeal pants. She put her tea mug down on the glass-topped coffee table, wiping away the liquid.

Rolfe conjured a napkin and was dabbing at her pants before she realized what was happening.

"Oh," she exclaimed as he applied himself to drying her off.

A surge of heat raced up her body, starting at her thighs, through her pelvis, pinging off her navel like a pinball machine, arcing towards her nipple, to the bone behind her left ear, and then straight out the top of her head.

Her scalp tingled.

It was like he'd flipped a switch, turning her on for the first time in her life. She felt hyperaware of everything, high-strung with expectation, and incandescent.

She fisted the front of his shirt and pulled him to her, his eyes and mouth, circles of surprise as she kissed him.

He moaned, his limbs liquefying fluidly as he dropped the napkin. He pulled her onto his lap, mirroring the way they'd sat earlier that evening, but this time, there was no hard bench, but a soft couch that molded to them.

Stella lost track of where she started and he ended, the warmth of their bodies blurring the edges between them.

They kissed and nipped to the music of the dancing fire, as Rolfe's hand skimmed along her waist, snaking long fingers under her shirt, caressing the arc of her ribs, causing her to giggle.

"Magnificent," he whispered.

The single world was the sweetest aphrodisiac Stella could imagine. She wanted to feel the hands and lips of someone who thought she was magnificent, all over her body.

She moved her hands to her waist to remove her shirt, but Rolfe placed his hands on her forearms, stopping her.

"Stella..." he said, his tone and gaze, haunted.

Her gut tightened, her survival instinct kicking in willing her to stay safe, to stay quiet, to stay in the vanilla marshmallow bland of the known.

She lifted his chin and stared into his inky eyes.

Magnificent, she thought. Drawing courage from the thought, she pushed away from her comfort zone in one strong kick and said, "I. Want. You." The unwavering strength of her voice surprised her, but it was true.

Although she and Rolfe were near perfect strangers, she felt like he saw her in ways that no one else did, even when she was trying to shrink into the oatmeal background; he'd *seen* her, and she liked the way she looked through his eyes.

With Rolfe she felt sexy, silly, and bold, and it was intoxicating. She could go back to smart, reliable, and staid on Monday, when she put on her white lab coat like a shield and locked herself away from the outside world for the next two months.

But tonight she was his.

She thought she noticed him shiver slightly as he blinked his eyes closed and leaned his forehead against her.

"I want you," he said, the words barely a whisper, his previously fluid body suddenly locking tight. He sighed. "But not like this."

Not like this? It seemed there were a million ways to interpret those three words. "What do you mean?" she asked, proud of herself for asking a question rather than jumping to any neurotic conclusions.

"I saw you at the club. I saw you walk in by yourself and noticed you immediately—"

"You did?"

He nodded. "I was standing up. I'm tall, so I could see over the crowd. Your clothes stood out in the dark club. It was like you glowed, and the glow didn't stop with your clothing, it extended all the way around you." He caressed her cheek with the back of his fingers. "You were luminescent."

Stella's body tingled with unexpected delight.

"But the expression on your face confused me. It was a mixture of anger and confusion, but there was strength too. And then suddenly, you were walking in my direction. That was when Ekaterina pulled me down and sat on my lap," he said, rolling his eyes. "But then I was blessed because suddenly you were in front of me and Nathan was introducing us. I felt like I'd been given a gift." He smiled at the memory, his eyes taking on an innocent glow.

A gift? Stella was certain that she'd never been given a gift as beautiful as Rolfe's words. She felt...she struggled to name the emotion, but then suddenly she knew how to describe it.

Adored. She felt adored.

She had the random thought that every woman—hell, every person—should be given this gift. It felt amazing.

He rubbed the back of her hands with his thumb, his eyes dropping. "When you went up on stage," he shook his head. "I've never seen anything like that. It was like you suddenly made sense. You looked so comfortable up there. I couldn't take my eyes off you."

Her face flushed, her hands and feet suddenly growing warmer.

When he lifted his eyes to her, they were hard, as though he was girding himself. "I *want* you, Stella, but more than that, I want to know you. If we are intimate tonight, it will define everything that comes next."

"What comes next?" she whispered. She knew what came next for her; thousands of hours creating and analyzing Western blots in a room kept at exactly the right temperature so as not to degrade the biological material she worked with. It was all very time consuming and exacting and she loved it.

He sighed, running a hand through his hair. He put his hands on her shoulders and she wondered if he was steadying her or bracing himself. "I know this sounds crazy. I know we've just met, but I feel like I *know* you, and I want to know you, well beyond tonight. I want to come to London and see you. I want you to come visit me here in Madrid."

Stella blinked in confusion.

He must have misread her face because he asked, "You don't want that?"

She paused as she considered his words, the time drawing out as she struggled to synthesize the foreign thought into her reality. "It's not that, I'm just, caught off guard."

Then her stomach growled.

His face brightened as though grateful for the distraction. "Are you hungry? There's a great restaurant nearby that is open twenty-four hours."

Although what she really wanted was to just stay in this cozy room with Rolfe, she *was* hungry. She hadn't eaten a full meal since lunch.

She glanced at her watch, it was a little after three. She hadn't seen the small hours of the morning since finals week in undergrad, however, she wasn't tired either. Being around Rolfe was too stimulating for that. "That sounds great."

They bundled up, Rolfe adding a light scarf of his to Stella's outfit. "It's probably chilly." After he wound the plaid check fabric around her neck, he laced his fingers through hers. Stella couldn't believe how erotic it felt to have Rolfe's fingers brush warmly against hers, the delicate skin between her fingers tingled with sensation, sending shivers of desire to her nipples. She moaned. Their foreplay on the couch had sensitized her entire body, making every touch a caress.

Rolfe's brows arched and his eyes darkened. "Did you feel that too?"

She would have blushed if he hadn't included himself in the sentence and she flushed with the pleasure that he was as affected as she. "Yes," she said, huskily, part of her still wondering why they were leaving his apartment.

Rolfe's face seemed to steel at her response, as though hardening his resolve. "Let's go," he commanded, opening the door for her and ushering her through, their hands never unclasping as he pulled the front door closed and locked it.

They walked silently into the misty dark, the streets still lit by the glow of lamps, people still walking the streets.

She couldn't remember the last time someone had held her hand, the familiar intimacy of the gesture was sweet. Although she'd technically been in a relationship for nine of the last ten years, in many ways it was like she'd been a monk. Her ex-boyfriend, Jonathan, and she had been high school sweethearts, and had stayed together despite choosing universities that were three time zones apart. Last year, when Jonathan finally decided that he wasn't ever going to return to the East Coast, they had finally broken up.

They passed a loud group of twenty-somethings singing at the top of their lungs. Rolfe squeezed her hand sending a tingle of delight up Stella's arm.

She already felt like she would miss Rolfe when she got onto the plane in twelve-ish hours.

The funny thing was, except for the loss of their daily emails— *Dear Jon, Hope you are good. Had a crap day in the lab, didn't wash the blots enough. Oh well, there goes two days of work. Talk to you Sunday! Luv, Stella*—their weekly phone calls, and their thrice a year in-person visits in New Jersey—Spring Break, summer, Christmas— breaking up with Jonathan had felt like a non-issue to her daily life. She didn't shed a single tear and she realized after the fact that they'd grown apart a long time ago.

Rolfe pulled her close beside him as they crossed a street, a necking couple crossing the opposite way, completely oblivious to everything around them, looking like they might be able to merge into one person despite the physical laws that made it impossible.

Stella sighed, wishing that was her and Rolfe.

Stella and Jonathan had parted so easily that part of her had wondered if she'd ever really loved him. Of course she'd cared for him, but now she thought that he'd been something of a placeholder; an easy excuse to become a recluse and lock herself up with her books and experiments. Certainly Jonathan had never looked at her the way Rolfe did; like she was his favorite dessert and he couldn't wait to lick the plate clean. She also had to admit that she'd never felt with Jonathan the way she felt with Rolfe, like her clothes were an unfortunate barrier that needed to be discarded.

She felt alive, desirable, and turned-on with Rolfe. It was intoxicating.

"Here we are," he said, pulling her into the entrance of a restaurant that looked and felt like an American diner. "One of the Americans in my language program turned me onto this place. They serve breakfast any time of day."

They walked through the door and Stella inhaled the smells of cinnamon rolls, frying potatoes, and fresh orange juice. She had a pang of homesickness.

Although they were lead to a four-person table, Rolfe slid next to her into a booth upholstered in sparkly red vinyl. He handed Stella a laminated tri-fold menu with a corner sticky with maple syrup.

Stella wiped off her hand, her stomach rumbling again. Scanning the menu, she wanted to order one of everything. Her mouth watered when she read blueberry pancakes, although she knew that she should probably eat something more nutritious, like eggs.

"Do you see anything you like?" Rolfe asked, laying a hand on hers.

A shiver snaked up her neck and she sighed. She didn't think she'd ever get tired of his touches. "Everything looks good. I'm so hungry. The blueberry pancakes are really calling to me, but I should probably get an omelet."

"Get both! I'll help you with whatever you don't eat. I'm going to get the *huevos rancheros*. They are my favorite."

When their server came, Stella ordered, "blueberry pancakes for the table," which Rolfe thought was a hilarious turn of phrase.

Then Rolfe pelted her with questions about her daily life, the arrival of their food barely slowing his pace. What time did she go to the lab? How many hours was she there a day? Had she done any site seeing in London yet?

If it hadn't been for his ever-present smile and the dark look of desire in his eyes, she might have thought she was being interrogated. Instead, she felt pleased that he wanted to know so much about her.

She was impressed at his grasp of science. For a layperson, he had an above average understanding of the work she was doing, laughing when she told him about her tendency to categorize people's dominant and recessive traits at first glance.

"What about me?" he asked, coyly.

She pretended to consider him as she chewed a bit of pancake, although she'd already cataloged his hours ago. She paused as a berry exploded in her mouth, the tartness a delicious contrast to the syrup's sweetness.

"Brown hair and brown eyes, dominant." Although she thought she'd never seen a more beautiful shade of bronze than his curls or a more refined shade of chocolate than his eyes. "Long eyelashes, dominant."

His brows quirked up. "Really? I would have thought they were recessive with what a big deal my mom always made about them."

She'd heard that before. "People confuse dominant and recessive with common and uncommon. However, just because a gene version—or an allele—is dominant, it doesn't mean it's common. For instance, six fingers is the dominant allele over five, however, it's rare in the human population, which is why you don't see a lot of people with that trait."

Rolfe held up his hand and wiggled his fingers as though seeing them for the first time. "Six fingers are dominant? I would never have guessed."

Stella smiled at his wonder, his interest detonating a burst of pleasure in her chest.

He sat up straighter. "What else?"

"Wavy hair, cleft chin, dimples, all dominant. Although I'm pretty sure you must have won some genetic lottery to get that specific combination along with long eyelashes. Broad, full lips, also dominant." Her body tingled as she studied his lips, imagining them on her own, on her neck, on her nipples, on her—

"You have beautiful lips," he said, as though reading her mind, his eyes lingering on her mouth even after he said the words.

She couldn't help but roll her bottom lip under her top teeth, his attention forcing her into action in that way you can't help but look when directed not to.

His gaze narrowed and he scooted closer until the outside of their thighs were pressed together.

She jumped, her lower torso felt heated.

"What about recessive?" he said, his tone suggestive, as though he'd just said, "I want to take you to bed," although maybe she just imagined that.

She cleared her throat and looked away. "Your height is recessive. In fact, dwarfism is actually a dominant gene expression. Your lack of an epicanthic fold is also recessive. That's something we share," she said, pointing to the inner corner of her eye.

"A what?"

"It's when the skin of the upper lid covers the inner corner of the eye. It's most widely seen in Asian, Polynesian, and Native American populations, however, since it is a dominant gene variant, it is found everywhere, although with a lower frequency." She felt herself calming as she spoke about science; it was a safe, neutral zone.

She took a final bite of her now-cold eggs and then placed her fork and knife at the five o'clock position on her plate and sighed. "I'm stuffed."

Rolfe chuckled. "You did well, and so did the table," he said, pointing to the empty plate where the blueberry pancakes had been.

Stella emitted a stifled laugh, moaning at the fullness of her stomach, and leaned against the back of the booth feeling drowsy. "What time is it?" She felt too lazy to even lift her wrist.

"Five forty-three."

She groaned. "I should *probably* go to Nathan's and nap before my flight." Although she said the words, she didn't mean them. She ached at the idea of not being in his presence. If he were to protest even the tiniest bit, her resolve would crumble.

She opened her eyes to see if Rolfe was as disappointed at the thought of their separation as she was.

Rolfe appeared thoughtful.

She started to say something, faltered, and then started again. "Will you spend the rest of my time here with me? I need to leave for the airport at three."

He gave her a rueful look. "I would like that, but I have an appointment with a study group at nine, and I'm feeling the effects of our sleepless night too." He brushed the back of his fingers against her cheek, and added, "It's probably best if we say goodnight now and put you in a cab. If I walk you home, I might not find the strength to leave you."

Her heart clenched.

He leaned forward and kissed her, a deep, sweet exploration that spoke of yearning and promise. She gave herself over to the kiss and soon they were wrapped up in each other like the couple they'd passed crossing the street, their surroundings falling away from them completely.

When they parted, she was certain she'd been drugged by his pheromones, for she felt as unsteady as a soufflé.

He swept his eyes over her face and then sighed.

She could almost hear him thinking the word "magnificent".

He took out his phone, handed it to her, and said, "Put your number in it. Give me yours so I can do the same."

After taking back his phone, he took out his wallet, threw some bills on the table, and then grabbed her hand. "We should find you a cab."

She didn't want to follow him, but her own need for sleep was imminent.

They walked to the nearest intersection, Rolfe folding her into his chest with one hand and raising the other towards the street. Within a few minutes, a white car with a red slash on its door had pulled to a stop. The sound of the engine seemed loud in the inky darkness; the surrounding black belying the fact that dawn was less than three hours away.

Rolfe opened the front passenger door and spoke to the driver for a moment, handing him some bills. Then he turned back to Stella and opened the rear door. He hugged her tight, pressing a final kiss against her forehead. "I'll come see you in London."

Promise? Stella thought, refusing to say the word, knowing it would come out as a pitiful plea. Instead, she smiled thinly and nodded. "Goodbye."

He closed the door, stuffing his hands into his pockets and watching as the cab pulled away.

Stella willed herself to not look back, staring straight ahead as her eyes grew misty.

She shook her head, unable to believe that she was tearing up for a man she'd only met eight hours ago, but there it was.

Although it wasn't her specialty, she knew enough about the science of attraction to understand the way endorphins, oxytocin, and serotonin were coursing through her brain and nervous system causing her to feel a connection to Rolfe, and its twin separation. However, even though she knew how the chemicals worked, it did not make her immune to their impact.

Her phone beeped and she opened it. It was a text from Rolfe: *I miss you already.*

She reread the text many times, her heart feeling lighter with each pass.

Resisting the urge to explain to him that he was simply feeling the drop in pleasant neurotransmitters, she smiled and—emboldened by his message—typed a reply: *I miss you more.*

Barely a second passed before her phone beeped again.

Impossible, he wrote. Another message pinged. *Enjoy my scarf. I'll come and retrieve it personally in London.*

She had forgotten about the scarf. She picked up the edge of the checked fabric and inhaled it, enjoying the reminder of Rolfe as a ridiculously large smile broke out onto her face and an anonymous cab whisked her through the streets of Madrid.

If you'd like me to write more about Stella and Rolfe, cast your vote by visiting SmartURL.it/KNB1survey
Thanks!

*Rolfe is a minor character in the **BECKONED** series and appears in parts 1 & 2. To read it now, go to SmartURL.it/AmazonAviva*

Anything. Really.

Soundtrack: Brutal Hearts by Bedouin Soundclash

"Anything. Really."

She reread the last two words of the email message, wondering if she'd imagined the zap of electricity she'd felt last week when she'd last seen their author.

It had been so long since she been attracted to a man; perhaps she'd mistook static electricity for physical chemistry.

"Anything. Really."

That could encompass a whole litany of sins.

She turned the possible responses over in her mind like marbles, wondering which color to lob at his salvo for just the right effect.

Was it the vibrant red marble? *Does 'anything' include us getting naked?*

Or maybe she should choose the cool blue marble? *That's kind of you to offer.*

Or maybe something in between, like the safe but flirty violet marble. *I'm sure you don't mean 'anything'.*

She sighed, running a hand through her hair as she inched closer to her laptop, trying to divine through proximity what she couldn't figure out through pure thought. After reading the email a few more times she slumped back into the ribbed leather of her Eames chair and pushed off with her foot, spinning around a couple of times before slowing to a stop.

Why is it so hard to select the red marble? The red marble was what she was feeling.

But the question was a rhetorical one. She knew *exactly* why she was hesitating.

And it wasn't for professional reasons, even though she liked to pretend that it was.

The moment she'd heard David Major pronounce her name—"Ee-saw-bell-uh" instead of the usual "Iz-uh-bell-uh"—a flame of heat had licked straight up her back. And that gaze…he looked at her like there was no one else in the room, even though they were always surrounded by a group of at least twenty other professionals. Men and women dressed in black and navy suits earning mid-to-high six figures, wanting to learn skills that would help them break into the seven-figure realm.

She was conducting a series of three evening workshops on public speaking for a local investment firm as part of their company's HR offerings. It was her usual gig: try to instill some life and energy into sales professionals to help them improve their numbers. As a ten-year veteran at the professional development firm Excellence International, she had spoken in front of tens-of-thousands of people—from schoolteachers to professional athletes—and never been flustered.

That all changed the first time she'd seen him…

Two weeks ago, she had been five minutes into her introduction when he burst through the door late, glanced at her name on the PowerPoint behind her, and apologized to her with his panty-dropping pronunciation of her name.

"Excuse me, Isabella," he'd said, with a dazzling smile, smoothing back his dark hair, before finding an empty black Aeron chair and silently slipping into it. Once situated, he straightened his red tie and gestured for her to continue.

She started and closed her mouth, not realizing that her eyes had been trained on him—and her mouth agape—while the rest of his coworkers' eyes had been trained on her.

The blood drained from her face.

She flushed at the memory, trying to figure out what it was about David Major—that was his name as she'd learned later—that entranced her. True, he was dashingly handsome with his olive skin, his closely cropped dark hair, and his wickedly twinkling brown eyes, so dark they were almost black, but it wasn't his looks that had initially caught her attention.

As someone who'd grown up her entire life having her name mispronounced—there just weren't a lot of Spanish speakers in her hometown of Eugene, Oregon—it always warmed her when someone said it correctly. Of course, it wasn't *just* his pronunciation that had turned her on, it was the *way* he had said it, rolling over each syllable of her name with a sensual caress.

Ee-saw-bell-uh, she thought, remembering how it sounded from his lips.

"Gah," she sighed, her head falling back in frustration. She pulled her leggings clad legs under her heather gray sweatshirt that read "Portland" in faded green and blue plaid letters.

Fantasizing about one's clients was definitely *no bueno*, as her mother would have said.

Growing up with a Polish-American father and a Mexican mother meant that she was fluent in three languages: English, Spanish, and Spanglish.

Then last week, during their second session, David had offered to distribute her handouts. When he took the sheaf of papers from her, his fingers grazed the side of her hand, causing her to drop the handouts, and leaving ellipses of heat in their path, the *dot dot dot*, a promise of coming attractions. She thought she'd caught him smiling to himself before he knelt to pick up the papers.

She'd never felt so out of sorts around a client before. It was most unsettling.

She grabbed one of the two squares of dark chocolate sitting in the shot glass on her desk, her nightly ritual to satisfy her sweet tooth, and gnawed on it as she reread his email.

Isabella,

What a lovely name you have.

You told us in class to email you for any reason, and I'm taking you at your word.

I wanted to thank you for the workshops. I've learned
so much and you are truly captivating. I'm only sorry
that we only have one meeting left.

If there is anything you need me to do: run your video
camera for you, distribute handouts, etc., anything so
that you can focus on what you need to do, don't
hesitate to ask.

Anything. Really.

David

Clearly, this wasn't a strictly professional email, but there
was nothing she could think to say that wouldn't violate her
company's policy about fraternizing with clients. Of course, in
six more days he wouldn't be her client anymore.

She sat up and jabbed at the keys, picking a variation on the
cool blue marble for a response.

David,
Thank you for the kind words.
Isabella

She reread her email and sighed. If she sent that, he'd think
she wasn't interested, but she was.

She deleted the email without sending it.

First rule of communication: think before you speak.

Or in this case: think before you type.

Her mentor at work had pounded that message into her during her first year with Excellence International, and she'd witness firsthand that it was better to send no message than the wrong one.

The next six days passed sluggishly, and no amount of masturbating, reading, or yoga could dull the ache that had been developing in the pit of her stomach ever since she'd set eyes on David Major.

Finally, the day came for her final seminar at David's company's office. She dressed carefully in a black pencil skirt with a slit that was just an inch higher than necessary, a silk ivory and black pinstriped blouse with a decadent ruffle that ran along the buttons, and black patent leather high heels that she usually reserved for dates.

Isabella closed her closet door and took a final look at her outfit in the wood framed full-length mirror hanging on the wall of her bedroom.

Perfectly tailored pinstripe blazer? Check. Pearl earrings? Check. Red lipstick? Check.

She smoothed a hand over her hair, held back in a sleek chignon and took a centering breath, wiping a stray bit of lipstick from her mouth with her ring finger. Her eyes alit on the bare skin; she hardly remembered what it looked like when there used to be a sparkler there.

That was a lifetime ago.

Her mouth felt dry, and she took a long drink of water from her stainless steel water bottle, avoiding putting her lips on the spot to keep her lipstick intact. Although she would have preferred some iced tea, she'd avoided caffeine all day to make sure her nerves were fully under control.

She faced her reflection in the mirror, distributed her weight evenly on her feet, and rolled her shoulders back. "I am confident. I am powerful. I am an amazing speaker. My clients will hear what they need to hear, and learn what they need to learn." She finished her mantra with a slight bow at her reflection, her words and power outfit fusing into a potent concoction that gave her the energy and gravitas to speak in front of thousands, as she had done on many occasions. However, although her preparation was always the same, tonight her audience was much smaller, although with David Major in it, she needed all the nerve-steeling preparation she could get.

She glanced at her watch. She had thirty minutes before her seminar started and the Portland office of the New-York-based investment firm she was presenting to was only a five-minute drive from her Pearl District apartment.

Better early than late.

She grabbed her purse, video equipment, monogrammed laptop bag, and headed out.

Throughout the workshop, Isabella struggled to avoid making eye contact with David, all the while feeling his hot gaze following her around the room like tractor beams, singeing her throughout the night. She could practically feel the burn on the back of her legs where her slit flashed just a bit of thigh.

However, she couldn't completely ignore him either. When he raised his hand to ask a question, she took a breath, girding her insides while hoping to maintain a calm exterior.

"Yes, David?"

"You said that it's important to create a connection with new clients. Can you elaborate a bit more on that?"

Although his question was legitimate, she thought she caught a hint of a smirk dancing on his lips.

"Yes, great question. People like to think that we make decisions for logical reasons. So for instance, your clients might think that when they are evaluating an investment advisor, they are picking you over someone else because you have a better track record, or more impressive educational pedigree. But the truth is, the part of the brain that forces humans to give priority to one piece of information over another piece, is the ancient part of the brain: the amygdala. The amygdala is incapable of reason or even language. It can only feel. And this is the part of the brain that you are appealing to when you create connections with your clients."

David nodded, his face now thoughtful. "That makes sense. And how do you make these connections?"

"By asking questions and then sharing relevant information about yourself. If your client says that one of their financial goals is to retire on a ranch, and you grew up on, worked on, or spent a summer on a ranch, then share that. But it has to be authentic, because if you lie, and the client calls you on the bluff by asking you a follow-up question you can't answer, then you've created distrust, which is the opposite of connection. However, if you ask enough open-ended questions, you will find something you can connect over."

"What if I have no personal ranch experience, but I have another client whom I've helped achieve a similar goal. Would that work?" David asked.

Isabella was impressed by his astute question. She nodded. "Yes, that would work. Obviously personal stories are best because you just have deeper knowledge, but any sort of connection is better than none."

He gave her a serious nod that made her wonder if she'd imagined the earlier smirk, then tilted his head down and began writing furiously in his notebook.

Glancing at her watch, she noticed that it was almost a quarter to eight; time to begin wrapping up. "I'm going to pass out an evaluation form. I appreciate all constructive feedback." She handed the forms to the two people sitting closest to her and gestured for them to pass them down the long conference table. "If you have any final questions, I'm happy to answer them now."

A few people asked questions, but most had begun filling out the form. It was usually that way with these after-work three-hour seminars; everyone just wanted to get home. She'd have a flood of email in the next couple of days asking tonight's unasked questions.

She spent the silence turning off the video equipment—she was required to record her presentations in case her boss wanted to review them—and other electronics.

People began handing in the forms, thanking her, and heading out into the night. Part of her wondered what she would do if David lingered behind, however, he handed her his folded seminar evaluation, gave her a final—smoldering?—glance, and walked out without a word when there were still eight people left in the room.

She exhaled with relief that she could stop sucking in her gut and holding her posture so perfectly. It had proved impossible for her to relax under his watchful gaze. However, there was also a part of her that was disappointed he had left so quickly, wondering if she had imagined the attraction on his side.

Once the last person had left, she locked the door and pulled her chignon out, running her fingers through her hair, taking off her heels, and sighing. After three hours of presenting, her feet were grateful to be released from their high-heel purgatory, and the place at the back of her head where the chignon had been, tingled with the released pressure. She sat for a few minutes, rolling her toes into the commercial carpeting and then started packing up her gear.

Once all of her equipment was packed, she grabbed the stack of evaluation forms, shuffling them together to fit into her bag, when she noticed David's; it was the only one that was folded. She unfolded it, noting that he'd given her all tens and written in the comments: *Isabella is one of the most captivating presenters I've ever seen. I learned a lot from this workshop. I don't have any recommendations because she was perfect.*

At the very bottom of the sheet, in bold capital letters, was written: *MEET ME AT THE KENNEDY SCHOOL, CYPRESS ROOM, 9:00PM*

She sucked in a breath, her heart taking off.

She glanced at her watch. It was almost eight-twenty.

The Kennedy School was a funky restaurant and hotel created out of a decommissioned public elementary school, and it was a fifteen-minute drive away, across the river.

There were dozens of places he could have asked her to meet at in the immediate vicinity. She wondered if he chose The Kennedy School because it was far enough away to guarantee that no one from his office would be there.

Or maybe it was because The Kennedy School was a hotel.

A tingling sensation spread out from her nethers, up her torso, pinging off her nipples.

She had just enough time to stop at her apartment before heading across the river to meet him.

Later on she would wonder at the fact that she hadn't even questioned that she was going to meet him.

She stuffed the papers into her bag, no longer caring if they were neat, and raced to the parking lot.

Thirty-five minutes later, she pulled up to the Kennedy School, the clock on her hybrid Lexus reading 8:57. She turned on the interior light and angled her rearview mirror towards her. Running her hands through her shoulder length wavy hair—never quite curly, never quite straight—she grabbed a nude lip pencil from her bag and dragged it across her full lips.

She then sat up straighter and gazed at her reflection, saying, ""I am confident. I am powerful. I am an amazing woman. Tonight is the night I break my dry spell." She nodded at her reflection, took a deep breath and readjusted the mirror before stepping out of the car, into the crisp spring air, which smelled of warming earth, the clean and crisp scent of winter no longer present.

The heels of her black, knee-high boots clicked on the concrete as she walked to the entrance of the school and pulled open the institutional double doors. The hallways were empty. Spring wasn't exactly high season for tourism; couple that with a weeknight and David's choice of location had seemed inspired if his goal was discretion.

The heavy door closed with a metallic crash as she walked down the hallways, which—except for the irreverent artwork—looked like an elementary school anywhere in the U.S., including the child-height white porcelain water fountains. She wound her way around to the Cypress Room, the happy, lilting tones of reggae music, beckoning.

When she entered the bar, she was greeted by potted greenery that was as tropical as one could hope for in Portland, with decadent silk and brass lanterns dangling from the ceiling. The strange mashup of Asian, Moroccan, and Caribbean made for an irreverently upbeat atmosphere, and the bar was filled with the bubbling conversation of a couple of dozen relaxed patrons.

She looked around the room, sucking in a breath when she spotted David, standing by the side of a booth in the back, his eyes trained on her like lasers…lasers that had just disintegrated her clothing with one look.

Her skin flamed. Any doubts she'd had about his attraction vanished instantly like droplets of water on a hot frying pan.

She took a deep breath and willed herself to walk, praying that she wouldn't trip and wishing she'd chosen flats. When she made it across the room without a single falter, she released her breath.

He closed the space between them, took her hands and squeezed. "You look amazing," he said, as he dragged his five o'clock shadow over her cheek, depositing a small, chaste kiss there.

The sensation made her legs quiver, depositing in her mind the image of him abrading her inner thighs with his stubble.

She pinked instantly.

"I love it when you blush," he said, licking his top lip. "Your nipples harden every time…," he added with a flick of his eyes to her chest, his gaze a mixture of humor and lust.

Her nipples puckered even harder, and she inhaled sharply. His words left no question as to his intent, and there was a part of her that wanted to just rip his clothes off right now and have him fill her until all thought left her, but he didn't know that.

She was going to have to take control and set some boundaries. "David—"

He raised his hands. "I'm sorry," he said, eyes wide. "That was too much, right?" He shook his head. "I don't know what came over me; it's just that ever since I met you..."

Her heart beat faster. She fluttered her hand, his earnest apology melting the last of her reservations. "It's forgotten, and...I know how you feel."

The color returned to his cheeks, and he gestured towards the booth for her to sit down.

She slid into the booth, watching as he waited to sit until she was situated.

So he's a gentleman after all.

The thought that his attraction for her was enough to overrun his manners turned her on immensely. She laughed inwardly.

"I'm so glad you came," he said, pulling at the collar of his black, pinstriped shirt, the dark burgundy lines accentuating the bronzed glint of his skin.

"Maybe it was just my interpretation of your note, but it felt more like a command than a request," she said, her thighs clenching at the thought of him commanding her somewhere else. The rogue image of going down on him, the feel of his veiny skin in her mouth, flashed through her head. She blushed hotter, wondering at the effect he seemed to have on her. Apparently she couldn't be within three feet of him and not think about sex.

It was disorienting.

He laughed, turning his palms up. "Maybe you're right. Maybe it was more of a command. A hopeful command."

Her traitorous nipples squeezed hard again, and she could tell by the way the corner of his mouth tugged upward that he had noticed.

His eyes bored into hers and she sensed that he was playing his own erotic fantasies of them on the theatre of his mind.

A fluttering in her gut told her that it had been too long since a man had looked at her that way. She hadn't been with anyone since her last boyfriend almost three years ago—

She shook her head to stop that train of thought. She only wanted to be here and now; wanted to mine the cave of desire that David had seemed to open up in her.

She could see the waiter heading over out of the corner of her eye and said quickly, "Let's get a room."

"Already have one."

Butterflies swirled in her stomach.

David stood, smoothly pulled out his wallet, and withdrew a twenty. He stood as soon as the waiter arrived at their table. "Sorry for taking up your time, but it looks like we're going to head to our room." He put the bill on the waiter's tray.

"Okay, thanks," the waiter said, sweeping the bill up quickly before David could change his mind.

David held out a hand to her, closing his warm fingers around hers gently. "Isabella," he said, a hard whisper that seemed to radiate up her arms and cascade delicious rivulets of heat down her entire body

"I love the way you say my name," she said.

"I love saying it," he answered throatily. "I plan on saying it a lot tonight."

Her legs faltered a bit, but she caught herself before she fell on her denim-clad knees.

He tucked her hand into the crook of his arm and led her towards the exit, his step, sure.

They crossed silently through the hallways, towards the courtyard, neither of them wanting to break the spell between them.

David stopped in front of a room and inserted a keycard into the door. He glanced at her, lifting his eyebrow in question.

She nodded.

He smiled and opened the door, ushering her in, pulling it closed behind him.

She looked around the room, taking in the masculine, scholarly decor, as though someone had raided an old library and brought the furniture here. It was a study in tufted leather and the warm burgundies and auburns of autumn.

A single warm bedside light illuminated the space, casting long shadows across the room, framing the bed with a border of black. An ice bucket with a bottle of champagne sat next to the bed, two flutes waiting pointedly on the nightstand.

She sucked in a breath. "Awfully sure of yourself, aren't you?"

He shrugged. "Not sure. Hopeful," he said, breathily. "I also really like champagne, so I was prepared to drink the bottle alone." He gave her his dazzling smile again, which she noticed was a bit lopsided.

The quirk of his smile warmed her heart, although it wasn't as warm as other parts of her body. She drank him in, the lean, confident cut of his clothes that seemed to accentuate the muscular physique underneath.

She glanced at the bed, grateful to skip all the fumbling uncertainty of dating. What she wanted was physical union, to feel a naked body gliding slickly against hers. To have her name called out in sensual agony. To give and take. It was honest. It filled a physical need for her. What had dating ever done for her but built up her hopes and then smashed them to pieces?

She pulled something out of her handbag before depositing it in the leather wingback chair, and shrugged off her blazer, draping it over the back.

He walked over to the ice bucket, his hand resting on the neck of the champagne bottle.

She sauntered over to him, scanning his face, committing to memory the way he was looking at her right now, pure possibility. "When was the last time you were tested?"

As though expecting the question, he said, "Last month, and I haven't been with anyone in almost six months."

She nodded. "It's been longer than that for me, but I'm clean too. I brought condoms," she said, holding up the foil packets for a moment before putting them on the nightstand.

She'd never trust any condoms but those she bought herself.

She'd learned that the hard way.

He exhaled sharply as she came to a stop directly in front of him, his eyes darting from her eyes to her mouth and then back again.

The tension between them was electric, like the air before a thunderstorm. She inhaled a long, tense breath, enjoying the sizzling of the space between them, and lingered for a second, relishing the final moment before she decided to jump and plunge into the unknown.

Fisting his shirt, she pulled him to her, his mouth opening in surprise as she kissed him hard, three years of need combusting into a heady embrace that swirled through her like a cyclone, tumbling her insides, leaving no cell untouched.

When they parted, he said huskily, "Cham. Pagne?" drawing out the word as though it took some effort.

Her hands found his belt and started tugging at it. "After."

"Thank god," he said, running his hands through her hair and pulling her mouth back to his, claiming it completely, his lips and tongue waging a sweet war with hers.

Although at first she'd been in control, she found herself quickly dissolving into his rhythm. He pulled her tighter, his need, hard between them as he chased her tongue, sucking on it playfully, and then longingly, his fingers dancing a fierce staccato along her spine.

She gasped, wondering if she'd ever been kissed like this before. It was like he knew her, knew her body.

They pulled each other closer, hands crossing over each other in an erotic game of Twister, tugging at one another's clothes, not wanting to separate for even a second.

Eventually, they managed to disrobe each other and tumbled into bed, a writhing mass of limbs.

She couldn't get enough physical contact from him, reveling in the scratchy feeling of his legs against hers, the tickling fuzz of his chest hair raking across her nipples, the erotic burn of his stubble against her neck and jaw. She pushed her neck harder against his jaw and he growled, biting down on her as his erection pressed against her thigh.

There would be time for more later, but right now she just wanted to feel him inside her. Remember what it was like to feel wanted.

She wrapped her hand around his veiny length. "I want you, now."

She heard his hand on the nightstand and then the telltale rip of foil, and stopped thinking, the anticipation of his throbbing cock within her driving all thought from her mind.

"Yesssss," she moaned.

He sheathed himself and she turned onto her to stomach, wanting desperately to be pumped from behind.

He groaned a sound of approval, trailing hot nips and kisses down her back.

He leaned in to her ear. "You're so beautiful, Isabella." The sound of her name rippled through her body and she lifted her hips, pressing back against his hot erection.

He bobbed slowly at her entrance, sweetly, hesitantly, and then, when his thick head slid against her slickness, he plunged in fully.

She gasped, pressing her ass against his pelvis as she stretched fully, welcoming him, the sweetness of it bringing tears to her eyes. "Yes," she cried.

"Isabella," he growled.

She pushed her face into the sheets, stretching her arms long. "Fuck. Me. Hard."

After a moment of hesitation, he did as she wished, fucking her with such sensual ferocity, his thrusts vibrating through her torso with erotic tremors.

She braced herself against the headboard, pushing back to give him deeper access, curling her toes against the mattress to keep from sliding back. *Fuck, that feels good.*

His warm palm anchored against her lower back, his fingers, wrapping around her hip and gently kneading her pelvis bone in time to his thrusts. Without pausing his deep, searching thrusts, he bent down, licking and nipping at her back, her name a constant prayer on his lips.

"Isabella."

She could feel him lengthening and hardening within her.

"Come," she cried, wanting to feel him pulse within her, wanting to know that she did that to him.

He removed his hand from her back, and steadied himself as he intensified his rhythm.

She squeezed his length with her pelvic floor, a tingle of satisfaction skating up her back as he uttered a muffled moan.

"Fuck, Isabella."

Droplets of sweat fell on her back as David cried out with a strangled moan, pushing her forward towards the headboard, his entire body convulsing.

Flushed with happiness she wrapped her arm backward around his ass and pulled him to her as he collapsed lightly onto her back, his arms enfolding her waist.

"Oh, Isabella," he said, breathlessly, feathering her neck with kisses.

She moaned happily.

After a few minutes of heavy breathing, he kissed her back, moved the hair out of her face and said, "Round two is all about you."

She nodded even though round one had been all about her as well.

But he didn't need to know that.

"I can't wait," she said.

If you'd like me to write more about David and Isabella, cast your vote by visiting SmartURL.it/KNB1survey Thanks!

The Goddess

One year after BECKONED, Part 6: Adrift in New Zealand

Nacho Sol adjusted his sunglasses and couldn't believe his luck.

Can this day get any better?

He was standing on Joatinga Beach in Rio de Janeiro, Brazil, his legs, ankle deep in soft white sand. He waggled his toes, a satisfying hum erupting from his throat.

Even though Nacho had grown up in the coastal village of Playa Hibisco, a tiny fishing town on the Pacific coast of Costa Rica, he never got tired of a beautiful beach. And this *was* a beautiful beach. And he wasn't the sort of person who thought that every beach was beautiful. Sure, there were plenty of beaches with nice sand and clear water, but it was the backdrop that set the gorgeous apart from the "just okay."

He'd seen enough "meh" beaches in his life to know that this one, with its crescent-shaped stretch of baby powder sand against a massive stone outcropping verdant with lush vegetation, was a showstopper.

The fact that he was there on a weekday, and the sand was practically empty, only made it more spectacular; like a hidden paradise.

The small beach was dotted with perhaps a hundred visitors; there were groups kicking a soccer ball around, others working on their tans as though it was a paying job, the random dog running around, seemingly ownerless. Among all of this floated the light tones of samba music, so faint, it was almost like it was a part of the wind, as though the very air of Rio was infused with it. And behind everything were the distinctive rocks of Joatinga, massive and majestic in their stoic glory.

And the magnificent view didn't stop there.

A stunning, leggy woman with black hair that fell to the middle of her back was perched on top of one of his surfboards, arching her back and making bedroom eyes that he could feel deep in his gut, and other parts of his body. Of course, all of her well-honed sex appeal was not for his enjoyment, but for the lens of the photographer who was shooting her.

Dangelo Mesquita's photographs had graced the covers of not just fashion magazines, but also sports ones, making him the perfect choice to shoot the inaugural sports issue of *ULTIMO* men's magazine

Nacho happened to have a ringside seat for the photo shoot, since Dangelo had chosen a surf theme and *ULTIMO* had requested Santos Surfboards new Sol Sister line as props for the shoot. As the exclusive distributor of Santos Surfboards for all of the Americas, Nacho was on hand making sure that his product looked good.

And boy, did it look good.

The leggy model was twenty feet from the water, caressing the top of one of Nacho's boards like it was her lover.

Nacho wished he could have switched places with the board.

Just then, Dangelo said something to the model who shook her head, her sultry face immediately taking on a spoiled look.

Dangelo lowered his camera, and raised his shoulders, clearly imploring the model.

She crossed her arms and lifted her chin in the air like a misbehaving poodle.

Nacho frowned. He'd never seen someone go from beautiful to ugly so quickly.

The photographer uttered a few more words and the model responded by turning away from him.

Dangelo handed his camera to a woman standing behind him, who was wearing a baseball hat and a safari vest that almost reached the bottom of her shorts, and then walked towards the brunette. Nacho couldn't make out what they were saying, but he could tell the photographer was trying to placate her, rubbing her on the back and using the tone one would use on a child. The model responded by standing up, brushing the sand off her hands, and storming away.

The photographer raised his arm and began yelling at the model, his voice finally carrying to where Nacho stood, "Get back here. If you walk off this set you'll never work for me again," he said in English laced with a strong Brazilian accent. He was turning red in the face and shaking his fist at her, but the model didn't even give him a second glance.

Dangelo cursed at the sky, kicking sand in the air.

The woman in the safari vest jerked the camera out of the way of the cloud of sand.

After a few minutes of walking in circles, Dangelo approached the woman in the safari vest and began talking to her, however, it was too quiet for Nacho to hear.

There were about a dozen people standing around assisting or watching the photo shoot. Nacho walked up to a guy with a long feather dangling from his ear who was holding a flexible disc as wide as he was tall, made out of gold lame fabric. He'd been using it to bounce sunlight onto the model.

"What's going on?" Nacho asked.

"From what I could gather, our supermodel didn't want to get in the water," Feather Earring replied, chomping on a fat wad of gum.

Nacho frowned. "It's a photo shoot about surfing."

Feather Earring shrugged, and blew a large bubble.

Nacho glanced back at the photographer who appeared to be in a heated debate with Safari Vest. Both of them were throwing their arms in the air, the mellifluous sounds of Portuguese contrasting with the angry tones of their voices. At one point, Dangelo wrapped his hands around the face of Safari Vest, bringing their noses within inches of each other. Nacho was able to hear enough to make out that the photographer wanted Safari Vest to do something that she didn't want to do. At one point, Safari Vest pulled her baseball cap low on her face, shoved her glasses up the bridge of her nose, and crossed her arms.

The photographer took a deep breath, put his hand on her back, and leaned in close to her face.

Safari Vest rolled her shoulders back and nodded.

Dangelo threw his arms around her, kissed her on the lips, and then gave her a friendly shove in the direction of the many tents set up on the beach for the shoot.

Dangelo shook his head and began walking towards Nacho.

"Is everything okay?" Nacho asked.

Dangelo nodded. "We got all of the beach shots I wanted with Irina," Dangelo gestured in the direction of the model that'd walked off the set. "Unfortunately, she failed to tell us that she can't swim, and I wanted to get some shots of the boards in the water." He turned to Feather Earring. "Tell the crew to take twenty, and then get the waterproof equipment. I think I came up with an idea that's even more brilliant than my previous one."

Feather Earring nodded like he'd heard that line before.

Dangelo held his arm out to Nacho. "Come get out of the sun."

They headed over to a couple of canopies set-up on the beach with chairs, tables, and food for the crew. Nacho filled up his reusable water bottle—printed with the word ULTIMO on it—from an iced beverage dispenser, skipping over the baked goods and candy, to grab a banana. Despite the fact that he had left his professional surfing career behind him over a decade ago, Nacho still had the body of an athlete, surfing or exercising at least five days a week. He rolled his shoulders back, wishing he'd had time to squeeze in a work out this morning; the combination of his flight yesterday and a hotel bed last night had made him tight. The shoot would wrap up by sunset; he could fit in a swim before dinner tonight.

Truthfully, he could have left the shoot now. His only responsibility had been to deliver the dozen Santos surfboards, now that he'd accomplished that, his presence was no longer required. Then again, why would he leave? He was in Rio for three weeks, and his first appointment, with the buyer for a chain of surf shops, wasn't for a couple of days.

He'd been working like crazy the last twelve months. Heck, if he was being honest, he'd been working like crazy the last three years, ever since he started working for his brother-in-law Joaquin Santos. However, the last year had been especially busy as he and his sister, current Women's World Champion of Surfing Elena Sol, had designed every board of the Sol Sister—her nickname on the professional circuit—series together. They had even come up with the artwork for the boards, which had been inspired by drawings Elena and Joaquin's son, Diego, had done.

He yawned. The flight from California had been long, and he'd been on the road for months. Although he stilled called Costa Rica home, it was more of an honorary title at this point. With no one to go home to, and a business to tend to, he was on the road for work two-hundred-and-fifty days out of the year. The days he wasn't working he usually traveled to wherever Elena and Diego were. With her competition schedule, they met more often on the road than in their hometown.

He was just thinking about going back to the hotel to take a nap, when the photographer shouted to the entire crew, "Let's get out on the water. We only have two hours of light left."

Nacho glanced up and caught sight of the new model, inhaling quickly. A bronzed goddess was having her mahogany waves sprayed down by a makeup person, while another person was fussing with her bikini, which matched the one the earlier model had been wearing. The make-up person tried to hike the bottoms up, exposing the goddess' curvaceous cheeks just a little more. The goddess swatted the woman's hand away, and readjusted her bottoms. When the dresser attempted to push back the top of her bikini to expose the swell of her breasts, The Goddess slapped her hands away and muttered something in Portuguese that Nacho couldn't make out. The make-up person merely shrugged as though she was just doing her job.

Nacho shook his head; modeling was a strange world. He'd much rather admire a woman's abilities than just her looks. A pretty face didn't count for much where Nacho came from; he'd take a woman who ripped on the water, burned up the dance floor, and played a mean game of chess. If she could match his above-average skills in the kitchen, even better.

Dangelo approached the new model and spoke with her, pointing out towards the water.

The Goddess squinted as she looked at him, her nose wrinkling up adorably, as her ringed, smokey eyes narrowed.

There was no way Nacho was leaving the shoot now.

The Goddess and Dangelo were standing over the surfboards Nacho had brought, and he decided to take advantage of the excuse to speak to the beauty. He jogged over to where they were standing. "Can I help you pick out a board?"

She didn't meet his eyes, instead looking somewhere just to his left.

"That would be great, Nacho," Dangelo said. "This is Joaninha; Joaninha, Nacho."

What a beautiful name, he thought, wondering how it was spelled. Although Portuguese and Spanish were both romance languages, the pronunciation of the letters were so different that the resemblance was easier to see in writing than in speaking. Based on what he heard, he would have spelled her name Zwaniya or maybe Zuania. Perhaps her name had an African influence. "Nice to meet you."

Joaninha nodded.

Dangelo waved a hand at her. "Ignore her, she's pissed at me."

Unsure who to address, Nacho asked Dangelo. "Is Joaninha going to actually surf, or just paddle?"

"I can surf," Joaninha answered in a haughty tone.

Dangelo nodded. "I want as much action as possible."

Nacho pretended to study Joaninha's figure in a detached manner, as though he was sizing up an athlete, but it was taking all his control not to linger on her almond-shaped eyes with their lashes that seemed to go on forever; her lush, pillowy lips; and her full, curvy hips. She didn't have the slender toned body of an athlete like his sister, nor did she have the slightly malnourished look of the woman who had been modeling earlier. She was just right.

Dangelo cleared his throat, perhaps Nacho had been staring too long. Joaninha, however, didn't seem to have notice. She was still gazing at a point behind him.

Nacho bristled. Did she think she was too good for him?

He glanced at the size of the surf and then picked an appropriate board. "Here you go."

Joaninha took the board without meeting his eyes. "Thanks," she said, uncertainly.

"Let's go," the photographer said, guiding Joaninha towards the water by her elbow.

They stopped at the water's edge where one of the crew handed Joaninha a bar of surf wax to apply to the brand new board. She listened as Dangelo spoke, occasionally nodding as she rubbed the wax onto the board's surface.

Nacho raked a hand through his curly black hair, which was held back in a short ponytail at the nape of his neck. He crossed his arms over his chest and watched Joaninha paddle out towards the water. There was no doubt that she knew what she was doing as she glided over the azure water with long, confident strokes, her head and back arched up in a sexy curve that he longed to run his hand over.

He cursed at the way he was ogling this woman who hadn't even glanced at him. Of course, now that he had a backside glimpse of her, he wondered how he'd missed her bodacious bootie that seemed to defy gravity with its perfect half-dome. Although he'd never considered himself an ass-man before, he realized that any man who saw Joaninha's backside would be forced to reconsider.

All thoughts of the workout he'd been hoping to do faded along with the sun. Nacho couldn't tear his eyes off the goddess out in the water, whose skin and hair seemed to turn into molten gold as the sun dipped further into the horizon. He wasn't going to leave until he'd had the chance to speak with her, find out if she was single and into men, and asked her out.

Thirty minutes later Nacho was still waiting, and Joaninha still hadn't emerged from the tent. The only person who'd come out of the tent had been Dangelo's assistant, the one in the safari vest, who dashed off towards the road like she had a fire to put out.

He sighed, walked to the tent, and called inside. "Excuse me. Is anyone in there?"

A woman with long black hair and fuchsia lipstick came to the tent's entrance. Nacho recognized her as the woman who'd been dressing the models. She gave Nacho a once over and smiled wider. "*Olá*," she said, in a rich Brazilian accent.

Although Nacho didn't speak Portuguese fluently, he knew a bit, aided by its proximity to Spanish. "Is the woman who was surfing still here?"

Fuchsia Lips shook her head. "*Ela já saiu*," and dashed one hand off the other.

Nacho frowned. Although that phrase sounded nothing like Spanish, he got that The Goddess had taken off in a hurry. Nacho scanned the tent, which was crowded with mirrored vanities, black boxes of equipment, and racks of clothes. Maybe there was a back entrance he couldn't see. "Will she be back tomorrow?"

The woman nodded and Nacho thanked her.

Guess I'm coming back tomorrow after all.

When Joaninha Oliveira woke up this morning, she knew it was going to be a bad day.

But I didn't know it would be this bad.

Not only was she going to have to move again in two days, but her bike got a flat tire this morning on the way to the photo shoot, and she'd gotten grease all over hands changing it. Naturally, the grease had ended up on her shorts, one of only two pairs she owned.

And now this humiliation.

"Two more waves," Dangelo said, as Joaninha paddled up to him, bobbing in the water with his life jacket, a woman bobbing behind him holding onto his jacket, keeping him safe and pointing him in the direction he wanted to shoot.

She couldn't believe that Dangelo had talked her into filling in for the model. Had she really sunk this far in life? She wanted to be a famous architect; responsible for making the *favelas* of Rio safer and more sustainable, but here she was, wearing a bikini that barely covered her lady bits for a photoshoot for *ULTIMO* magazine.

The shame of it.

"*Cuzão* Dangelo, you really know how to push your luck," Joaninha cursed, narrowing her eyes at the photographer, who happened to be her best friend, although she detested him at the moment.

"Come on, Bug," he said, referring to her name's literal translation: ladybug. "Three months free rent and I'll pay you? I think it's more than worth it," he said, referring to the deal they'd made earlier that'd convinced Joaninha to put on this ridiculous excuse for a bathing suit and allow Dangelo to finish the day's shoot.

She hooked her finger under the suit bottom and pulled it out of her ass crack for the fiftieth time. *How do women wear these things?*

Joaninha was a firm believer in one-pieces. They allowed her to surf and swim without worrying if a boob was going to pop out of place or whether she'd lose her bottoms on a big wave.

However, when Dangelo had offered him the use of his fabulous historic home in the Cosme Velho neighborhood while he was out of town, along with paying her to take care of his Golden Retriever, Amigo, she couldn't pass it up. Not paying rent for three months was a great way to save money, plus Dangelo's neighborhood was much nicer than anything she could afford.

But she couldn't resist trying to see what else she could get from him. "I want you to pay me that model's hourly rate for these last couple of hours."

Dangelo narrowed his eyes. "Joaninha..." he growled.

"I'm sure you aren't going to pay her for them. Don't tell me her contract won't deduct this time from her. It's only fair. And you need to let me move in this Thursday." It was only three days earlier than planned, but it would make her life so much easier. She pulled out her trump card. "You better hurry up and decide, the light is fading."

Dangelo cursed, his eyes almost black with frustrated amusement. "Yes. Fine. But surf as many waves as you can before the sun dips. Now paddle your ass back out to the break."

Joaninha whooped and swiveled on the board. When she caught the final wave, she gave it her all, carving for all she was worth. When she glided into the beach, the wardrobe lady ran up to her with a big thick bathrobe. "Thanks, Alicia," Joaninha said. "Do you have my glasses?"

"Sorry, *querida*, I left them in the changing room."

Joaninha looked at the tent in the distance, which was sharper than Alicia's face, given her far-sightedness. She hated not having her glasses on, always feeling defenseless without them.

Just then, a large figure loomed in front of her. She knew instantly that this wasn't someone she knew; years of wearing glasses had trained her to identify her friends' by recognizing their gaits.

"Excuse me," a low male voice said in an accent that told her he wasn't a native Portuguese speaker.

Joaninha reached out for Alicia, and grabbed the woman's arm, pulling her towards the tent. "Sorry, I have to go." Years spent growing up on the streets of Rio had taught her to be wary of strange men.

Once they were inside the tent, Joaninha turned to Alicia. "My glasses please."

A few seconds later, Alicia placed the chunky black glasses in Joaninha's palm and she stuffed them on her face. A wave of relief washed over her as everything came into focus. She glanced at her watch and cursed; it was almost five-thirty. "I have to get going, they are expecting me at Espírito da Favela in thirty minutes," she said, referring to the non-profit she worked part-time at.

Joaninha changed into her grease-stained shorts and shirt, threw on her vest with all the pockets, tucked her still wet hair up under her baseball hat and sped out the tent door. She jogged across the beach, scampering over the boulders and up a narrow path to where a rusted-out bicycle was chained, undid the lock and started peddling, her heart racing from the exertion.

She never needed to exercise to stay in shape; her life was exercise.

When she peddled up to the short, concrete Espírito building, the sound of young voices greeted her. "¡Joaninha *está aqui!*" they shouted over one another. *"¿O que vamos aprender hoje?"* They clamored. "What are we going to learn today?"

Joaninha giggled; the nonprofit was the closest thing she had to a family, and the children's cries of appreciation the closest thing she knew to love. She bent down and widened her eyes. "Today we are going to talk about how we can harvest rain water instead of relying on city water."

The children gave her dubious looks, as though that couldn't possibly be fun.

"And then we are going to make bubble solution and blow lots of bubbles."

The kids started jumping up and down. "Yay!" they cried.

A little before nine o'clock, Joaninha quietly opened the door to the small, concrete three-bedroom that she was staying at, silently wheeling her bicycle into a corner where she'd set up a hammock. Her "room" was a small ten-foot by five-foot corner, carved out of a living room by a sheet strung up along a line. It contained all her worldly possessions: a hammock, a bike, a crate full of clothes, three pairs of shoes, a dozen books, and her toiletries.

The non-profit helped her find families that would let her stay in their living rooms for a month at a time, in exchange for minimal rent or helping around the house. Living this way was what allowed her to pay for school. If she'd had to pay real rent money, she would have needed to work longer hours at a paying job.

But in just a couple of days she'd get Dangelo's apartment for a whole three months, and he'd pay her to stay there. It had been more than worth it to put on that ridiculous bathing suit for a few hours.

She got ready for bed, and laid back in the hammock, and dreamed of the impossible luxury of having her own space, if only for a few months.

The next morning, Nacho arrived at Joatinga Beach wearing surf trunks, a tank top, and a straw lifeguard hat, prepared to stay all day until he introduced himself to The Goddess. "Joaninha," he said, softly to himself.

He stifled a yawn. Although he'd gone to bed early last night, he didn't feel much more rested than he had the day before, which was why he'd worn trunks, hoping to expend some of his excess energy out in the ocean.

His attempts at sleep had been infiltrated by fantasies about Joaninha dressed in a gold lame bikini, riding the waves on a shell like a surfing Venus. In the dreams, he was on the beach, watching her, his feet stuck in quicksand. Slowly sinking, all he could do was watch as Joaninha seemed to mock him from the waves.

Eventually he gave up trying to sleep and went to the gym of his hotel, where he worked out for almost ninety minutes. That had served to cool his libido, at least temporarily. But as soon as he'd showered and eaten breakfast, his mind had immediately begun conjuring images of the bodacious woman who'd conquered the surf yesterday and hadn't even given him a second look.

He wasn't the kind of guy who got off on being ignored; he'd never chased a woman for the sake of "the hunt."

And he wasn't a vain man. He knew that he wasn't as classically handsome as his brother-in-law, Joaquin Santos, however, between his genuine love for women—most women said he was the sweetest man they'd ever known—and his sense of humor—childlike with a hint of wit—he'd also never had any trouble with the ladies.

Besides, at thirty-four, he was in better shape than most twenty-year-olds, his six-pack still well defined, and much more eager to please. He could just imagine the pleasure The Goddess would have at the mercy of his mouth and hands.

A twitch in his trunks made him realize the danger of this train of thought. The lightweight fabric of his trunks would not conceal any physical manifestations of his desire.

He closed his eyes and took a deep breath, forcing himself to think about a long-distance chess game that he was currently engaged in with a friend back home, and the next move he'd need to make to beat him.

"Hey, Nacho. You're back," Dangelo said, in faded black jeans, black cowboy boots, and pinstripe vest—no shirt. Thick wraparound sunglasses shaded his eyes, but Nacho guessed that the photographer was mid-forties by the crinkling around his mouth, then again, that might have just been the years of partying.

Nacho had heard from his sister, who crossed Dangelo's path many times on the surf tour, that Dangelo Mesquita was a hard-living man,

Nacho grinned. "I have a free day today. No work meetings until tomorrow." He was about to ask about Joaninha, when a woman in a robe strode up trailed by the woman with fuchsia lipstick from the day before.

"This is Gevenia. She'll be our model today," Dangelo said. "Gevenia, this is the rep from Santos Surfboards, Nacho."

She was only a couple of inches shorter than Nacho with black hair that hung to the top of her breasts, and emerald-colored eyes. She reminded him of the pouty model from the day before, almost generic in her physical beauty.

Nacho gave her a slight nod followed by his usual smile. "Nice to meet you."

Gevenia's green eyes twinkled. "You too."

The girl with the baseball cap and safari vest walked up to Dangelo and handed him a large camera, pushing her thick black glasses higher up her face.

Nacho held out his hand to her. "Hi. I'm Nacho."

"Jo," she said quickly, her smokey accent curling off the single syllable.

Nacho gave her a quick glance. With her bronzed skin and amber eyes, she looked Brazilian, but her American-sounding name was anything but. Jo arched a brow, her eyes magnified by her glasses shooting him a dare. "Nice to meet you," he added.

Jo crossed her arms and made a tsking sound under her breath.

A glimmer of a smile danced on Dangelo's lips as he took in the space between Nacho and Jo, then he turned to Gevenia. "Darling, I'm not sure what you heard about yesterday, but we got some brilliant shots out in the water, and I want to get some more. Do you surf?"

A frown marred her golden forehead. Gevenia shook her head. "No, but I've always wanted to learn."

"I could teach you," Nacho offered nonchalantly.

Dangelo's head swiveled. "You can do that?"

He shrugged. "In my sleep. Elena and I have taught surf lessons our whole lives. That's how we made money as kids. We'd teach the tourists who came to town."

Dangelo turned to Gevenia. "His sister is the current world champion."

Gevenia's eyes traveled over him, reappraising. "Your sister is Elena Sol? I saw her on the cover of *Peak Fitness* last year. She's amazing."

Nacho nodded. "Yes she is. And guess who taught her to surf…"

Gevenia's eyes widened. She turned to Dangelo. "I can't promise anything, but if you want me to try, I'm game."

Dangelo clapped his hands. "Shots of you learning to surf might be even better! Let's try." He turned to Nacho. "Just pretend like we aren't here. Teach her like you would teach anyone. I'll work around you. But before we can start, you have to go get made up by Alicia." He jerked his thumb to the woman with fuchsia lips.

Nacho frowned. "Whoa, dude. I said I'd teach her to surf, I didn't say anything about being photographed doing it."

Dangelo pulled off his sunglasses and trained the same smile on him that Nacho had seen him give to the other models when he wanted to convince them to do something. He put an arm around Nacho's shoulder. "You won't even know we are here. You just teach her to surf, and I'm going to document it." Dangelo pulled Nacho a little tighter. "And I'll pay you," he added in a low seductive voice.

Nacho shrugged off the other man's arm. "I'm not one of your models, Dangelo. You don't have to snake charm me."

Dangelo chuckled. "Sorry. Habit I guess." He seemed to mentally shift gears, adjusting to his audience like a true salesman. "So are you cool?"

Back when Nacho had surfed professionally, he'd been photographed numerous times for magazines. Maybe this wouldn't be that different. "Okay. I'll do it. We'll need some surf wax once we get in the water. I don't have any, and except for the board you used yesterday, none of them have wax."

"Great. Just tell me which boards you are going to use today and I'll take some pictures of Gevenia with them while you are in wardrobe," Dangelo said.

After almost forty-minutes of being fussed over by Alicia in the makeup tent, Nacho emerged from the wardrobe tent wearing a new set of trunks—red to match Gevenia's suit—and a whole lot of oil. His body felt strange without the friction that he was used to between his limbs and torso. It was like he was gliding, his arms threatening to fly right off his body with the slick movement. Alicia had also freed his hair from its rubber band, and the thick waves kept swinging in front of his eyes, distracting him.

He did a quick scan of the area, but Joaninha was still nowhere to be seen and he'd been so preoccupied thinking about the shoot that he forgot to ask Alicia about her. Maybe it was for the best that she wasn't around. She wouldn't have to see him fumble at his first modeling assignment.

He walked over to where his quiver of boards were standing, the whole time moving like a dog with gum stuck to its paws, annoyed and self-conscious at how ridiculous he felt. He grabbed two boards, tucked them under his arms, and jogged back to where Dangelo and Gevenia were standing about twenty-feet from the waterline. He bent down, arranging the boards on the sand side-by-side.

Dangelo pulled his camera away from his eye and studied the small digital screen. "Gorgeous," he said quietly. In a louder voice he added, "You just keep doing that and this is going to be a piece of cake, Nacho. The camera loves you and your big, shiny muscles."

"Okay," Nacho said, lifting his chin at Dangelo before turning to Gevenia. "You ready to get started?"

Gevenia gave him a nod, but he could tell by her darting eyes that she was a little nervous. "Are we going into the water right now?"

Nacho shook his head, trying to ignore the phalanx of crew tightening around him and Gevenia.

Today Feather Earring's gold lame disc would be trained on him. He laughed inwardly, his heart speeding up a bit.

Focus on Gevenia, he thought, needing to concentrate on her in order to distract himself from the camera crew.

He looked up at Gevenia, focused on her emerald eyes, and gave her a reassuring smile. "No. We start on the sand. We won't go into the water until you feel ready. I promise," he said, placing a hand on his heart.

His words seemed to reassure her, and she walked closer to him.

"This is your board," he said, pointing to the larger of the two boards. "Because it's bigger than mine, it'll be easier to stand up on and balance when we are out in the water."

She nodded, her face relaxing.

"Now just watch me and copy what I do." He put his chest on the smaller board, digging his toes in the sand for balance, and gestured for Gevenia to do the same. Once she was prone on the board, Nacho lifted his upper body into the air, curling up like a cobra, and moved his arms. "This is how you paddle. Chest as high as you can get it, back lengthened, legs activated but not tense."

Gevenia studied him critically, and then copied him almost perfectly.

"Very good. That's it. The next thing you have to do is get your feet into the right position. They should be up and—" he lost his balance and slid off the board into the sand.

Gevenia giggled, a tinkling sound that washed over Nacho, making him smile.

"I forgot the boards aren't waxed yet," he said, laughing as he stared down as his sand-coated stomach. "There's no way I'll be able to stay on an unwaxed board with all this body oil. Dangelo, can we towel off some of this body oil or wax up the boards?"

The camera was still fixed to Dangelo's face. He waved his hand at Nacho. "Do whatever you need to do. Pretend I'm not here."

"I need a towel," Nacho said, to nobody in particular, although a second later, a towel was shoved into his hands. "Thanks," he said. "Jo, right?" he said to the girl in the safari vest.

She nodded and turned away.

Not much of a talker.

Nacho toweled off his chest and rubbed the surface of his board. He handed the towel to Gevenia and tried not to stare as she did the same, rubbing her oiled-up breasts, stomach, and thighs; every move executed with sphinxlike grace. She seemed to have perfect control over every tiny inch of her body. It reminded him of a ballet dancer.

While she didn't evoke the same primal sensations in him that The Goddess had yesterday, he couldn't complain about the company. There were certainly worse ways to spend the day than teaching a beautiful woman how to surf.

He laid down on the board and they continued the lesson.

Joaninha watched as Nacho reached out, took Gevenia's hand and subtly corrected the angle of it so that she would paddle more efficiently in the water. She had to admit, the man knew what he was doing. He was a thoughtful, detail-oriented teacher, and he and Gevenia were going to be gorgeous in these photos together.

And for some reason, that bugged her.

She reached into the back pocket of her shorts, pulled out a bandanna, and mopped at her brow.

For a moment, she'd been amused that he hadn't recognized her from the shoot yesterday, but then—when she saw the way his gaze licked Gevenia's curves—her pride had gotten the best of her, and she'd misled him. "Jo" was the name she gave tourists; it was easier for English speakers to pronounce—the sliding sound of the "Joa" at the beginning of her name always confused non-Portuguese speakers—and it was her way of thumbing her nose at the man who hadn't thought enough of her to even remember meeting her.

She could tell Dangelo had been amused by the misdirection.

"*Jo*, can I have my gum please?" Dangelo called to her, overemphasizing her "name".

Joaninha reached into one of the dozens of pockets on the vest she was wearing. Although it was too big for her, having once belonged to Dangelo, it was perfect for her crazy life juggling school and however many jobs she was working at the moment. She could store everything she needed in it, and she loved amazing people by always sliding her hand into exactly the right pocket to extract whatever it was she was looking for, in this case: gum. She pulled out a stick of Dangelo's requested item, unwrapped it, and handed it to him.

He turned his eye away from the camera for a moment and winked. "Thanks, *Jo*."

She scowled at him and he laughed, before turning his lens back on Nacho and Gevenia.

Dangelo Mesquita was not just her sometimes employer, he was also one of her best friends. They'd met on the streets of Rio, and he'd taken her under his wing.

"Okay, that's good for the camera. Gevenia, do you feel ready to get wet?" Dangelo asked.

She bit her lip but nodded.

Joaninha had taught enough tourists to surf—it was the side hustle to her side hustle—to see that Gevenia was going to be a natural. She was graceful, and her slenderness hid a muscular strength that hinted at athleticism.

Dangelo spoke out of the corner of his mouth as Nacho and Gevenia began heading into the water, his large SLR clicking away the whole time. "So Nacho isn't even good enough for your fake name let alone your real name," Dangelo said, the rebuke clear in his voice.

She kept her eyes on Nacho and Gevenia. "Joaninha is my real name."

He *hmphed.* "Why are you misleading him?"

She shrugged, feeling foolish that Nacho got under her skin.

Before she could answer, he continued, "You want to know why I think you're doing it, Bug?" He didn't wait for her response, but continued, "You're keeping him at arm's length. Staying emotionally distant. It's the orphanage all over again."

Joaninha didn't want to own his words. She shrugged. "I'm just messing with him."

Dangelo knew her too well to bite.

He was her oldest friend, the first kid to befriend her at the orphanage.

When her mom left her there, she wouldn't speak to anyone. As an adult, she'd been able to name the reason why: shock. She'd been so stunned to be abandoned by her mother, for months she operated in a state of disbelief, until the day when one of the kids, fed up by her silence, started picking on her.

She'd been five-years-old.

"What's your name?" The twelve-year-old boy had asked.

When she didn't answer—or even meet his gaze—he repeated the question with increasing belligerence, finally giving her a shove that sent her reeling onto her butt.

That was when Dangelo stepped in. "Back off, Manuel."

At seventeen, Dangelo was one of the oldest and tallest kids; this, combined with his air of languid self-confidence, made him a leader among the orphans.

Manuel shrugged. "I just wanted to know her name. She's been here over three months. How can we call her anything if she won't tell us her name?"

Dangelo sat on the ground beside Joaninha, who hadn't moved since falling. He lowered his voice. "Do you want to tell us your name?" Something about the kindness in his voice had cut through her grief and shock and she shook her head. "Want me to give you a name?"

She inhaled quickly. She could have a new name, a new life; start over.

She turned to meet his gaze, her eyes taking a moment to focus. She nodded.

A smile tugged at the corners of his mouth. He stroked his chin. "Joaninha," he said, simply.

Later he would tell her he chose the name because she was cute and small, like a ladybug. She'd gone by the name ever since, picking her last name, Oliveira, for herself when she came of age; choosing it because it was the last name of her favorite singer, Simone Bittencourt de Oliveira, whose soulful, throaty rendition of *Procuro Olividarte* always brought tears to her eyes. She couldn't even remember the first time she'd heard the song it was such an old memory, but a mental soundtrack of a woman crying and the sound of a banging door seemed to overlay itself whenever she heard it.

"He doesn't deserve your torment. Nacho's a nice guy," Dangelo said, snapping her back to the present.

She colored under his reproach.

Dangelo was the closest thing to a father figure she'd ever known. When he'd left Rio at twenty-five, to pursue his dream of being an internationally famous photographer, her heart broke. She didn't see him for ten years, only receiving periodic postcards from wherever he was working. His cards introduced her to foreign-sounding places like Malibu, Zanzibar, and Uluwatu.

He might as well have been on the moon as far as she was concerned.

Although he'd filled the pages of his passports in the last fourteen years, she still didn't even have one. She hadn't even been outside the city limits of Rio.

However, now that he was well established, and could afford to work anywhere, he made Rio his base and Joaninha his assistant whenever his shoots were in town. On more than one occasion he'd offered to make her his full-time assistant, but that would require keeping up with his exhausting, and unpredictable, travel schedule. Gallivanting around the globe was not conducive to her dreams of becoming an architect and helping to fix some of the systemic problems of the *favelas,* that she and Dangelo had grown up in.

She pretended to search in a pocket for something to avoid answering him.

"Bug?" he prompted, firm but gentle.

"Okay, you're right. I'm being difficult for no reason." She zipped up the pocket she'd been rooting around in a bit too forcefully, the metal teeth catching. Taking a breath, she unzipped and then rezipped it slowly, the metal teeth closing smoothly. "It bugged me that he didn't recognize me." Although she still wasn't sure why she cared.

"Mario," he said, calling over one of the crew, and handing the man his camera. "Take some pictures as they paddle out." Dangelo turned the full force of his gaze on Joaninha. "*Carinho*, I barely recognized you yesterday, and your face is the one I know best next to my own."

She should have smiled but frowned instead.

He added, "But that doesn't mean you are any less beautiful than you were yesterday. He just doesn't recognize you. I'm sure 'Jo' could win him over as well as easily as 'Joaninha', with a little effort." Chucking her under her chin he added, "You're always hiding under all this," he waved his arm up and down her body.

She pushed her glasses back up the bridge of her nose and tugged on the edge of her safari vest, suddenly self-conscious.

Her hat, glasses, and baggy clothes were her armor, shielding her gender and diminutive size as she biked around the streets of Rio at all hours of the day and night. "It's functional and you know I can't spend money on clothes anyway."

"Ah. You reminded me," Dangelo said, as he reached into his jeans pocket and pulled out a wad of bills. "Here's your payment for modeling yesterday." He counted out four-thousand reals in paper money and handed it to her.

Her eyes widened. "What?"

It was enough money for three months' rent on a one-bedroom apartment, if she had one. It would have taken her two months to make the same amount of money between her four-ish jobs.

"Models get paid this much for a day's work?" her voice tight and angry.

Dangelo shook his head. "Models get paid twice this amount. You only worked half a day, remember?"

She didn't need to look up to know that he was giving her a self-satisfied look. He'd asked her to model for him before, and she'd always refused.

He'd never mentioned the money.

"Why didn't you tell me?" she said, feeling a bit breathless.

He put a hand on her shoulder. "You never asked, you stubborn, little thing."

If she did some more modeling she wouldn't need to take tourists surfing or pick up shifts at a local restaurant. She could finish school sooner and spend more time at Espírito, maybe even get a non-paying internship with an architect. "I'll do it."

"Do what?" Dangelo said, playing dumb.

She sighed, struggling to hold her excitement in check. "Modeling. Let me model some more. Please, Dangelo, please." Perspiration broke out along the top of her forehead. Breaking the paycheck-to-paycheck cycle she was stuck in was so close, she could taste it.

"Well...I didn't say I *need* you to model anymore this time..." he drew his words out languidly, like a cat playing with a mouse.

She smacked him on the shoulder. "Stop teasing me!"

Dangelo chuckled. "To tell you the truth, I was hoping you'd say that. The pictures of you yesterday were phenomenal. I'd love to get you back in front of the camera. Tomorrow?"

She brightened. "Yes. Absolutely."

Early the next day, Dangelo picked Joaninha up from where she was staying on the outskirts of Rio's largest, and some said safest, *favela,* Rocinha. Even though Dangelo was now a city dweller, or "of the asphalt", living with all the services a citizen would expect from its city, Joaninha was still "of the hill", choosing to stay in the *favelas* that she had grown up in and developed a love/hate relationship with, and yet, couldn't seem to leave.

It was almost eight a.m., and Rocinha was bustling with middle class activity; families walking to and from businesses including banks, restaurants, and a cable television station. Others were on their way to work or to drop off their kids at kindergarten and perhaps head to the local samba school.

Although Rocinha was quiet today, she was a mercurial mistress. Rocinha was controlled by a drug cartel called Amigos dos Amigos or ADA. Ironically, things were safest when a strong leader was in charge of ADA; it was during the "transition periods" when violence was prone to breaking out. That was when warring factions fought for the leadership position, and the gun fighting in the street lasted from dawn to dusk, young men patrolling the narrow, warren-like community with automatic weapons.

It was those days when Joaninha would bike to Dangelo's place in Cosme Velho, no matter how long it took her, and stay with him until she could find a place to stay that was safer. However, since Espírito was located in Rocinha, she always came back.

She threw her meager belongings—two small plastic crates of clothing, her schoolbooks, and a handful of toiletries along with her hammock and her bike—into his SUV. She was looking forward to moving into his place. Her one-month stay with this most recent family was ending today, and she didn't like to overstay her welcome by even a few hours.

Better to be the guest who left early than the one who stayed too long.

Dangelo removed his sunglasses. "You know," he said, taking a hard look around the graffiti-filled walls. "The offer still stands for you to live with me full-time, Bug."

Even though he was now "of the asphalt" he still looked comfortable in the hills, however, Joaninha noted that he had brought his beat-up, inconspicuous car to pick her up.

She closed the passenger door and sighed as Dangelo pulled out of the narrow, windy road.

This was a conversation they had at least twice a year. "You know I can't do that," she said, even though there were days when she wondered if that was still true. She was no longer a kid, and although thoughts of settling down or having kids of her own were not on the horizon, she also knew that she would never raise a child in the *favela*. She would rather be childless than live in fear for a child's life.

Dangelo slid his sunglasses back into place. "I know."

They wound down the hillside heading south, away from Rio's city center, back towards Joatinga Beach, which was so serenely beautiful, it was hard to believe it was less than fifteen minutes away from the hard life of Rocinha.

When they arrived at the beach, it was empty except for their tents and the two dozen security guards who had been hired to watch the gear overnight.

"I asked Alicia to come early. She's waiting for you in the wardrobe tent. You can have some time to get yourself ready," he said, pointing to his head, "Before the rest of the crew arrive."

She shot him a grateful smile at the thoughtful gesture. He knew she was nervous. "Thanks."

"You have your contact lenses, right?" He leveled a finger at her.

She made a face. He'd gotten them for her as a birthday present a few years back, but she only wore them when she was surfing. "Yes. I have them."

"Good." He started to walk away but turned back. "You were really great the other day. I'd like to try some new stuff today and I hope you'll have an open mind."

Yesterday Dangelo had said that if she was willing to model for him, he'd completely change the concept of the shoot and need her the next three days. She'd already taken the days off from Espírito to work as his assistant, so it was easy to say yes.

"For what you're paying me? You can count on it," she said, already planning what to do with the riches she'd be earning.

Dangelo gave her a strange look, like he was going to say something else, but then turned and walked into his tent.

Nacho arrived early at Joatinga, made his way down the steep and narrow path to the beach, and headed straight to Dangelo's tent, just as the other man had asked.

He hoped Joaninha would be at the shoot today. Although Gevenia had been a nice woman, it was the image of Joaninha ripping on the waves, bronze curls flying that was keeping him up at night. He'd decided last night that if she didn't show today, he'd ask Dangelo how to find her.

Walking through the tent flaps, he greeted Dangelo, "Hey man."

Dangelo looked up from the camera lens he was inspecting. "Nacho! Hey, you made it early. Good. There's something I want to talk to you about."

Nacho frowned at the serious tone, but sat in the director's chair Dangelo was pointing at.

Dangelo put his camera down and sighed. "Today I want to shoot you with Joaninha…"

Nacho's heart seemed to be in his gut. "What?"

"Is that a problem?"

"Yes. I mean no. No. It's not a problem," he said, rubbing his suddenly sweaty hands on his cargo shorts.

"Good. I just wanted to give you a heads up. Monday was her first day modeling, and she's a bit skittish, so I just wanted to warn you," Dangelo said nonchalantly.

Skittish? "Okay. Thanks for the warning. But what do you have planned? She's already an excellent surfer; she doesn't need any teaching."

Dangelo gave Nacho an inscrutable look. "Oh don't worry. I have something in mind."

Joaninha looked in the mirror, her mouth agape, barely recognizing herself.

Her curly hair had been teased so that it was three times its regular size, a halo of bronze and gold held back by a headband-cum-crown shaped out of gold triangles surrounding her face like the corona of the sun.

She was wearing a gold one piece that felt more revealing than a bikini, with large triangular cutouts on either side of her torso and a large gold ring holding the top and bottom together that centered on her belly button. A thick gold cuff wound up one bicep like a snake, and her body had been covered in elaborate gold stenciling that looked almost like body jewelry and alternately like tribal markings. Triangular webs of gold chain covered her hands and feet—jangling merrily while she walked—attached by small loops of elastic that slid over her middle finger and big toe and then secured around her wrist and ankle.

She was striking.

"*Nossa Senhora*," she said quietly, transfixed by the other-worldly being depicted in the mirror. She'd never seen anything like it.

"Do you like it?" Alicia said, her eyes bright with excitement.

Like it? Does one "like it" when they've been transformed into an impossibly gorgeous vision that defied imagination? "Alicia. It's stunning."

Alicia made a face. "*You're* stunning, Joaninha."

"Me?" But this wasn't her. This mirage in the mirror was certainly not her. And yet, when she moved her lips, the mirage followed.

She turned away from the reflection, it was simply too much for her brain to compute.

"How did you—" Joaninha started to say.

"Three hours of hair and make-up, *carinho*. I can turn anyone into anything, given enough time and resources." Alicia gave her a self-satisfied smile.

Joaninha nodded. "You're an artist."

Alicia's smile traveled to her eyes and she leaned forward, air-kissing Joaninha's cheeks three times. "Thank you. That means a lot." She glanced at her watch. "Dangelo is probably ready for you on set."

"On set?"

Alicia smiled. "Oh yes. Dangelo has completely reimagined this shoot. I think you'll be very surprised when you get outside."

When Joaninha exited the tent, she sucked in a breath.

Diaphanous white sheets had been rigged overhead and were rustling gently behind an assortment of straw mats and ivory-colored pillows that had been arranged on the sand. On top of the straw mats were three large, white plastic props, each about three-feet tall: a cube, a cone, and a sphere, that had been spaced apart from each other. An assortment of potted plants dotted the space, their vibrant greens a stark contrast to the surrounding white. The overall effect was of a room in the middle of the beach. Behind everything, the sparkling turquoise of the ocean shimmered.

It was stunning.

Dangelo walked up to her, his eyes, merry. "You look amazing, Bug. Do you like it?"

Her mouth agape, she raised her brows. "The set is…fantastic." She had more to say, more praise to effuse, and yet, words seemed to fail her.

Dangelo chuckled. "I wasn't talking about the set; I was talking about your hair and make-up. Do you like it?"

"What? Oh," she looked down at her feet and hands, the golden webs reminding her that she wasn't wearing her baseball cap and safari vest like usual. She shook her head. "I can't get over it. I didn't recognize myself at all when I looked in the mirror."

Dangelo smiled. "The magic of make-up and wardrobe. You know, the models I work with? None of them looks like the pictures in the magazines when they walk into the make-up tent in the morning. It's all an illusion, Bug. This thing I do," he gestured to the set and to her, "It's just dress-up. Make believe. I want you to use that to your advantage today."

She wrinkled up her nose. "What do you mean?"

"I want you to play pretend. Like we would do in the orphanage. Remember how you would pretend that I was your dad, and you would tell me what our house looked like, and all the toys you had? You would describe everything down to the last detail, and it was like we were really there."

Playing pretend had been a way to leave the orphanage, at least with her mind. She got to imagine that she had a father, something she'd never had in real life. It had been her refuge, her escape.

She nodded. "Okay. So what am I pretending?"

Dangelo's eyes brightened. "You're a goddess. The sun goddess. You've come to spend the day on the beaches and ocean that you grace with your loving gaze. Think of yourself as an extension of the sun. One of the sun's rays that has landed on earth, except today you are going to experience the earth, not just land on it."

"Experience it? How?"

"By falling in love with a human."

She frowned.

He continued. "A human man, who will start out wearing white trunks, just like the rest of the surroundings, but will progressively transform throughout the shoot until he looks a bit like you. Every scene he'll have to go back to wardrobe to change his trunks and get a bit of make-up. But the story of the shoot is that you and he are falling in love and by the end of it, you turn him into a ray of sun so he can join you. We'll place the surfboards in the frame of the shot, so we capture them too. At the end of the day, before the sun sets, you and your love will be on the waves. Since we'll be shooting during the Golden Hour, I imagine that the entire shot is just going to be a glorious glow of gold," he said, gazing out towards the ocean, clearly seeing the vision in his mind's eye.

"It sounds amazing, beautiful even." It even sounded doable to her. She could pretend to be the sun—that part would be easy, and fun—and although she had never been in love before, she could certainly pretend to *like* a man, and hopefully, that would be enough. "I'll do my best."

Dangelo smiled, moved as if to hug her, but then backed away saying "make-up" under his breath as a reminder. He clapped his hands together. "Great, this is really going to be great. This might be the best thing I've ever come up with and it's all because of you, *carinho*. Now we just have to execute my vision."

She wasn't sure how she had influenced his vision, but she nodded. "Okay. Where is this love interest?"

A contrite look passed over Dangelo's face, but before Joaninha could consider it further, a low voice called from behind her. "I'm ready."

She stiffened.

What had Dangelo done?

She turned slowly and came face-to-face with the man who hadn't remembered her. Although she remembered his name, she refused to acknowledge it, her ego still bruised by the fact that he hadn't recognized her.

She thought of all the money Dangelo was paying her and forced a smile on her face as she stuck out her hand. "Joaninha."

"Yes. We met on Monday. I'm Nacho, the rep for Santos Surfboards."

She arched a brow. She had to say one thing for Nacho, he was humble. He was the brother and brother-in-law of two superstars of the surfing world and yet, he never mentioned anything about it, referring to himself simply as "a rep." However, although "Jo" knew who he was, "Joaninha" did not, and she wasn't about to admit they were one in the same.

Let him figure it out for himself.

On the other hand, she also wasn't going to purposefully mislead him. That would be the same thing as lying, and she hated liars.

So instead, she opted to neither affirm not deny that she already knew who he was, and changed the subject. "I liked the board I rode on Monday. It was fast and nimble."

Nacho brightened. "That's Elena's favorite board in our new line. She likes a lot of rocker so she can really carve up the waves."

Joaninha couldn't help but be pleased that she had picked Elena's favorite board; it made her feel like she had something in common with the world champion, as though they might agree on many things in life since they liked the same kind of board.

She knew it was a silly thought, but she liked it anyway.

"Let's get started," Dangelo said, motioning for them to step onto the set. "I'd like for you to start with Nacho reclining on the mats and pillows like you are sunbathing and Joaninha, I want you to hover over him like you are the sun, purposefully shedding your warmth on him."

He turned to one of his crew and said, "Mario, once Nacho is situated, can you bring in the first board and put it behind him. Yes, that's it. Maybe angle it a little bit higher. Yes, that's perfect. Now Nacho, lay back as though you are completely unaware that Joaninha is paying any attention to you. You've just gotten off the waves, you're tired, and you're just soaking up some rays. That's it. Good. Yes, the sunglasses look great. I'm going to start shooting, just listen to my direction." Dangelo started clicking away, his camera fixed to his face.

"Try putting an arm behind your head, Nacho, and propping your upper body up a tiny bit. That's it. I know you are lying down, but can you flex your abs a bit more so we see the definition. There we go. That's perfect."

Although at first Nacho had seemed a little self-conscious, once Dangelo started directing him, he was too busy trying to follow instructions to be aware of himself. Joaninha knew Dangelo sometimes did that to get models out of their head. It seemed to be working for Nacho, who looked every bit the tired, laid-back surfer simply getting some sun. From her vantage point above him, it was impossible not to notice the way his muscles bulge. There didn't seem to be a muscle on him that wasn't shapely and well defined, and she took advantage of the fact that it was her job to stare at him all while trying to keep her face neutral.

"Now Joaninha," Dangelo said, turning his attention to her. "I want you to extend your arms and wave them in Nacho's directions like sun rays. Yes, that's great. Can you exaggerate the wave so I can see more of the bending in the shots? Maybe try waving them more vertically than horizontally. Yes, perfect, that's it. Now slowly walk towards him, very slowly, all while waving. Yes, great. That's beautiful. As you get closer, I want you to soften your face, as though you are suddenly noticing something interesting. Perhaps you find his face to be kind, or handsome, or intriguing. Or maybe it's his amazing six-pack."

For a split second, Joaninha was shocked at the fact that Dangelo was telling her to check Nacho out. However, she knew enough about photography to know that it would be impossible for her to feel that emotion without it showing on her face and therefore ruining his shots. She forced herself to stop thinking about Dangelo's direction and really be the sun, allowing herself to embody the vision he had so that the shoot would be a success.

So she took Dangelo's words to heart and really looked at Nacho, allowing her eyes to travel over his smooth bronze skin, the sprinkling of dark hairs on his chest looked inviting enough to touch. She imagined what it would feel like to run her hands over his broad chest, so firm and sculpted. She admired the deep curves of his abdomen, the deep lines delineating each muscle like rivulets carved into stone by running water.

As she had these thoughts, her heart began beating faster and her throat felt like it was tightening, causing her to breathe in short, shallow bursts; her chest heaving with the effort.

What's wrong with me? she thought, allowing a tiny part of her brain to observe herself, while focusing the majority of her attention on the instructions Dangelo kept volleying at her and Nacho, "Bigger eyes, Joaninha. Part your lips just a bit. Tilt your head as though in wonder. Kneel beside him and hover your hands just above his skin, but don't touch him."

She wondered at the strange sensations running through her body; her skin felt like it was prickling and tingling, hot and cold, flushing then puckering. She seemed to have lost all control over her breath, and was panting in short, hard bursts. This was not normal. However, she also recognized that she didn't feel unwell, in fact, there was something almost exciting about what was happening to her. The foreign sensations actually felt good...in a way.

It was all very confusing. She'd have to ask Dangelo about it.

She was now kneeling just a few inches away from Nacho—who was still reclining, sunglasses on, seemingly unaware of Joaninha's presence—her finger tips just an inch above his skin.

It felt like there was a tingling of electricity pulsing under her fingers as she slowly swept her hands over his chest and abdomen. She'd never wanted to touch anyone or anything so badly in her entire life. It was actually requiring some effort to keep herself from brushing against his smooth, oiled skin.

"Great. That was great," Dangelo said, then turned to the crew and raised his voice. "Scene change." He walked over to Joaninha and offered her his hand. "You were great, Bug, really great," he said as he helped her to standing.

She fluttered her eyelids, surprised at how absorbed she'd been in the fantasy.

Dangelo was searching her eyes, his own widening when she met his gaze. He dropped his voice, "How are you doing?"

She tried to speak but found she was parched. She licked her lips a few times and nodded. "I'm fine. Yeah. Good," she added, wondering why she was babbling. She'd always been a very concise speaker.

Dangelo squeezed her shoulder. "Have a seat in the shade." He then extended a hand to Nacho, who jumped up at the exact same moment. "Go change your trucks. Alicia knows what to do."

Nacho nodded and jogged off, his tan muscles rippling with the effort.

Dangelo then started barking orders at the rest of the crew who adjusted the scene slightly; adding and subtracting tiny details while the general equation of the set stayed the same. All it needed were its main variables now: Joaninha and Nacho.

Once Nacho returned—in identical trunks as before although the bottom cuff had been painted with just a hint of gold as had his feet and ankles—Dangelo asked them to return to the exact positions they'd been in before.

"This is the scene where Nacho's character, let's refer to him as 'The Surfer,' this is where The Surfer finally becomes aware of Joaninha's, let's call her 'The Sun,' her physical presence. The Sun is going to extend her fingers and touch The Surfer on the shoulder. When The Surfer feels that initial touch, I want his face to go from completely unawareness of The Sun's presence, to sudden shock that there's a person standing in front of him. It's like she's suddenly appeared out of thin air. Then I want The Sun to run her warm fingers—remember, think of your hands like sun rays—I want you to run your rays down his arm and then when you reach his hand, I want The Surfer to half sit-up and grab her hand, like you're afraid she'll disappear if you don't grab her. Got it?"

Nacho's face had returned to its usual earnest appearance, and Joaninha saw as his throat bobbed with a nervous swallow, her heart doing that funny, fast-beating thing again.

She tried to take a breath to slow her heart to normal, but found that once again, she didn't seem to be in control of herself.

"Surfer," Dangelo called, looking at Nacho. "When you reach her hand, you are going to be in a kind of jack-knife position. I want you to really squeeze your abs and flex your arms so we have all your gorgeous muscles popping out all over the place, okay?"

Nacho nodded, slipping his sunglasses back on and with it the appearance of non-awareness that he had for Joaninha. She didn't know why, but for some reason this made her sad.

Dangelo lifted his camera to his face. "Okay, Sun, do your thing. I want you to have a look of intense curiosity on your face. For some reason, you're drawn to The Surfer the way you've never been drawn to a human before, and this confuses you."

Joaninha didn't have to do anything to get into character this time; she knew exactly how The Sun was feeling. She extended her hands towards Nacho's skin, the tingling under her fingertips immediately returning. For a few moments, she just hovered there, wondering at the strange sensation as it traveled up her fingers, through her hands, and began ascending up her arms. She wiggled her fingers, arching and contracting them, but the sensation didn't dissipate, but strengthened.

"That's great, Sun, now slowly, hesitantly, reach forward and brush your fingers against his skin. If you can, I want you to be surprised by it. You're touching human flesh for the first time."

Again, Joaninha didn't need to pretend.

It felt like time stood still, and minutes passed as her fingers traveled millimeter by millimeter on a collision course with Nacho's shoulder.

She never imagined that the first time she'd purposely touched a man, would be like this, however, there was something wonderful about it because the situation removed any uncertainty or embarrassment from the equation. Joaninha was simply an actor, being directed by Dangelo, nothing more, nothing less.

And yet, it was *so* much more.

The tingling intensified as she drew nearer and at the moment when she was about to touch him, she hesitated, drawing back by a millimeter before taking a deep breath and plunging forward.

Contact.

She gasped, a stuttered breath erupting from her chest.

Her eyes flitted to Nacho's, which were hidden behind sunglasses, however, she felt like she was looking in a mirror, his mouth the same shape as hers.

Her fingers heated at the touch of his warmth, but then continued to grow warmer, that same warmth now replacing the tingling and moving up her fingers, hands, and arms until it reached her cheeks. She felt her face, neck, and scalp, flush at the contact.

She wanted to feel more.

She slowly dragged her fingers down the ridges of his arms, zig-zagging from side to side, not wanting to miss a single inch of his flesh. She watched her fingers as they moved, and became disconnected from her body again. Were these really her hands touching him? Her fingers looked familiar and foreign at the same time. She'd never seen them touch a person in this way and there was something mesmerizing about it.

So engrossed had she become in observing herself, that when Nacho reached out and interlaced his fingers with hers, she startled, her free hand flying to her chest.

"Yes, yes, yes," Dangelo cried. "That's perfect."

Her eyes flew to Nacho's face, finding that he'd removed his sunglasses with his other hand, and his eyes were now searching hers, as though trying to figure out what words were written on her heart.

She felt her breathing become shallow again, literally felt it, her hand feeling the short, rapid rise and fall of her chest.

Nacho was still studying her, his expression worshipful.

He's good at pretending. A bereft sensation flitted across her heart knowing that he'd never look at "Jo" that way.

"That's it. We got it. Perfect. You two are amazing." Dangelo looked around and shouted, "Scene change."

Joaninha blinked rapidly, coming back to reality.

She stood, pulling Nacho with her as she did.

When he rose, he was close to her, their bare skin separated by mere inches.

His chest seemed to be heaving too, but why?

When she looked into Nacho's face, his eyes were flitting around her face, as though he was taking in everything he saw.

Just then, Dangelo clapped his hand on Nacho's back. "Wardrobe change."

Nacho blinked rapidly and then gave the smallest nod, turned on his heel, and walked away.

Again, Joaninha was left with the strangest sense of loss.

They continued through a few more scenes, the ombré of gold on Nacho's trunks and body, increasing as the shoot progressed, like he was becoming infected by The Sun. Sometimes they'd lean against the large geometric shapes, using the props as things to be sat on, or kicked, or contemplated, all with the feel of playful exploration. A surfboard always hovered in the background somewhere.

They did a scene where they picnicked, taking turns feeding each other bits of fruit and nuts, and then another where they did a bit of dancing, Nacho's hands on her hips as though teaching her the concept of samba. The moment when her back brushed against his bare chest, her skin had exploded in delicious pinpricks, and a warm heat had unfurled in her belly.

Her whole body thrummed with a sort of nervous, excited energy she'd never known.

There were long stretches of the day when Dangelo said nothing, and it really felt like they were living the scene; The Sun and The Surfer, spending an impossibly beautiful day together. She laughed and giggled, enjoyed being fed by Nacho, and dancing with him. It was like being part of a waking dream, the way Nacho looked at her causing her to feel like she might catch on fire from the inside out.

As the day wore on, a tiny grain of an idea began to form in the back of her head, trying to remind her to keep her wits about her; this was an illusion, just a beautiful fantasy. But she was enjoying herself too much to pay the sensible side of her brain much attention. She'd lived with her wits about her—her survival instinct on high alert—her entire life. She didn't want to miss a single moment of this dream so that she could replay it every day for the rest of her life in perfect clarity.

"Just one more scene before we get in the water," Dangelo said.

The hour was late, the Golden Hour would soon be approaching, and Joaninha knew that it was important for them to be on the water at that time, because out on the ocean, Dangelo had no control over lighting the way he did here on land. He couldn't bounce golden light with a disc out on the waves; he needed the sun to do that for him.

Nacho went to change, and this time, when he returned—all but the very tip of his waistband was gold, and the paint on his skin had reached almost to his elbow, with just a hint of striping on his chest and neck foretelling his complete transformation into a sun ray—he reached out and took hold of Joaninha's hand.

It felt like coming home.

They'd been holding hands a lot for the last two scenes and somehow, it felt completely natural. It felt stranger when they weren't touching than when they were, as though there was something familiar or complementary in their physical proximity.

Dangelo approached them, the look on his face alerting Joaninha to the fact that he was about to ask them to do something different. "So," he said, clapping his hands together, the single syllable hung ominously in the air.

The hair on the back of her neck stood up, and she and Nacho gave each other uncertain looks.

"Okay. Look. I'll be straight with you," Dangelo said, running a hand over his hair. "I wasn't going to ask you to do this, but you are getting along so well," he said, pointing to their married hands. "And the way you relate to each other has been so natural and spontaneous. I was wondering if we might take things a bit further than I had originally planned.

Joaninha frowned.

Dangelo took a deep breath. "I'd like to take you over to the large boulders and just have you hold each other. I want to frame the beach and ocean behind you with your bodies."

Joaninha thought she saw a bit of color in Dangelo's cheeks.

"Basically I just want you to be embracing the whole time, running your hands through each other's hair, gazing into each other's faces, running your hands up and down each other's arms. As though you are trying to memorize one another."

That wonderful buzzing of her skin began again, and she felt her nipples tightening. It was so strange how something like that could feel so good.

"Then, if it feels right, I'd like for you to kiss," Dangelo said, as blasé as if he'd just commented on the weather.

Joaninha turned to look at Nacho, then Dangelo, then back at Nacho, her heart thumping out a loud staccato.

Nacho raised his palms. "Whatever Joaninha is comfortable with…"

Joaninha was at a complete loss for words, which might have been a first for her.

Dangelo raised his hands to her, as though calming a skittish horse. "Look, if it happens, great. If not, you can just lean your foreheads together and have your noses touch. I'm sure that will be lovely, okay?"

Joaninha nodded, words still failing her.

"Walk over to where Mario is, he's laid out some pebbles as marks for your feet," Dangelo said.

Nacho gave Joaninha a reassuring smile as they walked. "It's no big deal if we don't kiss. Don't worry about it." He squeezed her hand.

She took a breath, not realizing that she'd been holding it since Dangelo said the word "kiss".

Kiss Nacho?

The truth was, she wanted nothing more than to kiss him; to feel his mouth on hers, his full lips requesting permission to taste, suck, and lick her. She couldn't imagine anything better. However, she was also anxious about the prospect.

She'd never kissed a *man* before, and the couple of pubescent fumblings that she'd experienced had turned her off so badly, she'd avoided men all through her hormone-filled years.

Then she became an adult and had to fend for herself. That took up so much time that there was nothing left for dating, and the androgynous look she'd cultivated over the years helped ensure that men paid her no attention.

What if I'm a bad kisser? What if Nacho doesn't like the way I kiss? The thought of him being turned off by her inexperience was more disconcerting than the idea of kissing him.

What should I do?

By the time all of this had run through her head, she was standing near the pebbles that marked her location and Alicia was doing some last minute arranging and fussing of her and Nacho's make-up and attire—what little of it there was.

Nacho was staring into her eyes as though the most fascinating movie he'd ever seen was reflected in them. "Are you ready?"

She nodded, a lump in her throat.

"Don't think about anything. If it happens, it happens." He took her other hand in his and gave their fists a reassuring shake. "We are in this together."

She nodded. "Together."

She didn't think there was a more beautiful word in the whole world. Somehow, Nacho had found the one thing that she craved more than anything, belonging. By planting himself firmly on her side, he instantly swept away all of her fear and uncertainty.

They were in this, *together*.

"Wonderful, beautiful, you look amazing. This is going to be fantastic," Dangelo said. "Whenever you are ready…"

Nacho smiled, looked at their hands, and then raised them to his mouth and placed a kiss on each knuckle.

Joaninha's eyes widened and she sucked in a breath.

His lips had parted just the tiniest bit, leaving a warm, wet path in their wake.

Her legs felt weak.

"Touch me," Nacho whispered, his lips barely moving as he placed his last kiss.

Oh right! She'd been so entranced by his ministrations, she'd forgotten she was also supposed to move. She took a hand and raised it to his cheek, brushing back a lock of thick curls, enjoying the feeling of it springing under her fingers. She smiled.

"I love your smile," Nacho said, pulling her hands to his chest.

"You do?"

He nodded, bringing a finger to her mouth and tracing her lips. "It's so innocent. It's not the overly practiced smile of most models."

If you only knew how right you were. "I like your smile too."

He smiled big. "Really? Why?"

"Because it's so gentle."

She'd never met a man like Nacho before, so laid back, so kind, so powerfully built. It was like nothing bothered him, and he knew everything would work out. It was an attractive orbit to circle in. She'd always felt like everything was wrong, and nothing would work out.

He ran his hand down her cheek, along her neck, and over her shoulder, as Joaninha closed her eyes, her head lolling to the side as his caresses vibrated through her body, clicking on switches she hadn't known she posessed.

"*Nossa Senhora*," she half-moaned, completely oblivious to everyone and everything but Nacho and the feelings he was creating in her.

He pulled her closer, taking her wrists and placing her arms around his neck before he encircled her waist with his strong arms. "Can I kiss you now?" he whispered. "Goddess…"

Without thinking she nodded at him, and before she knew it, his warm lips pressed against hers, hesitantly, gently, the barest pressure possible.

She leaned forward instinctively and tightened her arms, wanting to be closer and deepening their kiss. The entire front of her body was an explosion of bells and fire and tingling heat as it came into contact with his, the edges between them blurring as his heat became her own and she melted into him.

But it wasn't enough, she wanted to open herself to him and take him in whole, but she didn't know how. Instinctively, she parted her lips and offered her tongue, and he took it, sweetly, slowly, lacing his own with hers.

For a few delicious seconds they were the only two people in the world, Adam and Eve, man and woman, yin and yang. She wanted the moment to go on forever—

"Great, I think we got it," Dangelo's voice cut through their passion like a bucket of cold water.

Joaninha went rigid, realization that she'd been kissing Nacho in front of the entire crew, suddenly dawning.

Nacho pulled away slowly, reluctantly. His fingers released her, he took a step back, cool air racing to fill the void he'd created.

Joaninha's heart panged at the separation.

The waking dream was over.

If you'd like to read Nacho and Joaninha's story, subscribe to SmartURL.it/BECKONEDfan
Their story, titled "BEYOND BECKONED: Roaring in Rio", will come out late 2019

Nacho is an important secondary character in the BECKONED series appearing in parts 5 & 6. To read it now, go to SmartURL.it/AmazonAviva

A Thousand Dreams

Soundtrack: Mozart Lullaby Turkish March – Relaxing Sounds of Nature (Start near end at "I'm sorry I've been such a git" line)

Two years after BECKONED, Part 6: Adrift in New Zealand

It was almost six a.m. and Conrad Jameson was finishing his morning workout with some twisting planks; holding the position on one hand until his abs burned and his arms felt like they might give out.

Forty-six, forty-seven, forty-eight, he counted in his head, before switching to the other side.

Usually he could hold it for much longer, but this last week he'd been working out twice a day, trying to numb himself with physical exhaustion.

He was just about to switch back to the other side when his work mobile rang.

As the London-based head of security for one of Europe's wealthiest families, Conrad was never really off the clock, which suited him fine. He liked to work, to obsess about details that most people never thought about, such as how many points of ingress and egress a building had. He'd discovered a knack for this kind of obsessing as a young man in the military, and even though he'd been doing it for almost thirty-five years, he still found it stimulating.

He noticed the caller's name on the screen of his mobile and smiled. "Soren, my boy. How are you doing?" He immediately stood up, grabbed a towel, and mopped his sweaty face; his mood lifting considerably.

"Conrad! I'm doing great—" Soren was cut off by the sound of a small voice saying "Papa".

Conrad's heart clenched. Although he'd never had children of his own, the man on the phone was a close approximation, and the child's voice affected him like a grandchild's might.

Rustling could be heard on Soren's end of the line, and then a loud intake of breath, as though Soren had picked up something—or someone—heavy. He began speaking again, only this time his voice had a stammer in it, as though he was bouncing as he spoke. "I should say that *we* are doing fine. KJ has started talking and I don't think I've ever been prouder. Even the time I bottled my first vintage here at the vineyard wasn't as exciting as my daughter speaking."

Conrad guzzled a liter of water in one go before saying, "You're a natural father, Soren. It makes me happy to hear that you're thriving," he said, noticing that it was the first time he'd felt this light in months. "To what do I owe the honor of this call?" Conrad asked. Although he and Soren saw each other quarterly—when his family traveled to London for board meetings—they rarely spoke during the months in-between. Soren had been in London less than a month ago for the last meeting, so there must be some other reason.

"Yes, well, I was hoping you could come to New Zealand. Celina and I are looking at some properties for potential wind and solar farms, and we wanted your expertise on security. Since we'll be selling the energy to the government, security is a higher priority on these projects than usual."

Conrad pursed his lips. The Lund Family had never asked him to consult in this manner before. His specialty was on keeping people safe, not property.

As though sensing his hesitance, Soren pressed. "Besides, you said you'd come down here when I saw you last. To meet KJ, remember? And I know Angela would love to see you."

Conrad's lips twitched up. The thought of going to New Zealand, and seeing Soren's young family, was too enticing to turn down. His London team was a well-oiled machine with nothing to do until the next board meeting; he wouldn't be missed. "I'll be there. When do you want me?"

"The sooner the better. Celina is already here, and we can tour the properties tomorrow if you like."

Conrad chuckled. "How about the day after? It's not a short trip getting to you, you know."

"Wonderful. Text me your details and I'll send someone to pick you up from the airport. See you soon," Soren said, hanging up the phone after Conrad said his goodbyes.

Soren switched his dark-haired daughter to his other hip, bouncing her as he walked, her dark curls bobbing to the rhythm as she smiled a toothy grin at him.

He crossed out of the library, across the tiled floor of the entryway, over to where the kitchen was located, led by the delicious smells wafting from there.

Opening the door to the kitchen, he smiled at his wife, whose long dark hair was in a messy braid hanging over one shoulder. Walking up to her, he placed a kiss on her neck and hugged her tight, extreme gratitude welling up in his heart.

Although Soren Lund was many things, ungrateful was not one of them.

Angela turned, flashing him her luminous smile, the same one their baby daughter KJ had. "Is he coming?"

Soren arched a brow and nodded. "He is. Are you sure about this?"

Angela shrugged. "Sure? I don't know if I'd use that word. Let's just say it's a hunch."

He'd known his wife long enough to trust her intuition. "Well, at the very least he'll be getting a nice vacation. I don't think he's taken one since our wedding, and that was over two years ago."

Angela frowned. "It'll be good for him." She wiped her hands on a kitchen towel, and looked at him with sparkling hazel eyes. "Dinner's ready. Why don't you go fetch Celina from the garden? Maybe you can convince her to pick-up Conrad at the airport." She arched a brow.

Soren narrowed his eyes. "I see you have me doing all of your dirty work, woman," he said lowly, giving her a playful swat on her ass.

Angela giggled. "Well, it would be rather suspicious if I invited Conrad to visit and told Celina to pick him up…"

"I guess you're right," Soren said, turning his attention to KJ. "Shall we go get Aunty Celina?"

KJ clapped her hands together in delight, her fat, rosy cheeks, luminous.

Soren walked with KJ to the other end of the kitchen to a door that opened directly onto a small cooking garden, planted with herbs, tomatoes, and lettuces. Soren's eyes surveyed the landscaped area beyond, his eyes sweeping over the formal rose garden, an allée of fruit trees that led to the pool, and finally landing on his sister's blond bob—its straw color so like his own—sitting on a stone bench in front of a tall fountain near some geometrically trimmed hedges.

She was sitting as rigid as if she were made of stone.

Soren carried KJ over to where Celina was sitting and the toddler called, "Tee Leena," as they approached, stretching her chubby arms towards Celina.

A myriad of emotions flitted across Celina's face, too quickly for Soren to interpret, but they hadn't all been good. His faith in Angela's hunch grew even stronger.

"Come here my love. Come to your Tee Leena," Celina said, pulling KJ from Soren's arms and then nuzzling her nose in the girl's blue-black curls as Soren sat beside her. "God she smells so good. Like heaven itself," she said, in their native Danish.

Although his sister had always been on the reserved side, Angela had pointed out that she seemed even more so on this trip. The only times Celina seemed to come alive was when she was holding KJ or talking about business. Other than that, she'd been spending a lot of time imitating a statue; staring off into the distance, deep in thought.

Maybe Angela was right; maybe Celina was lonely.

However, even though Celina had always been alone, she'd never struck him as lonely, until recently.

"Celina, dear," he said, catching himself. *I sound like our mother.* Then he realized maybe that was exactly what she needed, a little nurturing. He started again, "Celina, dear. Is something the matter? You haven't seemed quite like yourself this trip."

Actually, she hadn't seemed quite like herself a month ago in London either, Soren realized.

Celina turned KJ around so the child could face outward, winding one arm around her tiny chest. She sniffed, keeping her eyes trained on KJ's arm, which she caressed with her free hand. "Whatever gave you that idea?"

Soren noted that she didn't deny that something was wrong. "Well, you've been very quiet this trip—"

"I'm always quiet," she said, cutting him off, which was very unlike her.

Celina was usually the queen of politeness.

Now Soren *knew* something *was* wrong. He thought carefully about how to proceed because it seemed the direct approach was not going to work. "Guess who's coming to visit?"

Celina was pointing at something on the ground, directing KJ to look at it. She didn't look up. "Who?"

"Jameson," Soren said, reverting to Conrad's last name, which was how everyone in their family—except Soren—referred to the man who had been in their father's employ for almost thirty years.

For the first time since he'd sat, Celina's gaze met his, her eyes and mouth shaped in wide Os. "What? Why?"

Soren filed the reaction away; he'd definitely need to tell Angela about it. "I thought it would be wise to make sure our security measures are extra tight since we are pitching the New Zealand government on renewable energy projects."

Her eyes still wide, she answered, "But we've never brought Jameson in for something like this before? Why now?"

Soren shrugged, strategically pulling his daughter out of Celina's lap and standing so as to end the conversation. "I trust Conrad. I value his opinion." He turned, and held out his hand to Celina, pulling her to standing. "Now let's go have dinner. Angela has made mushroom and asparagus risotto and we shouldn't keep her waiting," he said, appealing to Celina's ingrained politeness.

Celina rose, although there was a decided hesitation to her bearing.

As they walked, Soren decided that Angela's analysis of the situation was dead on. There was something more to the Celina-Conrad dynamic than was obvious. He also thought that having Celina pick Conrad up at the airport was a good idea, but how to ask? He decided to wait until they were walking through the door of the kitchen knowing that if he asked in front of Angela, Celina would not be able to turn him down.

When they arrived at the kitchen door, Soren opened it, ushering Celina through. She walked in, head down, as silent as she'd been on the walk back from the garden.

"Oh good, you're back. The table is ready," Angela said as she untied the rose-printed apron and hung it on a copper hook before smoothing back her mahogany hair.

Although they'd been married a little over two years, Soren still felt like he'd won the lottery every time he looked at his wife. Their path to marriage had been fraught with detours and—what had seemed like—dead ends, however, it had all been worth it.

Angela approached him, grabbing KJ from his arms, and leaned in to kiss his cheek, quickly whispering in his ear, "Did you ask her to pick Conrad up?"

Soren gave her the barest shake of his head, but then lifted his chin in Celina's direction. "Celina, dear. Would you please pick-up Conrad at the Auckland airport tomorrow? Angela and I have some commitments at In Bocca," he said, referring to their wine estate located on a small island off the coast of New Zealand's North Island, which housed a restaurant, bed and breakfast, and vineyard.

Celina's misty face suddenly took on the same surprised expression she'd had in the garden, which was a fairly good imitation of Edvard Munch's *The Scream*. "Why can't you send a car?"

Angela—her back still to Celina—arched a brow at Soren and he continued, "Conrad is too good a friend to send a car. I'd meet him myself if I didn't have to be at the vineyard," he said, carefully modulating his voice to sound disappointed.

Angela handed KJ back to Soren, walked to Celina, and wrapped an arm around her shoulder. "Great, it's settled. Thank you so much for doing this, we really appreciate it. It's such a big help to your brother and me. Now, let's go eat. We don't want the risotto getting cold."

"Okay," Celina said quietly, the matter clearly settled.

Soren raised KJ to eye level and whispered. "You have to watch out for your mother, she's a crafty one."

KJ smiled and clapped her hands on Soren's cheeks.

Celina drove the sleek, black SUV off the car ferry and headed south for the Auckland airport, intimately aware of the fact that she had sweat through the armpits of her blouse, and hadn't brought a jacket to cover up with. "Guess I'll be keeping my arms glued to my side," she muttered.

The afternoon had not gone as planned. She'd allowed herself plenty of time to arrive early for Jameson's pickup, however, she just couldn't seem to find the right outfit to wear to the airport. She rolled her eyes. "You have no problem dressing in fifteen minutes for a board meeting, but take two hours to pick an outfit for this." She took a deep breath. "And now you're talking to yourself like an idiot. Get a hold of yourself, Celina."

At the next red light, she ran a hand over her blond hair, hoping to smooth her brain back into the calm, cool, collected CEO headspace it usually occupied. When it came to running a multinational, diversified company, she was unflappable, but the prospect of being alone with Conrad Jameson for two hours had her sweating buckets.

When she next stopped, she reached into the glove compartment, praying that she could find a tissue or napkin to dab at her forehead. Fortunately, there was a stack of napkins. She grabbed a few to mop the sweat from her face, the white paper turning shades of beige and pink as her makeup came off. "Bollocks," she sighed.

The day just kept getting better and better.

The moment Soren mentioned that Jameson would be visiting, her heart had taken off like a skittish colt. She'd barely slept a wink last night, the idea of seeing Jameson—especially after their embarrassing encounter last month—was more than she could bear.

Allowing her mind to wander, she remembered how beautiful he'd looked that day in the on-site gym in her family's home in London less than a month ago.

All four Lund siblings had converged at the Covent Garden home—a large, stone structure overlooking a park, nestled in the heart of London's theatre district—for the quarterly board meeting of Lund Enterprises. It was a quick, two-day trip from Copenhagen for most of them, although Soren was staying a few extra days to catch-up with friends from business school and spend some time with Jameson.

Ever since Soren had returned to the fold of their family—after a two-year estrangement caused by their father—his relationship with Jameson had changed into something more intimate and less transactional, even going so far as to address him by his first name.

"Conrad, I have some pictures to show you," Soren said, approaching Jameson with an arm outstretched.

Celina started. *What a terrible snob I am*, she thought, watching from the treadmill as Soren and Jameson chatted by a weight machine. *I've known the man most of my life, and never even knew his first name.*

The fitness center of their five-story London home was large enough that Celina could watch Soren and Jameson without them being aware of it.

All of her siblings were present, getting in some morning exercise before they headed off to the board meeting of the company founded by their great-grandparents of which they were its main shareholders. Although the company's roots were in real estate management, Lund Enterprises had diversified into clean energy under their parent's watch. A few years ago, their parents had gifted their children all of their shares and it was then that Lund Enterprises added hospitality and apparel to its interests.

Celina felt a swell of gratitude as she looked around the room at her tight-knit siblings. They hadn't always been this close, and she appreciated how running the family company together had brought them closer.

Her youngest brother, Filip, was using a rowing machine, pulling on the chain as though in the race of his life, all while chatting on his mobile phone, probably to one of the many women he was courting at the time. He'd always been a bit of a flirt. With his striking combination of dark hair and blue eyes, he stood out in a family of blondes.

Her youngest sibling, Isabel, was sitting at a recumbent bike busy reading some book that she'd probably been saving just for this trip; her life in Copenhagen included caring for her twin eight-year-olds, which often kept her from the pastime

Then there was Soren, who was a few years younger than Celina. For many years it had just been the two of them, and in some ways she felt closest to him because of it. He'd been like her own real-life baby doll when he was born, and their coloring was so similar there had been a period in their adolescence when people asked if they were twins.

Her adoration for Soren was such that even during the many years when their father had skipped over her, the eldest child, in order to groom Soren, the eldest son, to run Lund Enterprises, she'd never been able to feel jealousy towards Soren, only anger towards her father.

However, it had all worked out in the end. Although she and Soren legally shared the CEO title, she ran most of the company just by the fact that she was the one based in Europe where most of their business was generated.

"It's a shame Angela and KJ couldn't come with you," Jameson said, flipping through the pictures, handling them as though they were delicate.

Jameson's words snapped Celina back to the present.

The evident fondness Jameson had for Soren's wife and daughter was touching. One of these days she'd have to ask Soren what had caused the change in his relationship with Jameson. Maybe it would help her to create something similar. She would enjoy knowing him better.

Especially now that—

She didn't allow her mind to follow that train of thought. She had long ago accepted the fact that Jameson and she would never be anything more than they were: warm acquaintances.

"It's such a long trip from Auckland, and KJ has already been subjected to flights to Los Angeles and Copenhagen to visit her grandparents. But why don't you come to Auckland sometime? I'd love for you to meet her," Soren said, his smile bright. "And I know Angela would love to see you."

Jameson's lips twitched up, his eyes studying a picture with obvious affection. "I'd enjoy that."

Celina was riveted by their interaction, then again, she'd always watched everything Jameson did with interest; ever since the first day she met him when she had been a gangly eight-year-old headed for braces and he a strapping twenty-five-year-old fresh from the military with thick brown hair and sparkling blue eyes that were so light, they looked like ice. He'd immediately won her and Soren over with the offer of spearmint chewing gum.

At first, she'd just found Jameson fascinating, idolizing him as the perfect man: strong, handsome, debonair. But as puberty hit, the fascination turned to youthful obsession, and she had covered her physics and calculus notebooks with the words "Mrs. Celina Lund-Jameson." In her twenties the obsession turned to disgust—not with him but with herself—because Jameson never seemed to notice that she had blossomed into a woman, her teeth as perfect as three years of braces could make them. Then, four years ago, on the cusp of her thirty-fifth birthday, she'd found out he'd gotten married and her disgust turned to resignation that Jameson would never be hers.

After that, she'd settled into life as the spinster aunt, content to know that her heart would always be intact because it was locked up so tight with Jameson, that no other person could hope to find the key.

To this day, she couldn't taste mint without thinking of him.

Jameson returned the photos and both men turned back to their exercise; spotting each other on weights as they chatted.

A spike of jealousy pierced her chest watching as Soren conversed easily with Jameson. Celina always felt like she had marbles in her mouth when she tried to talk to the man, and usually managed no more than the barest pleasantries. Of course, Jameson never noticed because he was used to it. Her entire family had always taken Jameson for granted.

There was not a title that suited Jameson's station in their lives; he was at times a majordomo, a concierge, as well as his primary duties as London Head of Security. To Soren, he was a valued friend, but none of the other family members had this familiar relationship with Jameson, treating him instead like an admired and trustworthy stranger.

She shook her head, refocusing on the treadmill, which was clearly on too easy a setting since she was able to give all of her attention to these errant thoughts. Pushing some buttons, she raised the speed and elevation.

After five minutes, she was breathing heavier, a light sheen of sweat breaking out across her forehead, however, it wasn't enough to drive Jameson fully from her mind, so she pushed the buttons again.

She was at the highest elevation, running at level ten out of fifteen, and was just beginning to get used to the challenging pace, when the sound of loud grunting caught her attention. She glanced up and saw Jameson pulling down a chrome bar stacked with weights—his face red and dripping with sweat—the exertion on his back and shoulders causing his muscles to bulge and constrict with a life of their own.

Celina's mouth dropped open and suddenly—

"For helvede!" she shouted as she bounced off the treadmill, landing heavily on the ground. "Oww," she said, rubbing at her hip.

Commotion swirled around her as people lunged to her aid.

"Are you okay?" Soren asked, kneeling beside her.

Filip and Isabel murmured their own questions, their faces darkening with concern.

"Let me take a look at her," Jameson commanded, her siblings taking a step back, mobilized by the authority in his voice. "Does anything hurt?" he asked softly, his icy blue eyes paradoxically warm.

She shivered slightly. "Uh huh," she mumbled. Her brain empty.

"Where, Celina? Where does it hurt?" Jameson asked, strong and forcefully as though trying to get her to focus.

 She scanned her body. "Maybe my ankle, and my hip."

"Right or left?"

"Left ankle, right hip."

He nodded, lips pursed as he gently lifted her left foot, probing delicately with his fingers around the ankle.

The pain was minimal and quickly overshadowed by the sensual shiver that laced up her leg at Jameson's touch. A quiet moan escaped her lips.

"That hurts?" Jameson's brows knit tightly.

Celina blushed furiously. "Just a little," she said, barely able to push the words past the lump in her throat.

He continued probing, only this time, she was ready for it, and kept her lips clamped shut as another delicious shiver snaked up her back.

"And your hip?"

There was no way she was going to let him probe her there. Besides, she was sure her pride was hurt more than her body. "It's just going to be a nasty bruise."

He nodded. "I think your ankle is only sprained. Let's go to my office, we can put ice on it."

She was about to stand up and try to walk when Jameson swept her off the floor and into his arms.

"Oh." She glanced around at all the exposed skin and muscle and couldn't decide where to place her hands. It all felt so intimate.

Seeing her hesitation, Jameson said, "Sorry I'm such a sweaty mess, but if you put your arm around my neck it will be easier to carry you." A small smile danced on his lips.

She obliged, allowing her fingers to curve around his neck, her heart pounding loudly in her ears. She was sure that her face and ears must have been flame red.

Jameson started towards the exit, weaving around the machines, her siblings trailing behind.

"You don't have to come. It's nothing serious. Go get ready for the meeting," she said.

"You sure?" Isabel asked.

Celina sighed, looking skyward, her embarrassment complete. "It was just a clumsy stumble. I'm sure a little ice will fix it up straight away."

Her siblings nodded and stopped their progression and Celina was grateful when Jameson turned a corner and they disappeared from view.

He carried her silently and Celina struggled with where to train her eyes. When she looked at his face, he would flick his gaze in her direction, causing her to blush furiously. When she looked at his chest, the sight of his tight, white t-shirt—soaked through with perspiration—made a hot sweat break out across her forehead. Finally, she settled her gaze forward, in the same direction as Jameson's, so her body could no longer betray her.

Heading down a long hallway, Celina felt like she was walking back in time. She hadn't been to this part of the building since she was a child. When they were young, she and Soren used to visit Jameson in his office all the time, asking him for gum and rides on his back.

They arrived at a set of double wood doors with wavy, inset glass. Jameson leaned forward to twist the large brass doorknob, shouldering the door open. As they walked in, the lights automatically clicked on, illuminating a spacious office with a view of the walkway that led up to the building.

The furniture was gracious but minimal, with a large oxblood Chesterfield sofa—flanked by matching armchairs—dominating half the space, a glass and chrome coffee table in front of it. A wide mahogany desk, so long that it could have seated eight as a dining table, anchored the other half of the space. It was devoid of papers with only a thin silver laptop perched on its leather-covered surface.

Jameson placed her gently on the sofa and kneeled in front of her, his face full of professional concern. "Can I test your ankle again?"

The way he was looking at her was doing all sorts of strange things to her body; was it possible to feel ill and euphoric at the same time?

She nodded and he reached out, gentling probing around the knob of her ankle.

He sighed. "It's definitely swelling. Try standing and see if you can walk on it," he said, looping his arms under hers, supporting the majority of her weight.

She gingerly placed her foot on the ground, putting half of her weight, then three quarters, and finally all of it on the sprained ankle. "It smarts a bit, but it's tolerable."

A look of relief danced across his face. "Just a sprain then. Some ice and ibuprofen will fix you up." A strange look crossed his face, and he colored. "Celina, I have to ask you a personal question."

Celina blinked quickly, surprised by his embarrassed tone. "Go ahead."

"Are you pregnant or trying to get pregnant?"

She blanched at the strange question.

He must have sensed her discomfort because he hurried to continue, "Ibuprofen isn't recommended for women who are pregnant or trying to get pregnant, but it's my favorite pain reliever and since I'm not a woman," he said, gesturing to his torso.

Celina barked a short laugh, unable to imagine a less feminine form than the bulging mass of testosterone in front of her. Although she'd never been much of a biology buff, she would have loved to know the name of the muscles that caused all the delicious curves and valleys in his physique. She had no idea a man's thighs could be so alluring.

Jameson frowned. "Does your laugh mean you aren't trying to get pregnant?"

She was about to laugh again, but managed to turn it into a coughing sound. What was it about Jameson that she found so disarming? She was usually in much better control of herself; some of her employees even called her "The Ice Queen" for her ability to relay no emotion in tense situations. It was part of why she was so good at negotiation. "Yes, sorry. It's just a funny idea. I haven't dated anyone in years. Ibuprofen is fine."

Jameson frowned, but then quickly rearranged his face into a neutral expression, disappearing into an adjoining room and returning with ice, water, and a couple of reddish-brown pills.

She took the pills as Jameson lifted her foot and placed it on the coffee table, spreading the bag of ice over the top of her ankle.

Jameson stood and looked at his watch. "We have a couple of hours before the board meeting. If you ice your ankle now, you should still have time to shower and change. Did you eat breakfast?"

Celina shook her head.

"Why don't you have the kitchen send your breakfast here?" he asked, gesturing to a phone on an end table next to the couch. "You can eat while the swelling goes down."

"Good idea. Will you join me? What would you like?" She surprised herself with the force of her words, but she didn't want their time together to end.

Another inscrutable look crossed his face.

She would have paid good money to know what he was thinking.

"Yes, I'd like that. Please ask them to send my usual. Do you mind if I take a shower?" He jerked his thumb towards the door. "I'll be back before the food arrives."

"Please, go ahead. I'm sorry to be such a bother," she answered, growing annoyed at herself now that the emergency of her injury had passed and the realization that she'd fallen on her ass—while staring at Jameson—was surfacing. She propped her elbow on the rounded arm of the sofa and laid her head in her hand. *I'm such an idiot.*

She heard footsteps heading toward her. "Is your head okay?" Jameson asked.

She shook her head in disbelief, and then nodded, realizing that Jameson would misinterpret her original headshake. She looked up at him. "Yes, yes. Please go shower, Jameson." *And leave me to wallow in my oafishness.*

He gave her a quick nod and exited the room.

A whoosh of air escaped her mouth as she sighed with relief. Being around Jameson was exhilarating but exhausting. The opportunity to make an ass of herself, and the effort it took to avoid it, took all her energy.

But at least they'd get to have breakfast together. This would be the most time she'd ever spent with him alone.

She picked up the phone and dialed the kitchen, ordering a berry and granola parfait, and asking for Jameson's usual. Part of her wanted to ask what his "usual" entailed, but she figured she'd see it soon enough.

Closing her eyes, she leaned back against the stiff sofa, wishing for a throw pillow. Of course, Jameson's couch was probably used more for meetings with his staff than for lounging, which was probably why there wasn't a single pillow in sight. She rolled her shoulders and tried to run through what she was going to say in today's board meeting, however, try as she might, she couldn't recall anything.

Instead, images of Jameson grunting, his sweaty back glistening with exertion, kept popping into her head. Finally, she decided to stop fighting it and allowed herself to indulge in the vision, even imagining what other exercises she might have seen him perform if she hadn't fallen off the treadmill. Squats would have been excellent; she would have enjoyed seeing him work his legs. Today was the first time she'd seen him in shorts, and the sinewy shape of his thighs and calves were as sculpted as a marble statue.

A soft moan escaped the back of her throat as she imagined Jameson posed as a statue, his body arranged like Michelangelo's *David.*

"Excuse me, Ms. Lund? Where would you like the food?" A pleasant voice called Celina back to the present.

Her eyes flew open and she started in her seat. "Right here, thanks," she said, a bit too brightly.

The young man rolled in a cart and unloaded its contents on to the table in front of her: three covered plates, two espressos, her parfait, a mug of what looked like hot water, and a bowl of cut lemons.

When the man left, she took an espresso and sipped carefully, enjoying the chocolatey brew, although it felt strange to be enjoying her morning coffee in soiled exercise clothes. She shifted the partially melted ice around her ankle once more, satisfied that it didn't smart when she did.

Just then, Jameson walked in the door looking like his usual polished self: black suit, black mock turtleneck, salt and pepper hair almost military short. "I see the food beat me here," he said, pulling at his cuff as he walked to the coffee table and then squeezed all of the lemons into the mug of water.

"Just barely," she said.

He drank the water in one gulp and "aahhhed" with satisfaction. "Better?" he asked, pointing at her ankle.

She nodded. "Yes, thanks."

He looked relieved to hear it.

It was strange, but she liked having him concerned about her.

He removed the lids from the three plates and then glanced towards the desk, as though trying to decide where to eat.

"Sit here," Celina said, patting the tight leather of the sofa. "We can eat together." Putting her espresso down, she took the parfait glass and a spoon and lifted it towards Jameson like she was toasting him.

After a beat, he nodded and sat a polite distance away from her, arranging the plates of scrambled egg whites, breakfast sausage, and melon slices on the table with practiced precision.

Celina raised a brow. "Do you eat that every day?"

"Every day," he said, without looking up, cutting a breakfast sausage into thirds and forking a piece into his mouth. After he swallowed, he said, "I find that eating the same thing frees up a lot of mental energy while ensuring that my caloric needs are met and not exceeded."

"But doesn't that get boring?"

"I don't think about it. It's not that I don't enjoy variety in my food, but on a work day, this just helps keep me focused on what's important," he said with a quick smile. "How's your yogurt?" he said, in a decidedly British way.

YUH-gert, she thought, enjoying the sound of the word when Jameson said it. "It's good," she said. "The berries are really sweet."

"I'll have to ask the kitchen to substitute berries for melon. That would be a nice change," he said, offhand, focused on his eating.

The energy of their conversation flagged as Jameson ate like it was his prime directive, his movements quick and efficient. She searched for a new topic. "This isn't the office I remember."

This time, a big smile crossed Jameson's lips. "That office is farther down the hall. This is the 'big boss' office. Perhaps you remember the man who occupied it before me; Mr. McDonald?"

An image of a man with a mustache popped in her head. "Oh yes. I remember. It's been a long time."

"This has been my office for almost fifteen years now," he said, wistfully. "It's hard to believe how long I've lived in this building. I've resided here almost twice as a long as I lived in my parent's home."

Celina cleared her throat, hesitating to ask the next question, but hungry to know more Jameson's life. "Did…Anne like…living here?" she asked haltingly.

Jameson glanced briefly at his shoes and shrugged. "She didn't mind, but I don't think she ever liked it."

"Why?" Celina asked, twin thrills of curiosity and foreboding snaking through her, knowing that she was pushing into uncharted— and perhaps indiscreet—territory.

However, Jameson didn't seem to mind; if anything, he seemed to want to talk. "She would have preferred a house in the country; the Cotswalds or The Lake District. She wasn't much for the city."

Celina could sympathize; the London bustle was intense. "I'm sorry for your loss, Jameson."

He swallowed the bite he'd been chewing and then settled his eyes on her. "Thanks, Celina. In the end, it was for the best. She was in a lot of pain."

It seemed too sad that Jameson should have been married only three years and that almost half that time his wife had been battling the disease that would kill her.

"Had you known her a long time?"

"Most of my life. We went to high school together."

Her stomach dropped. "High school sweethearts?" She couldn't help the jealous pang she felt; Jameson might not have loved her back but she'd taken some comfort in the fact that she'd loved him the longest.

Jameson shook his head. "No, just friends. We were in the running club together. We ran at the same speed so we clocked a lot of time jogging and chatting. We lost touch for many years and only reconnected at a dinner held by mutual friends about six months before we married."

"So fast?" Celina said, her cheeks heating, wondering again why she had no control of what came out of her mouth around him. "I'm sorry. That was rude of me."

He smiled, the corners of his eyes crinkling, moving his hand as though he was about to pat her on the knee, but then thought better of it. "You can ask me anything, Celina. I don't have many secrets, especially from you Lund brethren. I feel very…" he glanced away as though searching for the right word. "Affectionate," he said quietly. "I have very affectionate feelings for all of you."

Paternal you mean. She'd seen the way he treated Soren, and it made her stomach churn to think he felt like a father figure towards her, when her feelings were so decidedly not familial.

Her emotions must have been visible on her face, because he said, "You look disappointed, Celina."

Why does he keep saying my name like that? The way he hissed the "c" and laved across the top of the "l" sent seductive shivers up and down her torso.

If she were a stereo equalizer, the green lights would have been turning red every time Jameson hit the "l" in her name.

She sighed. "I am disappointed," she said, her body tingling with nerves as she placed her empty parfait glass on the coffee table, removed the ice pack, and stood, not even noticing the slight tenderness in her ankle.

I'm going to say it. The thought made her feel stronger. She was finally doing something actionable, even if she was sinking the ship in the process; it felt good to be in control.

"You are?" he asked, wiping his mouth and fixing his eyes on her. "Why?"

Limping a couple of steps away, she swallowed hard past the lump in her throat as she clenched her fists. "Because, Jameson, I'm thirty-nine-years-old and the only man I've ever had feelings for still thinks of me as a little girl."

The color in Jameson's face drained and he became as still as a statue, his jaw, severe.

"Now if you'll excuse me, I'm going to go shower," she said, and walked out of the room without a backward glance.

A line of red brake lights told Celina that she was entering the arrivals area of Auckland Airport. The dual-pull of her responsibilities for Lund Enterprises coupled with the opportunity to visit Soren's family meant that this was her eleventh visit to New Zealand in less than three years and she was intimately familiar with the airport's layout.

"I guess it's time to face the music," she sighed, turning the SUV towards the international terminal.

Her cell phone rang and she accepted it, hitting the speaker button. "Hello?"

"Celina, it's Jameson."

She froze at the sound of his voice, her body, once again no longer under her control. She took a deep breath. "Go ahead," she said, knowing she sounded colder than she meant. Maybe he didn't notice.

She thought she heard him sigh before he said, "I'm at the curb in front of the baggage claim."

"Okay. I should be there in five minutes," she answered, ending the call when he didn't reply.

She took a deep breath hoping to martial her business skills. Maybe if she thought of him as a business associate she could tap into her innate politeness and calm. *He's a third round interview candidate, and I want to offer him a job.* The muscles in her neck and shoulders began to release. This was familiar territory, an interview she could handle; being cooped up with the only man she'd ever loved, now *that* was scary.

As she approached the baggage claim, she emptied her mind of expectations. *I'm picking up a stranger. I've been told to look for a fifty-something man with salt-and-pepper hair and military bearing.* She scanned the crowds lining the sidewalk, not looking for Jameson, but for a fit man with good posture. She passed a woman wearing red, holding a baby; then a couple in shorts paging through a guidebook; then a slouchy man in a suit wearing dark sunglasses. "Military, military, military," she muttered, the illusion of looking for a stranger was working. She felt markedly calmer.

Finally, she saw a man with military bearing, but he was in his thirties. "Not him."

A gesture caught her attention. Someone was waving to her.

She slowed down and moved towards the curb as a fiftyish man approached wearing a black crewneck and black jeans, looking as fresh as though he'd just emerged from a shower, his outfit somehow both formal and casual.

So complete was the illusion she had created, she had to remind herself not to ask him his name.

She unlocked the doors, and braced herself for the sound of his voice saying her name.

Jameson opened the back door, threw in his bag, and then joined her in the front. "Hello, Celina," he said, hesitantly.

His tone surprised her. Celina was certain she'd never heard Jameson sound uncertain. She was so thrown off, she didn't even notice the beautiful way her name sounded from his lips.

"Hello, Jameson," she said evenly. She immediately turned her eyes back to the road, needing to concentrate anywhere but on that face she knew as well as her own. She waited for the click of his seat belt and put the car into drive, easing away from the curb.

The airport traffic was a welcome distraction, easily occupying her mind as she wove in and out of the lanes and then navigated back towards the road to Auckland.

Jameson sighed once they were cruising along. "So…" he said, the single word hung heavy in the air.

She prayed silently that he wouldn't bring up the last words she'd said to him in London, and flipped on the radio.

Jameson settled into his seat, resting his hands on his thighs. "You have something on your face."

"What?" She swiped at the cheek facing him and felt bits of rolled up paper, detritus from the napkins she'd wiped her face with earlier. She sighed inwardly. The day just got better and better. "Thanks."

Neither of them spoke as the radio station cycled through songs and commercials, none of which Celina actually heard, her own inner dialogue about Jameson was taking up all of her mental bandwidth.

After five minutes, Celina grew a little warm, suddenly becoming aware of the awkwardness of her muteness.

Should I say something?

Out of her peripheral vision, he looked like a sphinx, his body motionless, his face blank, eyes staring straight ahead. He could probably remain that way for the entire drive if he wanted.

After ten minutes, Celina grew warmer still, undecided if she was embarrassed or angry.

How dare he not talk!

After fifteen minutes, fiery ice ran through Celina's veins.

If he's not talking, I'm not talking!

"Celina."

She jumped at the sound of her name.

With a quick flick of her gaze, she took in Jameson's face full of kind concern, his voice beseeching. She turned back to the highway; they were approaching a short bridge.

"Celina," he said, firmer this time. "We have to talk."

There was no doubt this time; he was definitely pleading.

She sighed heavily.

"Turn off here," he said, motioning towards the next exit.

She chafed at his commanding tone. She wasn't one of his underlings to be ordered around. However, her curiosity was piqued. "Why?"

He sighed, exasperated. "So we can talk, Celina. I don't understand why you are being difficult."

She pursed her lips. The tight quarters they were sharing was causing her frustration to fester. She *was* being difficult and to be honest, she wasn't sure why. Certainly her embarrassment over what she said in London didn't warrant icing Jameson out. Deciding to check her attitude, she turned off at the next exit, entered a roundabout, and took the turn that read "Auckland".

They entered a wide street that rose quickly up an incline through a residential area. She gripped tight to the steering wheel, trying to keep all irritation out of her voice as she asked, "Where do you want to go?"

She could practically feel the frustration dripping off him as he opened the glove compartment and rummaged around. He unfolded a map and scanned it. "Stay on this road for a few more kilometers. I'll tell you when to turn right." His voice was commanding again, the previous annoyance, gone.

She withheld her desire to "tsk" loudly, not sure why he was getting under her skin this way. Her interactions with Jameson had never had any sort of anger or animosity to them; it felt like they were fighting. *But why?*

"Turn right here," he said, his voice calm but authoritative.

She bristled again, but thought carefully about what she could say. She didn't want to provoke him for no reason. "You could say it more nicely."

He sighed and ran his hand back and forth through his hair a few times. "I'm sorry. You're right. *Please* turn right here," he said, his tone apologetic.

She rolled her window down and sighed. The combination of fresh air and his apology dissipating some of her resentment.

He directed her up a street and into a park that wound its way uphill past gnarled olive trees and wide pastures with cows and sheep grazing. It was as if they had driven out of the city and into the countryside, however, long vistas of the town below were visible off to her right as the land around her rolled and dipped.

Finally they arrived at a small, round parking lot, cars looking like time markers on a watch face. Jameson must have thought the same thing because he said, "There's a spot at two o'clock."

She pulled into the space and pointed to a café a few hundred feet away. "Coffee?"

Jameson's seat belt unclicked and he said, "I'd prefer a walk if that sounds good to you. Need to stretch my legs."

"Of course, I forgot you've been stuck on a plane. A walk sounds nice."

"By the way," he said, clearing his throat. "I didn't want to distract you while you drove, but you still have a few more bits of paper on your face."

Celina colored. If God was trying to tell her she needed more humility, the message was coming through loud and clear. "Thanks," she said, turning the rearview mirror and picking at least a half-dozen bits of napkin from her face. *What a nightmare!*

Once she was done, she exited the car and inhaled the fresh air, immediately feeling her spirits lift. Her day had nowhere to go but up.

Spotting a copse of trees, she said, "How about we walk over there?"

He nodded. "Perfect. Lead the way."

They started walking, Celina admiring the late spring foliage of the trees, the mild afternoon sun, and the sweet scent of flowers in the air. Traveling to New Zealand was always slightly disconcerting, as though she'd missed a season or two during her flight. When she'd left Europe it had been mid-fall, the air just starting to turn colder, but here in the Southern Hemisphere it was mid-spring just beginning to turn warmer.

She didn't need to turn her head to know exactly where Jameson was located in relation to her; her body was uniquely tuned-in to his particular frequency. He was half a step behind her to her right, however, his gaze must have been taking in the lush greenery as well because she couldn't feel the heat of his eyes.

"Beautiful," he murmured, his voice softer than she'd ever heard it.

Not wanting him to drive the conversation, she decided to finally satisfy her curiosity about Soren and Jameson's relationship. "Tell me, Jameson," she said, turning his direction. "When did Soren start calling you Conrad?"

His brows lifted. "It started in Costa Rica," he answered quickly, as she knew he would, his memory sharp and swift.

Celina imagined that nothing escaped his notice, which made her even more certain that he had understood her meaning in London. However, it was now her turn to be surprised. "You went to Costa Rica?" perhaps a bit more incredulous than she'd meant it.

He smiled at her tone. "I've always felt an affinity for Soren, however, the summer between his two years at business school—when he lived at the Covent Garden building—we grew closer. And you know, that's the summer he and Angela began their…thing…" he trailed off, waving his hand in three quick arcs, like a stone skipping across a pond.

Celina understood his difficulty choosing the correct term to describe Soren and Angela's romance; it was simply too much to encompass with a single word.

She nodded for him to continue.

"I knew how he felt for her; had seen it for myself. So when I learned he ran away to Costa Rica, I became concerned. I felt like I was a party to their relationship, perhaps the only person who really knew what she meant to him, and as such, I had a responsibility to check on him. I'm part of the reason he chose to settle in New Zealand, and look how well that turned out," he said with a self-satisfied smile.

"You? How?"

Jameson glanced down at the grass, accidentally kicking a mushroom free from its stem, but the spell had been broken. His face became closed. "I think it's best if you ask Soren that part of the story. It's not really mine to tell," he finished, his thick sense of propriety cloaking his words. "Ever since then, Soren has called me Conrad." He gave her a sideways glance, a bit of color coming into his cheeks. "He's almost like a son to me."

Does that mean I'm like a daughter? A metallic taste rose in her mouth at the unwelcome thought.

They had reached the beginning of a low stone wall, like the kind she'd seen run for miles in countryside stocked with animals. They turned slightly, following the direction of the wall.

"Celina," he said heavily, his tone full of meaning.

The hair on the back of her neck stood up.

She wasn't sure she was ready for this talk. Perhaps it was enough that the frustration and anger that had built between them in the car had dissipated. She could finish the ride back in a composed fashion. Glancing at her watch, she forced a smile. "We should get going. We need to leave now to make the next ferry."

Not waiting for his response, she turned and started walking back to the car. If Jameson protested, it was lost in the wind as he quickly caught up to her and walked back with her in silence.

Once back at the SUV, Jameson said, "I can drive if you like."

Thinking that might keep him from asking any probing questions, she agreed.

She dropped the keys into his hands and they climbed into the car, Jameson driving the SUV as smoothly as if it had been a sedan, his years of experience instantly visible.

Celina sighed and leaned back, instantly put at ease by the capability Jameson exuded. It was impossible not to feel safe and cared for with him around. He was so skilled, so unflappable; he inspired confidence with his mere presence.

Jameson also relaxed in the driver's seat; it was a position he was accustomed to and his training instantly clicked into place.

Allowing his instincts to take over, he scanned the mirrors unconsciously, treating Celina as though she was his job. It was easier this way; turning on his work brain forced the questions he had for her to the back of his mind.

However, the silent calm only lasted the thirty minutes it took to arrive at the dock and park on the ferry. Now they had at least ninety minutes, with nothing to do, as they waited for the boat to take them to Waiheke Island. Now that driving no longer occupied him, the unasked questions flitted annoyingly in his brain like mosquitos at dusk, looking for an opportunity to draw blood.

Was it possible that Celina had feelings for him?

Had feelings for him all her life?

Was he the reason she'd never married?

He wasn't sure which question pained him more.

Celina and Soren had been the first children he'd ever spent time with. Long before he became an uncle—when his younger brother had kids—he experienced the joy and responsibility of having young charges on their visits to London.

Celina had been a chatty and inquisitive eight-year-old who seemed as responsible and competent as an adult. Soren had been five and serious, always looking to see what his older sister did or said before he committed to anything. When they met, Jameson had been new to the security detail and his boss had been fine with him spending time with the Lund children especially since their parents had encouraged the arrangement.

Watching them grow up had been like watching a time-lapse movie of a sapling turning into a towering oak, sped up because of the quarterly nature of their visits. When they went away to university, the time-lapse became more extreme as the Lund offspring would only come to London during summer.

There had been one period where Celina stayed away from London for two years, going from twenty to twenty-two. When he saw her again, he couldn't believe the woman that she had become; so poised and confident. He'd almost been able to forget the eight-year-old who'd stolen his heart when he looked at her, although their vast age difference, and the fact that she was his employer's daughter, was so ingrained in him that he'd never thought of her as a woman who could be interested in him romantically.

However, ever since last month when she'd walked away from him—stunning him into silence by her cryptic admission—he'd lost many hours of sleep turning her words over; inspecting them from every possible angle, no nuance left unconsidered.

Because the only man I've ever had feelings for still thinks of me as a little girl.

His first reaction was anger, wondering how any man could think of Celina—so elegant, so brilliant, so composed—as a little girl was beyond him. Celina had been mature in spirit even when she was young in years, and it pained him to think that someone she had feelings for could have such a misguided opinion of her.

Then he wondered who this jackass could possibly be.

At first his humble nature made him wonder who Celina was talking about. Was he supposed to know who this alluded to man was without her naming him directly? He considered this idea for many minutes, finally admitting that he knew relatively little about Celina apart from her work with Lund Enterprises, and absolutely nothing about her dating life.

Finally, he considered if Celina was referring to him. Even thinking that thought had required considerable energy, his brain rebelling against the idea. However, there were simply no other options left; Celina had made the statement to him because it was *about* him.

A cold shiver swirled up his back causing him to shrug his shoulders as it lanced up his ears.

Celina has feelings for me.

Once he came to terms with what her words meant, two days after she had stated them and a day after she'd returned to Copenhagen, he sat in stunned silence at his desk, staring off into space. He sat this way for at least two hours, until one of his junior staffers roused him with a request for a signature.

Of all of the words to come out of Celina's mouth, he never would have guessed at those.

His first reaction, once the ability to string a coherent thought returned to him, was concern; had he done something to encourage her? It was impossible to remember all of the interactions they'd had over the years, the vast majority of them too short and transactional to even leave an actual imprint on his memory.

However, after going through his recent memory, he could say with certainty that there had been nothing in them that would have led her to construe that he harbored anything more than platonic feelings for her.

However, the more troubling concern of his was the reaction he had to her words. As someone who had worked personal security most of his life, it had been hardwired into him to think of his clients with professional disinterest. Of course, he'd met Soren and Celina when he was still new to this business, and their age and innocent curiosity had somehow snuck under his defenses.

The truth was there was a part of him that was flattered that the smart, lovely Celina Lund had even noticed him. It was easy to feel a bit like living furniture in his line of work, and the fact that he had somehow managed to be worthy of the friendship and admiration of not one, but two Lund children, meant a lot to him.

However, there was something else—

He had forced that errant thought from his brain with sheer force of will—until now.

All of these thoughts dashed through his brain in the time it took Celina to unbuckle her seat belt, open the door, and exit the SUV. She walked away without a word, the ends of her spring coat flapping in the wind; her elegant gait somehow even more graceful in her withdrawn silence.

They needed to talk, but he wasn't sure what about.

Celina was still his employer, not to mention a woman he'd known as a child.

There was something about that which bothered him, although he couldn't quite put his finger on it.

However, she was also a woman whom he admired and cared about, and he wanted their rapport to be repaired; to go back to how they used to be.

Satisfied with his analysis of the situation, and his decision to act, he got out of the car and followed her to an upper deck where she was leaning against a railing, looking out at the sea ahead although the boat was still docked firmly in place.

He leaned against the railing and wove his hands together, mirroring her. Clearing his throat, he said, "Celina, I'd like us to be able to interact without this tension between us," he said, gesturing with his closed grip to the space between them.

She sighed, tilting her head down. "I'm sorry, Jameson. It's my fault." She rubbed her forehead with her fingers, her lashes fluttering.

He'd never seen Celina so uncertain, so vulnerable.

Even when she was a little girl, she'd been extremely sure of herself. He laughed as a favorite memory bubbled to the surface. "Remember that time you marched into my office, you must have been about twelve, and you said that I had been poisoning you?"

She gave him a quick sideways look and shook her head.

He stood up straighter, the joy of the memory forcing a smile onto his face. "You said that I was poisoning you with the spearmint gum I always gave you because it had aspartame in it."

Celina's mouth lifted. "I think I remember."

Jameson turned to her and mimicked her twelve-year-old self, putting his hands on his hips. "Jameson! Do you know what you've been feeding us?" he said in a ridiculously high voice. "Poison!" he said, lifting up one hand as though he was clutching a pack of gum in it. "This gum has poison in it!" He stamped his foot and pouted his lips together, impersonating the vision of her from his memory.

Celina couldn't help but laugh. "I don't think I stamped my foot or pouted like that."

Jameson shrugged and relaxed back into his normal posture. "Probably not. It has been a long time, but I remember you were definitely horrified and shocked that a responsible adult would be feeding you aspartame."

She sniffed. "You should have been locked up," she said, with a lift of her brow.

He nodded solemnly. "They should have thrown away the key. Endangering the life of innocent children."

After a beat, they both laughed, and just like that, the tension lifted; blown away by the cleansing breeze of humor.

Jameson reached towards her and plucked something from the hair surrounding her face. He showed it to her, it was another bit of rolled up napkin.

She shook her head. If she'd had any pride before this day had started, she officially had none left.

"I think that's the last of it," he said, his lips quivering with the effort to control a smile.

She laughed and he joined her.

Loudspeaker announcements were made and the ferry began to move away from the dock, the wind picking up with their movement.

"I'm sorry I've been such a git," she said quietly. After a moment she added, "I was embarrassed."

She looked so forlorn at that moment, that Jameson felt honor-bound to reassure her. He closed his palm over her hand, which was clasped on the railing. "You have nothing to be embarrassed about."

Celina's eyes flicked to his hand as surprise flitted across her face before the corners of her lips turned up slightly, although the smile didn't reach her eyes. "Thanks, Jameson, but I do. I've put you in an awkward position, and I've done it for no other reason than because I wanted to get something off my chest." She gave him a weak smile as she removed her hand from the railing, effectively forcing him to withdraw his own.

Jameson felt a sense of loss at the movement.

She sighed and added, "It was inconsiderate of me."

"It wasn't inconsiderate, it was brave," Jameson said, surprised as the words left his mouth.

Celina shook her head. "You're just trying to make me feel better."

He wanted to reassure her, and he knew there was a way, but it meant acting unprofessionally which went against his very nature. But when she looked up at him with those sea-blue eyes, the painful longing displayed there, disarmed him. "If things were different, Celina..." he said quietly.

Her eyes flickered. "What does that mean?"

He sighed, torn between leaving the wall up between them, or pulling it down with a single stroke. "Ce-li-na," he said, his voice a warning growled out in three long syllables.

Her eyes flashed. "Don't 'Celina' me. You can't just say something like that and let it dangle out there in the ether," her nostrils flaring.

He'd never seen her so angry, and there was something thrilling about it.

The realization made him pause.

Maybe there was more truth to his half-sentence than even he suspected, but what could he possibly offer her? She was an heir to one of the wealthiest families in Europe by birth, and the CEO of a multinational company by merit, not to mention one of the smartest and most sophisticated people he'd ever met. What could he have that she would want?

He shook his head. "I shouldn't have said that."

"Bloody hell, Jameson," she said, throwing the words at him, before whipping her head around and walking away from him, her hand gripping the railing like she wanted to throttle it.

"Celina," he called, walking after her, but when he reached for her hand, she pulled it away as though she'd been burned.

"I'm a grown woman, Jameson, I don't need your pity." She said his name like a curse, and for the first time it felt like a boundary between them.

"Please, call me Conrad," his voice conciliatory.

Her eyes widened and lips parted, as though she was about to say something, but stopped. She blinked a few times as the earlier flash of anger, melted away.

Her next words were hopeful, her face soft. "Conrad," she said, to the wind, testing the feel of it.

Conrad. Just thinking it felt intimate, as though it gave her some power over him.

She turned it over in her head like a secret, each incantation making her stronger. There was something he wasn't saying, and asking her to call him by his true name was the key she needed to unlock this door.

"Conrad," she said, enjoying the percussive "C". It was a good name; a strong name. His parents had named him well.

He watched her carefully, his face open while also betraying nothing.

"Conrad," she said again, carefully this time. She needed to finesse her request. She decided to revert to logic. Unconsciously, she fluttered her lashes, unaware of how it made his heart beat faster. "We are both adults. I'm almost forty. If you have something to say to me, I deserve to know it all." She paused and licked her lips. Then with a slight plea she added, "If there is any chance you return my feelings, don't let me go on like this. I've spent my whole life trying to find your equal, and now I know he doesn't exist." It was the closest thing to an outright admission of her feelings that she'd ever made, and her heart beat loudly in her ears with the effort.

Time seemed to slow down as she waited for Conrad's response, her knuckles turning white as she gripped the handrail for support. She didn't even notice as unaware strangers walked by them, close enough to touch. It was like they were in a bubble of their own making, as though a force shield—forged of her hopes and fears—separated them from everyone else in both space and time.

His eyes wary, he said, "Celina—"

She held up her hand and shook her head. "Just be honest, Conrad. That's all I ask."

His shoulders caved and he shook his head as though he was going to regret what came next. The words came out gravelly, as though they'd had to fight their way out of his mouth. "Of course I have feelings for you, but it's impossible. I work for your family."

Tears pricked in her eyes as relief flooded through her body like a hot white light. She felt suddenly lighter, as though her unspoken love for him had been a weight she'd had to bear.

Releasing her grip on the railing, she took a step closer to him.

He seemed to tense up as she approached.

Keeping her eyes trained on his, she said quietly, "I'm about to do something I've been thinking about for fifteen years, maybe longer..."

His head moved infinitesimally and she couldn't tell if it was a nod or a shake. She took another step forward, and he tensed more.

"If you want me to stop, just say the word," she said, closing the distance between them.

Her eyes flitted to his lips and back to his eyes. She didn't want to miss a moment of this waking dream. She leaned forward and pressed her lips gently against his.

Although his lips were as still as stone, he didn't try to step away.

Still staring into his ice-blue eyes, she kissed him harder, a thrill of disbelief racing through her.

Am I really kissing Jameson? Conrad? Conrad Jameson?

It was her dearest wish in the flesh.

Conrad's face was serene, but his eyes seemed to be weighing concerns that she could only imagine.

She wanted to tip the scales in her direction, and had been emboldened by his acquiescence. She grabbed one of his hands and wound it behind her back, and then repeated the action with the other, pressing against him, chest to chest, thigh to thigh, toe to toe.

A low moan escaped the back of Conrad's throat.

"Stop overthinking it and kiss me," she murmured.

The skin around his eyes tensed and then relaxed, and he pulled her closer, covering her mouth with his.

Celina sighed the relief of a thousand dreams at the sweet pressure of their bodies together. If she never awoke from this moment, she would be content.

I love you, Conrad Jameson, she thought, as she pulled him closer, deepening their kiss.

__If you'd like me to write more about Celina and Conrad, cast your__
__vote by visiting SmartURL.it/KNB1survey Thanks!__
Celina and Conrad are both important secondary
characters in the __BECKONED__ series and appear in almost
all of the books. To read it now, go to
SmartURL.it/AmazonAviva

<u>Scene Setting</u>

Nadine read the last sentence of the chapter, her body hot and tingling.

Oh my, she thought, as she turned off her tablet, laid it on her nightstand, and slid lower under her covers.

She turned on her side and studied the silhouette of her husband of fifteen years.

"Rick," she whispered softly.

He didn't move.

She traversed the landscape of his ears, neck, and shoulders with her gaze; familiar territory that she'd explored countless times.

Could she? Would he? Maybe this was exactly what they needed.

The hardest thing about growing older is mourning your former self.

She remembered how they used to lay together, their limbs falling into a perfect mosaic, a tessellation pattern of pleasure.

She tried to remember how the puzzle pieces of their bodies had fit together, but it was no longer a perfect fit, now they were a weathered, cardboard jigsaw puzzles whose pieces no longer seemed to join together easily.

She wanted to fit again.

When they were young, their passion had never failed them; their lovemaking had been effortless and mutually satisfying. Sometimes, when she thought back to the hours they would spend in bed, orgasm after orgasm, it was hard to believe it had been them.

She lay back in bed, trying to figure out when their sex life had become so mundane. Certainly having a child had been a part of it, but he wasn't the only reason. There didn't seem to be a reason or a moment. On the rare occasion they did have sex, it was still good—albeit shorter—and she was still attracted to Rick and knew he felt the same.

And yet, there was no doubt there was plenty of room for improvement.

She thought about the early days of their courtship, back when they couldn't get enough of each other. She used to call her best friend and say, "I had eight orgasms today!" Those days were so long ago, it was as though it was another person; a person she longed to tap into, and maybe—just maybe—she'd found a way to do it.

She turned her head to glance at her tablet and thought about the book she was reading, which had surprised her to her core.

The book had popped up in her email as a freebie she might be interested in, and the thousands of ratings, along with a 4.5-star average, had convinced her to give it a try. After all, there was nothing to lose, despite the fact that it was about a topic she'd never been interested in reading about: BDSM.

BDSM, a broad acronym that included a myriad of erotic practices including bondage, discipline, dominance, submission, and sadomasochism was a topic she'd only heard about peripherally, however, she had to admit that the title alone left a bad taste in her mouth. It was not a lifestyle that called to her. However, reading the synopsis of the book had made her curious because it followed the life of a young woman becoming educated about BDSM and was written by a woman who had lived that lifestyle for over twenty years.

It sounded practically educational; like *National Geographic* for sex.

As she read the book, she was not disappointed, it was as illuminating as she had hoped, the author skillfully bringing the reader along on the heroine's journey from being someone as ignorant of "the lifestyle" as Nadine, through a number of boundary-pushing "lessons" that transformed her into a woman who embraced the BDSM lifestyle fully.

Nadine devoured the book, and although it didn't inspire her to become a BDSM acolyte, it did inspire the desire to improve her and Rick's sex life. What had been most fascinating for her was what she saw as BDSM's hyperfocus on communication, necessary to ensure a pleasurable experience for all parties, as something that her own relationship would benefit from.

Nadine yearned to be able to say "yes" or "no" with the certainty that the book's heroine had shown, so completely aware of what she liked or didn't like. She wanted to explore things she'd never done, so that she knew where her boundaries actually were, just like the heroine had. And just like the heroine, she only wanted to do this with one person, the love of her life, her husband.

When was the last time Rick and I vocalized our desires in actual words?

Did we ever?

Just the thought of talking more about sex sounded like a good place to start.

Her mind was made up. Tomorrow she'd talk to Rick about it.

The next day, she and Rick were at the off-leash dog park with their Labradoodle, Benny, and six-year-old son, Lukas.

"So, I've been reading this book," she began, holding her insulated coffee mug to her mouth, and taking a hesitant sip. The warm brew was mild and soothing, with just the hint of chocolate that a good Americano had.

"Hm? What's new?" Rick harrumphed.

She pursed her lips. Sometimes he said that she seemed to like her books more than him. She steeled herself to keep going. "It's about BDSM."

His eyebrows lifted and he turned to look at her, his dark gaze, questioning.

That got your attention, she thought smugly. She took a deep breath, gripping her mug through her leather gloves, the crisp late autumn air hinting of the coming winter. "It's been very surprising..." she gauged his reaction; he seemed to be waiting for her to continue. She looked to where Lukas was running with Benny, making sure they were out of earshot. "As I understand it, in the BDSM culture, an 'encounter'," she said, emphasizing the word with an arched brow, "is called a 'scene', and before a scene happens, the people involved have a conversation about what each of them wants to get out of it. Likes, dislikes, boundaries, they agree on a safe word. Then they engage in the scene and then there is a period of 'aftercare' where the players debrief..." she trailed off, not sure where she wanted to take the conversation from here, and deciding to wait until Rick said something.

After a thoughtful sip from his coffee mug, he said, "That sounds very honest," his deep baritone, thoughtful and—to her ears—open.

She sighed, her shoulders relaxing. "That's what I was thinking. It struck me that maybe any relationship..." she cleared her throat, she was being too indirect. "Maybe *our* relationship, could benefit from such open communication." She came to a full stop, hesitating, about what to stay next. She rolled back her shoulders and plunged forward. "There are times, when I really want to cuddle, but I don't initiate it because I don't want it to go any further than that and I feel like you will try and push it further, and so I do nothing at all," the words spilled out quickly, fighting to get out before she closed the floodgate.

She recognized the honesty of the words, and the fact that they'd been bubbling under the surface of their sex lives for at least six years, maybe longer.

Why was it so hard to be honest about this with the man she called her lover and friend for almost twenty years, husband for fifteen?

But it was. It was *hard*.

She could feel the effort it took in the cramped muscles of her neck and back. Another part of her felt ashamed to say these words out loud. It was embarrassing.

She wasn't good at talking about sex because she hadn't been taught how to talk about sex; it was as simple as that. But she knew she had to say it; had to say something. They needed to become good at talking about sex. They were only in their forties, she didn't want to spend the rest of their lives with a sex life that neither of them was satisfied with. Rick had been saying for years that he wished she wanted him more, and she'd wished it too. Especially now that Lukas was older and didn't cling to her like a baby monkey. Her body finally felt firmly like her own again, and she missed the sensual being she used to be.

Now was the time.

Rick shuffled his feet, looking down. "I had no idea you felt that way."

Nadine nodded, feeling bad for the glimmer of regret that flitted across Rick's dark features. She knew he'd never want to make her feel uncomfortable purposefully, but she simply hadn't known how to speak to him about this, but now she felt like she did.

"Damn, Nadine. Why didn't you say anything?" His volume rising.

She felt her neck hair bristle, but willed herself to stay calm. "I'm saying something now," she said with finality, ignoring the flash of shame she felt, old enough to recognize that she wasn't going to be held back by American culture's weird love/hate relationship with sex. He was her husband, they were consenting adults, they could do whatever they wanted in their bedroom.

There was something inside of her that knew this was the right thing to do and she clung to that knowledge. However, her "comfort zone" was not making it easy; flashing red neon lights across her brain, *"Danger! Danger! Turn back now!"* She breathed deeply, trying to mitigate her flight, fight, freeze response as she'd learned in a meditation class she once took.

Slowly, the flashing red lights dimmed and then disappeared and the tension in her body followed.

He took the hint, checking his tone. "I'm sorry, honey. That came out wrong. I just feel bad thinking that you ever felt pressured. He reached out as though to caress her shoulder but then stopped.

Now seemed like the perfect time to be more communicative, even if it felt strange. "You can touch me," she said.

He gave her a grateful look and squeezed her shoulder, a tender gesture that spoke of regret, but also hope. "So you want to talk more, before we," he struggled for a moment, "before we are intimate." His voice rose, uncertainly.

She sighed, her shoulders relaxing even more. "Yes. Why not? You always say you want me to touch you more, and I would do it if I knew it didn't mean that we *had* to have sex. However, more touching will lead to more intimacy, which will lead to more sex, *eventually*. At least, I think it will. It certainly can't hurt," she said, unable to remember the last time they'd had sex. Ever since Lukas had been born, their sex life had been about as regular as a board meeting: quarterly. "So let's see if it helps..." she said, with a hopeful shrug.

So they did, and it did help, and then one day, Nadine wanted to go further.

There had been a passage in the book when the heroine had been encouraged to test her boundaries. The heroine's mentor had said that she'd never know where her boundaries really were if she didn't test them.

Nadine was ready to test her boundaries.

They were cuddling in bed, naked, Nadine spooning into Rick's side as he stroked her back in long languid passes; Lukas fast asleep in his room across the hall. Nadine was enjoying the affectionate touching more than she had in a long time because she knew that was all it would be unless they explicitly discussed taking it further. Both she and Rick had been surprised at how transformative a little extra communication—and a little ego checking, not allowing themselves to be offended when the other didn't want the exact same thing—had been for their relationship.

It was early Saturday morning and the long winter rays of sun filtered in through the pleated window treatments, softening the interior light perfectly. Nadine felt so sexy like this, lying next to her husband, knowing that her needs would be met while her boundaries were not crossed.

It felt safe.

Safe enough to risk testing said boundaries.

"I finished that book I was reading."

Rick looked down his nose at her. "The kinky one?"

She pursed her lips. There had certainly been moments in the book that were kinky, but her major takeaways had been about the circumstances and rules that BDSM fostered, and less about the kink. It was the structure that allowed BDSM participants to investigate what turned them on safely, and that was what intrigued her most. "The BDSM one," she corrected, feeling surprisingly protective about the book, which had helped them bring a new honesty to their relationship with each other, and even to her relationship with herself.

Honesty was freeing.

Nadine had always downplayed her sensual side. As a curvaceous woman she'd gotten more than her share of unwanted attention from men over the years. She could remember being leered at by adult men when she was only thirteen and already filling out a D-cup. The BDSM book had helped her realize that her dislike of being objectified by strangers had somehow colored her entire relationship with men, as though Rick was an extension of the catcalling men from the street. This had become especially true after giving birth to Lukas. There had been times when Rick came on to her that made her feel dirty and shameful, as though being a mother somehow elevated her above sex.

She had no idea where these feelings/beliefs came from, but what did it really matter? They were a stranglehold on her sex drive, a sex drive that she wanted to reignite.

If she had learned anything these last few weeks, it was that honesty was a game changer. Honesty was paradoxically an emotional solvent and adhesive all in one. She'd felt how it had dissolved the barriers between her and Rick while simultaneously strengthening the bonds.

She wondered if honesty could help her dissolve the thoughts and beliefs that were holding her back. So she tried, but it wasn't like she did it consciously. She didn't sit on her couch and do this, or meditate in a quiet room, or journal about it. She might as well have been in the shower, or driving to the grocery store, or in the grocery store looking at the ridiculously comprehensive cheese selection. Because as soon as the epiphany of using honesty in this way came into her mind, she started to run through the beliefs she no longer wanted in her brain and began naming their positive opposite.

Not all men objectify women and Rick has never objectified me.

My sexual desires are healthy and deserve to be met.

As long as two consenting adults are enjoying their sex life, there is no reason to feel shame about anything.

She recognized the beliefs, named them, and felt lighter as the negative beliefs seemed to dissipate, evaporate away under the sanitizing light of honesty.

It was as simple, and as difficult, as that.

She was creating a safe place where all of her needs and desires could be addressed, where her voice could be heard, and it was liberating.

And now that she'd been liberated, there was something else about BDSM that she wanted to try.

"Please..." she implored, batting her eyelashes playfully and feeling absolutely zero guilt about it.

Rick chuckled, but said nothing.

She pressed on. "Did you know BDSM isn't always about sex? Couples can have a 'scene' where nothing that vanilla people—people like you and me—" Rick snorted and glanced at his skin. She rolled her eyes. "That's what they call people who are not in their subculture. Anyway, there can be 'scenes' where nothing that you or I would consider sexual occurs. Some of it is actually very playful, whereas, some of it sounds painful to me, but again, the focus is just on what turns each individual on, and sometimes that's not intercourse."

Rick arched a brow but continued to caress her back, this time stippling his fingers from side to side in the way she had told him she preferred.

"Just like that. I mean, would you have touched my back like that if I hadn't *told* you I liked it so much?"

He shook his head. "No, I would never have thought of this on my own," he said, a tint of understanding in his voice.

"Exactly. Anyway, there are parts of BDSM that are very sensually stimulating," she paused, realizing how loaded the word "sensual" was. "What I mean is a lot of the scene setting is designed to stimulate the senses. That's what I mean by sensually stimulating."

He frowned. "I'm not sure I'm tracking."

"Well," she started, collecting her thoughts. The idea she was trying to express had not been stated directly in the book, but was something she had synthesized. "They do a lot of setting up for their scene. Lighting, music, attire, props. If you think about it," she hesitated, trying to cobble her words together to express this new thought. "If you think about it, each of those items stimulates a sense: sight, hearing, touch. You could even stimulate smell and taste if you wanted to."

"Hmm," Rick uttered.

"I was just thinking about how, you know, when a relationship is new, the newness and the unknown fuel the passion, but of course, that wears off. But what if we could recapture that? What if we could create passion and excitement on purpose by stimulating our senses? Like Pavlov's dog."

Rick stopped caressing her back; his eyes widening. "How would we do that?"

"By picking items that trigger desire in our brains. For example, lingerie…"

It had always been a point of contention in their vanilla sex life. Lingerie felt patriarchal and seemed like a waste of money; what was the point of spending a hundred dollars on something one wore for two seconds? However, she loved costumes, and lingerie, in the context of experimenting with BDSM, felt like a necessity. She couldn't play the part if she didn't have the right clothes.

Rick cleared his throat, about to interrupt because he'd always tried to encourage her to wear lingerie, but Nadine kept speaking, "_But_," she said, emphasizing the word. "I can see the value of it if it stimulates you visually, and as a costume, it can help me get into character."

Rick continued to stroke her back, satisfied that his point of view was being addressed.

Nadine continued, "And I can see how, if we address as many of our senses as possible, it could help us to respark some of the excitement that has faded over the years."

"Sold," Rick said, kissing her hand, his voice full of anticipation.

They agreed to try on their next "date night" and discussed what senses were triggers for each of them. For Rick, sight and touch were important. He wanted to see Nadine in lingerie and touch her, and pretty much nothing else mattered. However, the more Nadine thought about, the more specific she was able to get about how she wanted to be stimulated. She liked music, but only slow, deep music, preferably without words; low lighting, but not pitch black; and light, teasing touch, especially during foreplay. She also realized that she was turned on by being squeaky clean, and told Rick that both of them being freshly showered was a must. She also had a turnoff: perfumey scents and candles and especially perfumey scented candles, so there would be none of those.

They agreed that for this experiment, Nadine would "set the scene" or as she liked to called it "play set decorator", procuring the necessary items and setting up their bedroom. They agreed that next time, Rick would be set decorator.

The most time consuming aspect of preparation was finding the right costume, and she intuited that it wasn't going to be had at the mall. Nadine wanted lingerie that was sexy as well as supportive, since one of her main complaints about frilly bras was that they weren't comfortable for large, real boobs like hers. She wanted her costume to be edgy but elegant, rock and roll but not trashy. Like a black leather pencil skirt, she wanted something that walked the line between these seeming dichotomies.

After hours of searching online, she found just the thing on a website dedicated to artisan entrepreneurs: a strappy black number—that had the feel of a spider web—with a sheer mesh material that covered her breasts and a sturdy halter that hooked around her neck in addition to the typical shoulder straps.

When her bra arrived in the mail, she immediately tried it on and was pleased with her reflection. The seductive coverage of the mesh gave her support while also giving the illusion of nudity, her tawny nipples clearly visible through the filmy fabric. She noticed that the fabric was cutaway on the sides so she could easily disrobe her nipple by pulling the fabric in either direction, while the web-like straps of the bra still kept her bust supported.

Nice! she thought.

She had also found some hosiery that she knew Rick would like, whose naughty construction turned her on as well. They were crotchless fishnets with a built-in garter belt, the "belt" and stockings a single unit made out of an incredibly stretchy material that she pulled this way and that, impressed by how it didn't snag or lose its shape. She could keep them on no matter what they did.

It was like active wear for sexperts.

Perfect!

On the appointed day, Rick took their son and dog to his mother's while Nadine prepared their room.

Thinking about the five senses, she moved around the room.

Sight. She frowned as she looked at their beautiful four-. post bed with sheers hanging on all four sides. She'd seen one similar to it in a Cate Blanchett movie, and had fallen in love. It was already quite romantic, but how could she make it feel "different" than their everyday bedding?

Opening the linen closet, she rediscovered a bedspread-like piece of material that a man had sold her on a beach in Europe to spread out over the sand. The coarsely woven cotton, with a red and blue mandala-like pattern block printed in the center, brought back the happy memories of that Mediterranean vacation.

"Perfect," she said, pulling it from the cedar scented closet. She walked back to the bedroom and spread the coverlet over their existing bedding, admiring how it seemed to transform the bed from a place of sleep to a place of activity. She got a thrill just looking at it.

She could tell this bedspread was going to be like Pavlov's bell for her.

Next she changed out the lightbulb in her nightstand to an orange-colored LED light that gave the room a candlelight glow, and closed the blinds against the late evening sun, taking in the warm incandescence the room was bathed in.

Sound. She grabbed her phone, considering what type of music to play, and typed the word "tantra" into the search bar, multiple playlists appearing before her eyes. She scrolled briefly, choosing the one that described itself as perfect for hours of sensual lovemaking. She gave it a listen and—liking what she heard—turned up the volume, immediately filling the space with low drums and the earthy sensual sound of an instrument that she couldn't place. The music sounded like desire and yearning, it was just what she wanted.

Smell. While not a positive trigger for her, she knew that Rick enjoyed the sensuality of warm, spicy scents, and she opened the essential oils she'd purchased for tonight, mixing clove, cinnamon, and orange oils in a clay vessel on his nightstand. The fragrance was subtle and earthy, and she found that she actually liked it.

Touch. She grabbed the clean make-up brushes she'd washed the night before, and placed them on her nightstand.

She studied the room, satisfied with the scene that she'd set. There was nothing left to do but shower and put on her costume.

A cold shiver ran through her body, this was it; they were on the precipice of taking their sexual relationship to a new place. She felt like she was on the end of a diving board that was just a couple of feet higher than she was comfortable with. It was exhilarating.

Just then, she heard the door to the garage open. Rick was home. She wanted them to have their scene-setting conversation before they changed.

She walked into the living room, just as Rick did, and they flashed each other awkward smiles, like teens who'd been caught kissing. Nadine couldn't remember the last time she'd felt that feeling; it was rather exciting to experience it again.

She palmed her neck and pointed to their mid-century couch. "Let's do our negotiation here, before we change."

At the word "negotiation", Rick's eyebrow shot so high it looked like it was trying to leave his face.

Silently Rick took her hand and they sat close together, thighs touching, fingers intertwined. She already felt closer to him than she had in months, the honesty—and its resulting trust—opening up a pathway she hadn't known was blocked.

The space between them vibrated with an uncertain energy; a potent mixture of fear and excitement, trepidation and anticipation, the unknown and the familiar. It was a heady, visceral combination and Nadine recognized how thrilling it was going to make everything that followed.

Rick cleared his throat. "We need to set our expectations, right?"

"Yes, exactly." She was pleased that he remembered this. She smoothed out her jeans, collecting her thoughts. "There's an aspect of BDSM that I'd like to incorporate tonight. All of this self-analysis about what turns me on and off has made me realize that it's a turn-off for me when we check in with each other *while* we're being intimate—"

"Isn't that what this pre-negotiation is for?" he interrupted.

"Yes, this should help. But I have another idea that I think will be even better. It's something called 'power play'. It's kind of like BDSM light. It would involve the scene discussion—which we are doing right now—the scene itself, and then the debrief, just like I described, but because neither of us is a natural dom or sub, or top and bottom, which are the terms some BDSM people prefer, we could take turns with the roles."

Rick stiffened.

"It's not as scary as it sounds," she said, softening her voice, hoping she didn't lose him here because she thought this could really spice things up for them.

Rick scrunched up his nose. "But isn't the dom supposed to whip the sub and stuff like that."

Nadine shook her head. "That's the common misconception. Look, instead of dom and sub, let's call it..." she paused, searching for the right word.

Suddenly she had an epiphany. "Let's call it 'director' and 'actor'. The dom/top/director is responsible for setting the scene and moving it along. The sub/bottom/actor is responsible for doing what the director says. The dom/director could say 'kneel with your thighs spread and your arms behind your back' or 'lie down and spread your legs so I can take you in my mouth'."

Rick sucked in a breath and his eyes widened. "Damn, that was hot." He shifted a bit in his seat. "Okay. So who do you want to be?"

She blushed, looking up at him through lowered lashes. As the more extroverted and opinionated member of their marriage, she knew that he wasn't expecting the next words to leave her mouth. "I want you to be the director, and me to be the actor."

A look of surprise flashed across his face, followed by one of naked desire. "What else?" he said, his voice catching.

She squirmed under his gaze, heat building between her thighs. "I left some makeup brushes on my nightstand. I'd like you to use those on my body."

He narrowed his eyes, looking positively predatory. "Anything else?"

She swallowed. "I want to leave all my clothes on."

His brow lifted in question.

"Don't worry, it won't be a hindrance to anything," she added quietly.

A growl rumbled in his throat. Rick nodded again, his lips tight.

"How about you. What do you want?" Nadine asked.

"Want? Honey, I just want to have sex with you."

Nadine laughed, the honesty of his comment catching her off guard. "Okay, that's a start. I'm okay with having sex too, but not right away. After forty-five minutes and at least one orgasm on my part, followed by lots of cuddling, some touching of my back, and some kissing on my shoulders."

Rick blanched. "There's a timetable?"

"It's not a strict one, honey. I just don't want it to be a quickie," she said, remembering most of their sex over the last few years.

Rick colored, the excitement of the past few minutes, fading.

Nadine squeezed his hand, the honesty of talking about their sexual shortcomings made her feel closer to him than she had in a while. She needed to feel emotionally close to be turned on, and right now, she was feeling both. "There's nothing to be afraid of. We are just playing, testing boundaries, experimenting. How can we know what we like if we don't try? If you don't like, we never have to do it again." She ran a hand over his chest, and watched his torso ripple under her touch. She felt a self-satisfied spark within her.

Maybe she'd like playing the seductress more than she realized.

Rick's face was inscrutable.

"Honey, let's just leave our egos at the door and admit that our sex life these last few years has not been what either of us wanted it to be. If we can admit that, then we can let it go…it's in the past, and we can focus on making the future better. But if you don't admit that, we are stuck."

Rick looked at a spot on the floor a few feet away, his brow rippling. When he looked back to Nadine he said, "Agreed. Okay then, I want you to tell me if you like things as I do them."

Nadine shook her head. "Absolutely not. That's exactly what I don't want. For this 'scene'," she said, making air quotes with her fingers. "I want us to do all of our verbal communication out here, and then none in the bedroom, unless I ask you to stop, of course. You will know that I like things by the moans I make, by the way I move, and by not telling you to stop. I want to be in the moment. I want you to pay attention to my non-verbal cues. You get the freedom and excitement of deciding what happens and I get the freedom and excitement of not knowing what will happen."

"Okay. I think I understand."

She smiled. "Look, it's not going to be perfect, okay? Let's just release that expectation. We are just playing, having fun, experimenting. Be playful."

"Be playful," he said, as though reminding himself. "I like that. Thinking of it as playing somehow takes the pressure off."

"Good. That's good. Play is fun. Pressure isn't. Sex should be fun, right?"

He nodded. "I don't think I need anything else. As long as I can have sex with you, and by sex, I mean intercourse."

Men.

They really are that simple.

Or at least her guy was.

"Remember, the goal here is to communicate. I'm telling you exactly what I want so that you can please me and vice versa. That way, everyone is happy at the end of the day. Isn't that a worthwhile goal?"

He nodded, the light coming back into his eyes.

She sighed. There was one more thing she needed to say. "I don't know if we need a safeword. I mean, I have a hard time imagining you'd want me to do anything I'm not comfortable with." She'd read that some subs didn't have safewords because they trusted their doms ability to guard their safety while simultaneously arousing their pleasure. She felt like she and Rick occupied that space of implicit trust as well.

Rick nodded, running his hand over her shoulder reassuringly. "Why don't you pick one anyway," he said, protectively.

She smiled, happy he was playing along while also knowing that he couldn't possibly think of anything she'd need a safe word for.

Unless…

Perhaps he'd been doing his own research.

She swallowed hard. "How about 'ow'."

He smirked. "Good one. But I'm not sure it's distinct enough from 'oh', which you might be saying a lot."

Heat coursed through her body. Rick was really getting into this. "Okay then. Let's just go with 'vanilla'."

He smirked. "Anything else?"

She shook her head. "But I'm literally not going to do anything if you don't direct me, understand? I'll just be a body on the bed until you tell me what to do."

"Understood," he said, his face a strange mix of being turned on and restrained. Then he held up his finger, as though he'd just remembered something. "My mom asked us to pick up Lukas by nine, and I know you wanted to debrief, so what are you thinking in terms of time?"

Her heart panged at his thoughtfulness. "Right. Good catch." She pursed her lips. "I'd like to chat for twenty or thirty minutes after we've had a good cuddle, so I suppose our scene should," she paused, looking for the right word. "Conclude," she said, starting again. "Around eight, so we have enough time to chat before you go pick him up."

She was glad they were chatting about this logistical, parenting stuff now. It would definitely put a damper on the mood in the bedroom if they'd had to bring it up there.

He nodded. "I'll keep my watch on."

Nadine gave his hand a squeeze and stood up. "I'm going to shower in our bathroom, you can use Lukas'. I left clothes for you to change into in his room," she said, thinking of the tight black t-shirt and jeans she'd bought for him. He was going to look like a hot ninja in the bedroom.

He stood as well, his face, questioning.

She brushed her lips against his. "It's going to be fun."

Rick chewed his lower lip and nodded.

She turned away, feeling his eyes following her as she headed down the hallway.

He was probably already trying to imagine her in lingerie.

Although they'd been together for a long time, Nadine never doubted her husband's desire for her. He had always been very vocal and demonstrative about how much he wanted her, no matter what she was wearing, how much she weighed, or whether she was wearing make-up. Her weight had fluctuated over the years, some gray was starting to color her dark hair, and she knew she was far from the size-6 twenty-four-year-old she'd been when they'd started dating, however, his desire for her had never wavered.

If anything, there were days when she wished he could admire her for all the other things she did. She was a great mom, a talented ceramicist. She threw wonderful parties, and made the best chocolate chip cookies on the planet. She always found the best deals on everything, and she welcomed him at the door every day.

Why couldn't he admire all those things about her too?

Then again, she'd never asked him to, the way she was asking him to be her "director" today. Maybe she would bring those things up tomorrow, more opportunities for honesty.

She smiled as she got into the steaming shower and thought about all the ways a little book about BDSM had improved her marriage. Today was a new beginning. Perhaps increased honesty in the bedroom would lead to increased honesty outside the bedroom too.

She showered carefully, cleaning every inch of her body because she was open to having every inch of it explored by Rick. When she got out of the shower, she chose to use flax oil on her skin instead of her usual lotion so that if Rick licked her he wouldn't taste lotion.

Deliberately preparing for sex was a new experience. She'd never approached it so purposefully before, and it was definitely turning her on.

When she walked back into their bedroom, she was greeted by the scene she had created earlier.

The room seemed to pulse with sensual promise.

Damn this is hot.

She pulled a silver cardboard box from the top shelf of her closet, removed the lid and pulled back white tissue paper, fingering the filmy fabric of her new bra and the texture of the stretchy stockings.

Her heart sped up.

She placed the box on the bed as though it was a totem that could help guide her as she prepared, and sat at her vanity, putting on just enough make up to set off her eyes; a sweep of powder to enhance her brows, and then layer of mascara to make her lashes stand out. Adding a layer of clear lip balm, she pinched her cheeks and gazed at her reflection. "Ready," she said to her reflection, a statement, not a question.

She pulled out the custom bra, admiring the intricate engineering involved in its design, which reminded her of a trapeze harness. Removing her towel, she held it up, trying to figure out which way to put it on. When it had arrived in the mail, the neck and back clasps had been hooked together, and now she knew why. Without the guidance of the closed hooks, it was impossible to tell the difference between front and back, top and bottom. After a few moment of consideration, she found the largest holes and put her arms through them arranging the smaller hole around her neck and clasping it, and then reaching around to clasp the one on the back.

Laughing inwardly, she raised her eyes to the full-length mirror; she was already transformed. Staring back at her was a woman who knew what she wanted, standing there in a bra that was made for sex, the rigid webbing designed to support without cups, the sheer mesh stretched over her breasts designed to entice rather than support, the halter neck giving the sensual hint of submission.

Her face flushed. She couldn't remember ever having stated her wants as clearly as she had half-an-hour ago, and she was surprised at how disconcerting it had been; she'd become so used to putting herself last. However, looking at her reflection now, she had finally figured out how to put herself first.

She winked at herself coquettishly.

She grabbed the hosiery, sliding her hands through the waistband and into the legs to stretch the material over her toes, calves, and thighs before pulling the waistband up. She plucked at the garter-like width of material that connected the waist to the stockings and lifted her right leg out to the side. The fabric moved with her, stretching and flexing like a seductive second skin. It felt strangely empowering.

Turning once more to the mirror, she took in her reflection and had to admit that she looked hot.

I'd do me!

She did a quick pirouette, giggling that her bare ass was hanging out. She didn't feel submissive at all; she felt powerful, confident, and excited.

Rick was going to go insane when he saw her.

She gave the room a final survey and felt her nipples pucker and her sex, clench.

Mission accomplished.

She heard Rick moving around in Lukas' bedroom. It was time to arrange herself for his entrance.

She had done a bit of research about positions for submissives and had picked a specific pose for just this moment. Approaching the bed, she kneeled on the mattress and spread her thighs into a deep open vee, welcoming. She straightened her back, chest high, shoulders back, chin level to the ground. Her hands dangled softly on the side of her thigh, palms up, like a bird prepared to take flight. Her eyes were trained downward at a spot on the center of the bed. Everything about her body was soft, waiting, open.

She took a deep breath and exhaled loudly.

She was ready.

A few minutes later, their bedroom door cracked open, and Nadine resisted turning her head, feeling her breath tighten in her throat. Her body was humming, veins thrumming in anticipation, the excitement of not knowing what was going to happen had her tingling with nervous anticipation.

She heard Rick inhale audibly and felt a ping of desire vibrate through her sex and moist warmth begin to gather.

The rustle of Rick's jeans seemed loud as he entered the room, her senses heightened, his bare feet padding on the wood floor as he walked to the side of the bed.

Out of her peripheral vision she could see him standing there and feel his gaze wandering over her like she was a glass of water and he was drinking her in.

Her nipples puckered.

Damn, she thought, surprised at how aroused she was becoming when nothing had happened. She'd read a bit about the erotic effect of anticipation, however, experiencing it for herself was something else altogether. Their scene had barely begun and already she wanted to do it again.

Heat pooled between her legs, her skin felt like a keyboard waiting to be played.

"You look beautiful, Nadine," Rick said, his words a low, heavy caress.

She could hear the want in his voice, and she shivered.

"Open your legs wider," he said, his normal voice edged with just a hint of command, as though asking permission to speak to her this way.

She immediately obeyed.

"Arch your back a bit more," he said, with more certainty. "Yes, yes," he said, his breath catching. "Just like that. That's good. So beautiful."

She couldn't ever remember feeling this aroused and he hadn't even touched her.

He licked his lips, the sound a sensual promise. "Raise your hands and touch your nipples." His voice was in full command now. "That's it. Gently, gently. Barely touch them, like a teasing feather."

She gasped, he was using her own hands to do the exact thing she most wanted. She was turned on by the creative thoughtfulness of it.

Using her middle finger she slowly circled her nipples, the pads of her fingers slipping over the mesh fabric, barely a hint of friction reaching the skin, and yet it was enough.

She gasped.

"Yes. That's it. Do that a bit more. Light and fast."

Her teasing touch was beginning to frustrate her. She wanted to arch into her hands, her body craving more pressure. When would it happen? When would he command it?

The uncertainty was delicious.

"Now on the count of three, I want you to pinch your nipples hard, but only one time. Do you understand?"

She nodded.

"Yes, *sir*," he commanded.

She felt liquid lust dripping from her labia. *He had done some research.* "Yes, sir."

She heard him suck in a breath and felt an answering vibration in her vulva.

Fuck she wanted him!

If he had bent her over and started pumping, she could have died a happy woman.

But this was only the beginning.

He moved behind her, brushing his fingertips across the tops of her shoulders and then into her hair, running his nails across her scalp sending cascades of shivers down her back. He stopped abruptly and stepped away. She could hear him walking towards the corner of the room where her vanity stood.

What's he doing?

Part of her wanted to turn her head and satisfy her curiosity, however, the other part of her wanted to see how good a "bottom" she could be. She knew Rick probably wouldn't care if she turned, however, she decided to make it a personal challenge to try and be as submissive as possible; to empty her mind of ego and just be flotsam on a wave of desire.

By the time Rick returned, she had almost forgotten he had walked away, so successful had she been at emptying her mind.

After his feet came to a halt behind her, she felt a pressure on her scalp and suddenly Rick was brushing her hair with the boar's hair brush she kept on her vanity.

"Aahh," she sighed.

She could have purred she was so happy.

He brushed her hair with firm but loving strokes, making her scalp tingle with friction as the blood rushed in. After a few minutes, he parted her hair into three sections and plaited it lightly, laying it over her right shoulder when he was done. Then he kissed the base of her scalp and rubbed his stubble over the delicate skin.

She giggled at the abrasion.

"This is so much better," he said, his voice gravelly. "Now I can get to that lovely neck of yours."

She gasped. *Who the hell was this guy and what had he done with her husband?*

They'd been together two decades and he'd never brushed or braided her hair. The act was so incredibly tender and loving, that her heart felt like it doubled in size.

She heard him pull something out of his jeans pocket and then everything went black, as he secured one of his silk ties around her eyes.

"I read that depriving you of one sense, can heighten your physical sensations," he said. "Lay on your stomach."

Now that her sight had been taken away, his voice seemed louder and more nuanced, flavored with calm authority and caged excitement.

She sucked in a breath as she slid slowly forward on the bed, arms over her head, making a show of it as she arched her back deeply pressing her ass high in the air.

"Naughty, naughty," he said, clearly enjoying the show. He pulled on the "garter" that connected the waistband of her hosiery to the leg. "What do we have here? My goodness, Nadine, you've outdone yourself." He caressed the slope of her bare ass with slow, deliberate movements, skirting the edge of the hosiery like a barrier just waiting to be breached.

She squirmed as curlicues of pleasure and desire wound through her body.

"Oh, you like that do you?"

"Uh huh," she gasped into the coverlet, conscious thought no longer easy, her mind overwhelmed by sensation. She felt like she was floating in some sort of erotic purgatory.

When his fingertips brushed the border of her vulva she sucked in a quick breath.

Before tonight, she wouldn't have thought torture could taste so sweet.

He continued to trace up and down the hills and valleys of her thighs and ass, occasionally brushing her labia, but never probing any further.

She wished for his fingers to delve into her and satisfy her squirming urges, but he resisted, stroking her excitement higher with every taunting caress.

Finally he stopped, and walked to a nightstand.

She tensed, excited for what she knew would come next.

Soft butterfly touches began skating across the skin of her back, so light, she might have imagined it.

He was using the make-up brushes to tease and tickle her, and their feathery edges were an even better weapon of erotic torture than she had imagined.

She sighed into the coverlet, enjoying the attention, the pent-up frustration that Rick had been building beginning to ebb into a delicious relaxation. At that moment, Rick switched to a smaller, denser brush than the first and raced it up the side of her torso, sending a thrill straight to her nipple. He mirrored the gesture on her other side and again, her nipple puckered.

"Holy mother," she whimpered.

"What's that?" he asked, tauntingly.

"Nothing, sorry..."

"Nothing...what?"

"Nothing, sir," she said, striking just the right tone because he sighed with approval.

"That's right, *mon coeur*," he said, his voice full of longing.

He switched to a bigger, but denser brush and quickly swept it up her labia, causing her to gasp with surprise. He did it again, and again, and each time, elicited the same gasp.

The gasping must have pushed him over the edge because suddenly she felt the pressure of his weight kneeling beside her on the mattress and then his hand was at her entrance and then—

"Yes.." she gasped, as he filled her with his fingers and she rocked back to deepen the thrust. "Yes, yes," she said, her vocabulary suddenly robbed of anything more than that single word.

He thrust again, his lips at the shell of her ear. "Do you like that, *mon coeur*?"

She moaned and gasped again. "Yes."

He gave a low chuckle. "Turn over."

He helped her roll over, his fingers never leaving the warmth of her sex.

When she was on her back he moved between her legs and brought his face down to his hand.

"You smell so good. I wonder how you taste?"

She whimpered at his words. She loved hearing him talk like this.

A coolness hit her clit as his tongue flicked over the most sensitive skin.

"Mmmm," he said, like he was tasting the sweetest fruit.

She made a guttural sound, which seemed to spur him on because suddenly he assaulted her sex with his mouth and hands like a man possessed.

She was already so wound up that her orgasm bore down on her quickly. She breathed in stuttered gasps as he licked, sucked, and pumped her higher and higher until she crashed, riding his fingers as wave after wave of her orgasm convulsed through her.

Holy fuck!

He read her body, his mouth and fingers still sucked and probing, but slower, and then slower, and then sweet, sweet stillness.

Sometime later, Nadine returned to her body to find herself in Rick's arms, cuddled in the curve of his chest.

He was caressing her forearm with the tips of his fingers, his chin fitted into the crook of her neck.

"Did I pass out?" she asked.

She felt him nod. "You had the most amazing, most fantastic, most orgasmic orgasm I've ever seen. If I hadn't given it to you, I might be a little jealous," he said, with pride and awe in his voice. "*La petite mort.* It was the most beautiful thing I've ever seen." He kissed her on her shoulder.

"Oh my. It was amazing. I've never felt anything like that. But we aren't done, are we?"

Rick showed her his watch and she saw that they had just enough time to chat for a few minutes before one of them— hopefully Rick because her legs still felt too wobbly to walk— would need to pick up their son.

"Debrief?" she asked.

"Yes. You first."

She shook her head. Words felt inadequate for the love that she felt for her husband. How to explain? "It was perfect. I wouldn't change a thing."

She felt him smile into her neck. "I agree. What did you like?"

She shook her head. "I loved it all. I love that you did some research. It was fun calling you 'sir' and the blindfold really heightened all my other senses. All of the teasing with the brushes was even better than I thought it would be." She paused, trying to pull out moments from the fog of her post-orgasmic mind.

"Oh wait." She grabbed his hand and kissed it. "I absolutely adored how you brushed and braided my hair. It made me feel so cherished; so wonderful," she paused as tears welled in her eyes. "It made me feel so loved."

"Oh baby, I do love you."

"I know. Especially now. I don't think I've ever felt closer to you or loved you more than this moment. I also loved hearing you talk. It wasn't even dirty, but it really turned me on."

"Fascinating," he said, hissing on the "s." He pulled her closer. "I love how free, and brave, and honest you were. It was so erotic to watch you just give yourself over to pleasure so fully. I had no idea how exciting that would be."

She felt like she was glowing at his praise.

"And I love this," he said, snapping the waistband of her sexpert hosiery. "Where on earth did you find this outfit?"

"The internet," she said, smugly.

"Of course. All hail the internet." He glanced at his watch. "I really should go."

She nodded. "We can continue when you get back."

"Continue?"

"Why not. We've had sex when Lukas was asleep before. It wasn't like we were being loud, or anything."

He kissed her shoulder. "Sounds great. I'll be back in a flash." He started to get up and then paused. "One thing though."

"Yes?"

"Keep this outfit on."

She smiled. "Okay."

He hesitated again. "One other thing."

She laughed. "What now?"

"I order you to masturbate and have at least two more orgasms before I get home."

Her nipples puckered. "Yes, sir."

__If you'd like me to write more about Rick and Nadine, Cast your vote by going to SmartURL.it/KNB1survey Thanks!__

Comprehensive Sex Education

Dear Readers,

As a woman and mother, I've worked to educate myself about sex. Sex is a loaded word that can refer to many things: gender identity, human biology, the act of procreation, the act of physical intimacy, however, all of these things are neither negative or positive, they just are.

There are studies that show that Comprehensive Sex Education (CSE) leads to fewer unplanned pregnancies, fewer sexually transmitted diseases, higher rates of gender equality, less physical violence, and higher satisfaction with one's sex life. These all sound like good things to me!

If you would like to learn more, here are three resources that I recommend to help give you the Comprehensive Sex Education that is considered a human right in some countries and which can use improving in ours.

1. NON-FICTION **"Come as You Are: The Surprising New Science that Will Transform Your Sex Life" by Emily Nagoski,** https://amzn.to/31tO6nc : This non-fiction book is the sex-ed class we all needed and deserved. I can't believe how much I learned about the female body, even though I've lived in one my whole life. Also includes information on how to heal oneself from sexual trauma.

2. NON-FICTION **"Beyond Birds and Bees: Bringing Home a New Message to Our Kids About Sex, Love, and Equality" by Bonnie J. Rough,** https://amzn.to/2KpXba6: This non-fiction book compares and contrasts one family's experience with sex ed while living in both America and Holland. It offers compelling thoughts on how American parents can advocate for CSE in their schools (and even places of worship!) and includes many fantastic resources.

3. FICTION **"Brie's Submission" by Red Phoenix,** https://amzn.to/2WBhdWA: Red Phoenix has lived the BDSM lifestyle for decades. This book follows the life/training of a young woman curious about the BDSM "lifestyle." It is definitely "kinky", however, it is not violent. If you read it, you will learn about how important consent and mutual enjoyment are for BDSM practitioners.

Fuck Fear

Fourteen years after BECKONED, Part 6: Adrift in New Zealand

She stared in the mirror, pulling out her omnipresent ponytail.

Fingering her shoulder-length sunshine-blond hair—the color of her childhood courtesy of a bottle—she considered her reflection. The last time she'd changed her hairstyle had been over twenty years ago, since before she got married, surely it was time for a new look.

"Mom? Mom! We're leaving," her twelve-year-old Maxwell called from the front hall of her three-bedroom rental house.

She sighed, walking from her bathroom between towers of unpacked moving boxes to where her two sunshine-blond sons were standing, both of them already showing the height they inherited from their father.

Her eyes started watering.

"Ah, come on. We'll be here all the time," Finnegan, her ten-year-old said, already sounding like a teenager.

She pulled them in and hugged them tightly. They didn't squirm. Thank god, she didn't know if she could take any more rejection. She'd once carried an American Express Black card that she'd earned on her own, and now she could barely qualify for this house.

Times had changed.

"Thanks for helping me move," she sniffled, into the top of Finnegan's head since Max was already taller than her.

Maxwell sighed. "It's okay mom. We'll be here all the time. Remember? Fifty-fifty split," he said, patting her on the back in a way that felt much older than his years.

They pulled away from her and stepped out her door, walking towards her ex's black Audi. Her ex raised two fingers off the steering wheel in a sign of greeting. She reciprocated the greeting and watched as her boys got into the car and drove off, returning—without her—to the home she had lived in for the last thirteen years.

She closed the door, glanced at the stacks of boxes, and sighed. "Might as well get started," she said, and walked to her kitchen to brew some coffee.

Six hours later, Therese Hartley, formerly known as Therese Hartley-McDowell, although she'd dropped her ex's last name as quickly as legally possible, was sitting in her favorite armchair looking through photographs. The first box she had chosen had held pictures and she had made the rookie mistake of allowing herself to wallow in memories, instead of unpacking, or going out to buy furniture, or going grocery shopping to fill her new fridge.

Just then, she heard a knock at her door.

Who could that be?

She looked through the peephole and spied a huge floral arrangement that was blocking the delivery person's face. When the person lowered the flowers, it was the face of her best friend: Angela Holguín.

She opened the door.

"Oh my god, what are you doing here?" Therese exclaimed, kissing Angela's cheek as she grabbed the huge arrangement filled with tuberose and blush-colored roses.

"I came to help you unpack," Angela said, looking around for somewhere to put her handbag, but since the only piece of furniture in the living room was the armchair Therese had been sitting in, she decided on the countertop of the open-floor-plan kitchen.

"From New Zealand?" Therese asked, putting the flowers next to Angela's bag as she stared at her friend in disbelief.

Angela nodded and then pulled Therese into a hug. "Therese, you helped pick me up more times than I can count. I'll always be here for you. Besides, Soren can handle the kids. He's got their *abuela* with him. He's fine."

Therese sighed, grateful her old friend had turned up, the weight on her shoulders, suddenly lighter. "How long are you staying?"

Angela smiled. "Two weeks. And if you want, I'll even stay here so I can help you more. I came straight from the airport, so I have my bag in the car." She studied Therese's face for a reaction and then added, "If that's too much, I can always go to my place," she said, referring to the L.A. home that her New Zealand-based family lived in for part of the year.

Therese pulled her old friend back into another hug, blinking back tears. She had not been looking forward to sleeping in an empty house tonight. Although she and her husband, Ian, had been separated for almost two years, it was Ian who had moved out of their home while they "figured things out", while Therese and the boys had stayed put. However, part of the divorce settlement included Ian buying Therese out of the house, which was why she'd been the one to move out. "I'd love it if you stayed here, it'll be like our college days, roommates again!" she said, feeling a genuine bit of cheer for the first time in months and a sudden pang for the simplicity of life as an undergrad.

"Great! What should we do first?" Angela asked, looking around the room as she pushed her long mahogany hair behind her ears.

Therese looked at her watch; it was almost four p.m. "I need to buy furniture for the boys' rooms so they can stay with me next week. Let's go to IKEA."

Angela clapped. "I haven't been there in forever. Let's go."

They drove thirty minutes to the big-box retailer and then wandered around the maze of room tableaus, catching up on things, soaking up the joy of being with someone you love and don't get to see as often as you like.

Angela threw herself into a beanbag chair. "You've got to get them one of these, right? Who doesn't love a beanbag?"

Therese screwed up her face in thought. "Sure, why not. Grab a tag so we can take it to the cashier."

"Come join me." Angela patted the empty beanbag next to her and Therese plopped down, inhaling the sharp tang of the cured leather. "Too bad we didn't have one of these in our dorm room."

"There wasn't room! We barely had enough space for our beds and desks."

Angela cried out as though she'd forgotten. "God that was a fun time. I can't believe we've been friends almost been thirty years." She turned to face Therese and repeated, *"Thirty* years!"

Therese covered her face with her hand. "Don't remind me. And don't age me either. We are forty-five."

"You are forty-five my friend, I already turned forty-six."

Forty-five. How was it possible? She could still vividly remember the day she met Angela at Trojan Hall, the honors dormitory at USC. She had been a shy and quiet transplant from Northern California. Angela had been a sparkplug, always dragging her out; excited to share her hometown of Los Angeles with Therese.

"So. Have you thought at all about dating?" Angela asked, waggling her brows.

Therese sighed and blushed simultaneously. "Yes." She and her ex hadn't shared a bed in over three years, the last year of their "marriage" they'd hid an air mattress under the bed for Ian to sleep on, so the boys wouldn't suspect anything. She missed physical intimacy and felt like she was withering on the vine, a ripe fruit still juicy for the taking.

"I sense a 'but'," Angela said, crossing her denim-clad legs, red patent oxfords on her feet.

Therese sighed. "It's just a strange new world out there. It's all about apps and swiping these days. I have to have pictures taken—"

"I'll take your picture!" Angela pulled out her smartphone and snapped a photo before Therese could say anything.

Therese grimaced. "They are supposed to be of me doing stuff."

"You're shopping at IKEA, I think that qualifies."

Therese rolled her eyes. Angela was one of the most motivated, "get-things-done" people she knew. She could also be incredibly bossy and steamroll you if you let her. As college roommates, Angela had been an excellent lesson in learning to say no to someone. "Not shopping. Photos of me hiking, or biking, or wine-tasting, or whatever stupid hobbies I'm supposed to have to attract a guy in this day and age."

Angela stood up and offered her hand to Therese, pulling her up as well. "So we can take lots of photos. No problem."

Therese took her shopping list out of her bag.

"Did we get everything?" Angela asked.

Therese looked at the list: bed frames, nightstands, reading lights, desks, desk lamps, bureaus, hangers for closet. All the basics. She could furnish the rest of the house slowly, with vintage and antique furniture, which she preferred. "We're done."

"What about mattresses?" Angela asked.

"I ordered those ages ago. The natural latex ones with organic wool and cotton. I can't sleep on anything else. The only furniture I moved into the house with was a bed frame for me, my favorite armchair, and a bureau I inherited from my grandmother. The boys' mattresses are wrapped up in plastic at the house just waiting for the frames."

"Smart." Angela nodded as they walked towards the checkout line. "Look. Why don't we make a point to take your pictures and get your profiles filled out while I'm here? We'll go do our favorite hike, go out to eat, maybe hit a museum. I'm sure we can pull together a dozen decent photos while I'm here. Besides, you're still hot as hell, Therese." Angela said, waving her hand up and down at Therese. "I mean, really, you have the flattest stomach I've ever seen on a mom of two."

Therese knew better. She was the proud owner of some extra skin around her belly, but she knew Angela wasn't completely off base. She'd always been into exercise and healthy eating and was still able to fit into all of her pre-pregnancy clothes, even if her tush was a bit rounder than it had been before, which wasn't necessarily a bad thing since her pre-baby bottom had been a bit flat for her taste.

They got into the checkout line as Angela nudged Therese in the ribs. "Come on. Say 'yes' and I'll take you out to dinner."

Therese knew Angela wasn't going to leave it alone. Then again, she wanted to date again, so what was the harm? "Okay. But I get to pick the restaurant."

Angela flashed her megawatt smile. "Deal."

Twenty minutes later, they were sitting on the patio of a restaurant that was somewhere between casual dining and fancy sandwich shop.

Angela opened up their wine menu, adjusting her lightweight wrap around her shoulders. "Hey. It must be good. They carry our wines."

Therese winked. "That's why I picked it."

Angela's face melted into a look of adoration. "I love you. You're the best. I'm so excited we have two weeks together."

The waiter, a tall, lean guy in the tightest jeans Therese had ever seen, blue eyes, and a sandy mustache that matched his tousled hair, approached the table. "Hello ladies. Can I get you started on a beverage?"

"Yes," Angela said. "My lovely single friend here can go first."

The waiter turned to Therese and arched a brow.

Therese started, a mild heat rising in her face. "Um, do you want to get a bottle of In Bocca?"

"Oh, In Bocca al Luppo is one of my favorite vineyards," Tight Jeans said. "Their Syrah is fantastic with any of our grass-fed beef or forest-raised pork dishes. Personally, I love to pair it with our pulled pork sandwich."

"I like this guy already," Angela said, snapping her menu closed. "Let's get the bottle of In Bocca Syrah; I'll get a pulled pork sandwich. Do you want to share the kale salad to start? It has dates and beets in it."

Therese nodded. "That sounds great. And I'll have the blue cheese and steak sandwich."

"Lovely ladies, I'll get that going for you," he winked before walking away.

Therese admired his tight jeans as he retreated. The view was even better from this side.

"He's cute," Angela said, following her eyes.

"He's a child. He can't be more than thirty. I couldn't have a relationship with someone that young."

Angela shrugged. "Just have fun. Don't go looking for a relationship. When you met Ian you weren't looking for anything serious, it just happened. Do the same thing."

Therese frowned. "Yeah but it's not really the same thing. I have two kids. I have to think about them."

"Absolutely. You'll think about them when you meet a guy that you like enough to have a relationship with. For now, just have fun. I only have one piece of dating advice," Angela said seriously, stopping herself as the waiter returned with their bottle of wine.

The two friends stayed silent as the waiter uncorked the bottle, pouring just the slightest bit out for both of them to taste before pouring full glasses.

Once he walked away, Angela took her glass and swirled it, smelling the bouquet. A small smile crept on her lips. "It smells like home."

Therese followed her lead, but all she smelled was an excellent Syrah with strong chocolate notes. "You'll have to send me another case. I'm all out." She took a sip and enjoyed the smooth silkiness of the wine as it spread across her palate.

"So my one piece of advice is this: hotel rooms. Don't go to his place, don't go to your place until you become serious. You don't want him knowing where you live until you know he's not a creeper," Angela said, pointing to her temple.

Therese's eyes widened. "Good point."

They ate their meal, their conversation devolving into silliness as they finished their bottle of wine. They were just intoxicated enough that neither of them felt safe to drive, so they decided to walk to a local movie theatre and catch a show.

As they walked, they passed a number of bars, but it was only a Thursday, so they weren't as busy as usual. They were just about to pass another bar when Angela pulled Therese to a stop and pointed at a sandwich board sign that had the words "SPEED DATING EVERY NIGHT. MONDAY: FF, TUESDAY: anything goes, WEDNESDAY: MM, THURSDAY: HETERO," with an arrow pointing towards the door.

"Speed dating! I've heard about this. And look, it's hetero night. Come on," Angela said, pulling Therese inside without waiting for an answer.

"Excuse me," Angela said, to the young woman standing at the host stand. "Where's the speed dating happening?"

"It's in the back room," the hostess said. "You better hurry. They are starting in ten minutes."

Angela started walking to the back, her arm still looped through Therese's.

"Wait a second," Therese said. "I didn't say I wanted to do speed dating."

"Oh come on. It'll be fun. I'll do it with you," Angela said, slipping the rings off her left hand and putting them into her coin purse.

"You'll do it with me?" Therese asked, wondering how intoxicated her friend was that she was saying that and how intoxicated she was that she was considering going along with it.

"Sure? It'll be fun. Besides, then you can get a second opinion on the guys." Angela lifted her neck, looking around the room. "I think we sign up over there. Let's go."

She pulled Therese towards two women with clipboards.

Therese sighed. She'd forgotten how strong Angela's gravitational pull could be, especially when it was trained on only one person.

"That will be thirty-five dollars each," one of the clipboard ladies said.

"My treat," Angela replied, whipping out her wallet before Therese could even process what was happening.

They signed in with the ladies who gave them each a piece of paper with the numbers one through fifteen written on it, followed by blank lines and then two check boxes under the words "YES" and "NO". In the top right corner of Therese's paper was the number fourteen written in permanent marker with a circle around it.

Therese's stomach turned with nervous anticipation. She hadn't seriously looked at another man as a potential love interest in almost fifteen years. She turned to Angela who gave her a reassuring smile.

"Relax, just have fun," Angela said. "Pretend it's research for one of my books. You can help me write the scene later, okay?"

Angela was an author of both children's books and adult literature.

Therese nodded, but she was only half listening to Angela, her gaze, wandering the room at the men holding identical sheets of paper to hers.

She swallowed hard.

Why am I nervous? I'll never see these guys again, and if no one picks me, I'm no worse off than I was before.

Her pep talk helped a little bit until her knees started to quiver.

She couldn't believe it. She was actually afraid.

She hadn't been this nervous since the first time she'd entered a courtroom as an attorney. She had been the second chair to a senior partner. The partner had turned to her and said, "You know what my mantra is when I'm afraid, Therese?" When she shook her head, the partner said, "Fuck fear. I say it nice and loud in my head. It always makes me feel better."

Fuck. Fear. She thought hesitantly, taking a deep breath.

Fuck fear. She thought, with a little more conviction.

The partner had been right, she did feel better.

FUCK FEAR! She yelled in her head.

Damn! That felt good.

At that moment, a forty-something woman with a severe red bob took a microphone and said, "We are about to start our speed dating. Hetero night is always the hardest because the numbers are never perfectly even." There were murmurs of laughter. She continued, "We have fourteen women and twelve men tonight, so the men will each have two more speed dates, but ladies," she paused, and looked meaningfully at the women in the room. "Once you are done meeting all the men, feel free to hang out and mingle while the last two women complete their round." She held up a piece of paper like the one Therese held. "When you start your first eight-minute date, start with number one and write your date's name on the line. Then, when the timer goes off, simply check 'yes' or 'no' and if both of you match 'yes', we'll send you an email with each other's email address tomorrow and you take it from there. Be sure to put your own name at the top of the sheet, next to your sign-in number, right now."

Therese wrote her name at the top of the sheet next to the number fourteen.

"Okay, please come line up in the order of the number on your paper, men to my right, women to my left."

Therese was last, and Angela was penultimate, which suited Therese just fine because they would get to watch what happened for the first couple of rounds.

"This is perfect," Angela whispered. "I can vet all of them for you." She gave Therese a thumbs-up.

The redhead said, "When you hear the buzzer go off, the round has started. When you hear it go off again, please thank each other and men, take a step to your right. Gentlemen: when you reach the last lady, circle back around to the front of the line until you've met everyone."

The buzzer went off and the room filled with the loud hum of twelve conversations starting simultaneously.

Angela leaned over. "Check out the guy with the Joe Manganiello look about halfway down."

Therese followed her eyes to where a tall man with salt-and-pepper hair was talking to a brunette. He had very expressive eyes and hands, and looked like he was explaining something complicated to his "date".

Therese frowned, wondering if he was an actor.

She did not want to get involved with anyone in The Industry—as the entertainment business was known—and in Los Angeles, the pretty people usually were.

She looked farther down the line and saw a serious looking man with wavy black hair and just a touch of gray at the temples. He was the only guy wearing a blazer, and he was staring at his date with such intensity, that Therese could practically feel the heat from here.

The buzzer rang, and the men sidestepped right. Angela was now talking animatedly to a guy who must have been at least a decade younger than her, but she already looked like she was having a good time; always the life of the party.

Therese had been so grateful when she met Angela the first day of college; being paired with an outgoing roommate had been a blessing. Therese had been pushed out of her comfort zone a lot by Angela that first year. She laughed inwardly as she remembered the first time she ever went to a club with Angela. She'd picked out a knee length dress with long sleeves edged in lace. Angela made her change immediately lending her black leather pants and a sheer turquoise blouse that she'd worn over a tank top.

The buzzer rang, and Therese forced a smile on her face as Angela made wide eyes at her and subtly shook her head.

"Hi, I'm Tom," Tom said, shoving his hand into Therese's.

"Hi, Therese."

"Don't forget to write my name down on your list," he said, dutifully writing her name on the third line of his sheet of paper. He'd checked the "yes" box for both Angela and the woman before.

"So, what do you do?" Tom asked.

Therese should have been prepared for this; it was the standard opening question in L.A.

What do *I do?*

She used to be a lawyer, on track to be one of the youngest partners at her firm before she got sidetracked by Ian and motherhood. She'd continued to work after her first baby, although her heart hadn't been in it, and when she'd gotten pregnant the second time, she had been grateful when Ian suggested that she mother full-time.

But she knew "I'm a mom" wasn't the answer anyone was looking for when they asked, "What do you do?"

But she was proud of being a mom. What's more important than raising the next generation?

Fuck fear! She squared her shoulders. "I'm a mom."

Tom blinked rapidly and clapped his hands together. "Really? A mom? How great." The lift on his voice a little too high.

Therese had a feeling he would have sounded exactly the same if she'd said she shoveled elephant poop for a living. *Really? You shovel elephant poop? How great.*

Therese could see he had already checked out of their encounter, but she realized that it was a blessing in disguise. What would be the point of wasting a nanosecond with a guy who didn't want to date a mother? It's not like it was something she could change, even if she wanted to.

Tom spent the rest of their time talking about his work as a brand manager for a local packaged foods company.

The buzzer rang setting off a string of actions like dominos falling that were echoed by all the other speed daters: "Thanks for the date." Check a box. Men shuffle right. Extend hand and introduce yourself.

"Hi, I'm Therese. I'm a mom," became Therese's new way of introducing herself; might as well lead with the fact that would quickly weed out the mice from the men.

She noticed that not all the men shut down at that statement, of her next five "dates", two of the men had kids as well, and one guy, although he didn't have kids, said that he would prefer a girlfriend with children because it meant she wouldn't move out of town.

Therese wasn't quite sure what to make of that comment.

Her next date would be with Joe Manganiello's doppelganger, and she didn't even have to look to notice his proximity, she could tell he was next by the way her palms were sweating. She tried to listen to what "Joe" and Angela were talking about and barely noticed what the man across from her was saying.

"Oh, a personal trainer? No wonder you're so fit," Angela said, a bit too loudly, as though she wanted Therese to hear. "No kids, but you were married once. Well, that isn't uncommon, is it? You like to cook? There's nothing like a man that likes to cook."

Therese perked up when she heard he wasn't in The Industry.

The buzzer rang and Therese's date held his hand out. She glanced at her paper to remind herself that his name was Jay. "Thanks, Jay."

He winked, his long blond eyelashes grazing the top of his cheeks. "Don't forget to check the 'yes' box. A date with Jay will be a-okay," he said in a sing-song voice.

Therese gave him a thumbs-up as he slid to the right, quickly checking her "no" box.

"Dante, this is my dear friend, Therese Hartley. I think you two will really hit it off. Therese is a marathoner," Angela said with a big smile before turning to her next guy.

"A marathoner, huh? Impressive," Dante said, raising his brows.

Therese waved it off. "Former marathoner. I haven't competed in three years." It had been one of the things she'd given up when things got tough with Ian. She missed it.

Dante frowned. "Never dismiss your accomplishments. You've done something you should be proud of. You. Are. A Marathoner." He gave a somber look, his dark eyes sparkling. Although not the tallest guy she'd met tonight, he was definitely the broadest, the curve of his back feeling like it gave them some privacy, blocking out everyone else who was around. "Come on. Say it back to me. I. Am. A Marathoner."

She gave a nervous giggle, but the look on his face made it clear he was serious. Finally, she said, "I. Am. A Marathoner."

He clapped his hands together and nodded. "Good. Now Angela tells me you're a mom of two boys. Are they athletic too?"

Therese practically swooned with relief. Now *here* was a topic she could talk about. "They love sports. My eldest is trying to convince me to let him go to a special sports camp in Wisconsin so he can perfect his basketball free throw. He's obsessed."

"Healthy obsessions should be encouraged. I wish someone had encouraged my interests in sports and nutrition; I would have become a trainer much sooner if they had. Instead, I spent five years as a consultant and hated every minute of it," Dante said, his face serious.

Therese's brow lifted. Dante was proving to be more than a pretty face.

"So what do you do when you aren't parenting?" Dante asked, an encouraging smile tugging at his lips displaying teeth that were startlingly white.

Therese liked the way he phrased the question. It left her room to talk about anything, like her passion for public schools, TED talks, and antique maps. But she decided to go the more traditional route. "I was an attorney until I had my second child. Corporate law. I think I'd like to get back into law, but maybe a different part of it. I love animals. I volunteer with a number of rescues. I love to be outdoors—"

"What are your favorite outdoor activities?" His eyes, brightening.

"I like to run, swim, hike, bike, ski; the usual I guess."

"Do you sail?"

Therese couldn't help but smile at the hope in his voice. It felt like they'd made a connection. "I took a sailing class in college and loved it, but it's been a long time."

They chatted a bit more, but the buzzer rang sooner than expected.

Therese checked her watch, surprised that it had been eight minutes.

Dante shook her hand and leaned in. "I'll definitely be checking the 'yes' box."

A spiral of delight swirled up Therese's core. "You'll just have to wait and see if I do the same."

He lifted a brow and smiled, before sliding to his right.

Her next couple of dates were nice, but paled in comparison to Dante. He had set the bar high. Who knew eight minutes could be so fun?

On her tenth date, Angela made a point of introducing the man again, making Therese take notice. "Peter, this is my friend, Therese, I think you'll find you have a lot in common," Angela said with an encouraging smile before turning away.

It was the serious guy with the blazer, whom Therese had noticed earlier.

"Hi, Therese, I feel like I know you already. All Angela did was talk about you," he said, shaking her hand enthusiastically, the fabric of his corduroy blazer wrinkling at the inner elbows. He had gray-green eyes, and dark, wavy hair that seemed to stay perfectly in place.

"Really? What did she say about me?" Therese asked.

Peter pursed his lips thoughtfully. "She told me you were recently let out of a maximum security prison, that you burn toast, and that you collect dryer lint in the shape of unicorns. Is that about right?"

Therese laughed. "Sounds like she covered all the bases."

Peter laughed as well, a comforting baritone that relaxed Therese immediately. "Just so that we are on a level playing field, let me tell you a little bit about me."

Therese listened as he told her about his previous life as an attorney and current existence as a manager for jazz musicians; he'd been divorced twelve years and had a daughter in high school, and about his experiences dating in the modern era. The more he talked, the more she realized that his seemingly serious exterior hid an impressive depth of personality. She felt like she could have listened to him for hours.

"I'm sorry, I just keep talking. How long have you been divorced?" he asked, lifting his hands towards hers as though he wanted to hold them, and part of her wished he would.

"Legally divorced? Only a week, but we've been living separately for two years. This is actually my first attempt at 'dating'," she said, making air quotes with her hands.

He pursed his lips and nodded. "Speed dating is very efficient. I've only been doing it a few months, but I feel like you know right away if you connect with someone, versus with all the online stuff and the apps." He mimed swiping on his phone.

"I haven't tried any of that yet. Angela is trying to convince me to get on them."

Peter tilted his head in Angela's direction. "Oh. Your married friend? That's nice of her to come speed dating with you."

"How did you know she's married?"

He pointed to his ring finger. "She's got a serious tan line on her ring finger. I'm guessing she just slipped them off for this event, right?"

Therese nodded, impressed by his attention to detail.

"Look, the buzzer is going to go off in about twenty seconds, but I'd love to see you again. Be careful on the apps, there are some creepers out there." He gave her another of his warm, genuine smiles and the buzzer sounded.

By the time Therese finished all twelve of her dates, she was exhausted and stone-cold sober. As she and Angela walked back to where they'd parked the car, they chatted about all the men they'd met.

"Well, we didn't make the movie, but did you have fun?" Angela asked.

Therese had totally forgotten about the movie. "I did. I mean, there were some real duds in there too, but it felt good to just do something proactive, and I liked Dante and Peter."

The next morning, Therese felt like a teenager, checking her smartphone to see if an email from the speed dating organizers had arrived.

It hadn't.

She brewed coffee and then started unpacking in earnest with Angela's help, blasting the oldies radio station that Angela said had played Elvis when she was a kid and now played Fleetwood Mac, Queen, and Prince.

The furniture from IKEA was arriving later, and Therese needed to have her sons' bedrooms set-up so that when she picked them up from school on Monday, they'd have somewhere to sleep.

She and Angela bopped around the house in capri-length denim and long-sleeve shirts, perfect for the overcast fall day, their hair pulled back in ponytails. Therese could almost pretend that it was move-in day their freshman year.

"Remember the first day we met?" Therese asked as she unwrapped dishes in the kitchen.

Angela looked up from a built-in bookcase where she was unpacking and shelving Therese's books and photo albums. "Of course. I couldn't believe that I'd been paired with a judgey girl from the Bay Area."

"I wasn't judgey; I was shy!" Therese said.

Angela wiped her forehead with the back of her hand. "I know that now. I'm just saying, when I met you, I was prepared to never speak to you. Fortunately, that changed," she said with a smile.

"What was our resident advisor's name?"

"You mean the one we never saw? Julie," Angela said, turning back to her shelving.

"Right. Julie. You know, before you, I'd never met anyone who was multiracial, and then when I met you and Julie in the same day, my mind was pretty much blown."

Angela laughed and walked towards the kitchen with her coffee cup, wiping the back of her hand across her forehead. She poured herself some more coffee. "Well, you hid it well. You weren't like all the other kids who kept asking me 'what I was' every other second. You've always been good at thinking before you speak. That's what made you a great lawyer." She raised her mug in toast, took a sip, and threw her arm around Therese's shoulder. "You are handling this like a champ, my dear. Grace personified."

Therese shrugged. "Our marriage ended a long time ago. This is really just a change in living arrangement." But she wrapped her arms around Angela and hugged her, grateful for the person who had helped eased her into adulthood being there to help ease her into this new— still unnamed—season of her life.

Angela glanced at her watch. "It's after one. I'm starving and the furniture should be here any second."

Therese grabbed her phone from her back pocket to make sure her ringer was on. It was. There were no missed calls from IKEA. *Maybe the speed dating email came through.*

Reading her mind, Angela said, "Have you checked your email again? I think I'm more excited than you are."

Therese unlocked her phone, swiping to her email, and reloaded. She waited as her new messages populated. Something from her kid's school, a newsletter from her old firm, a dog rescue email, and then her eyes noticed an email address she'd never seen before with a subject line that read "Your matches from last night."

"It's here," Therese said in a whisper.

"What's it say?" Angela practically hissed.

Therese opened the email.

Dear THERESE,

*We are so glad you could join us last night for SPEED
DATING: HETERO. We hope you had as much fun as we
did!*

*This email is to confirm that you matched with DANTE
VALLENS and PETER MURTAZA. Their emails have been
provided below.*

*There were THREE other MEN who also selected you as a
"Yes", however, because the match wasn't reciprocated,
we will not be sharing their names. However, if there was
someone that you were on the fence about, you could email
us back with HIS name and if there's a match, then we can
share HIS information.*

*Thanks again for joining us. If you'd like to register in
advance for next week's event, click this link and receive a
30% discount.*

Angela was reading over her shoulder and pointed at the bolded
words. "That must be the form generation program. Need to be sure
they collate all the names and pronouns properly. Welcome to the
modern world."

Therese reread the email, her heart beating faster than it had been before she'd opened it. She'd taken the first step in her new life and it had actually been fun.

Angela pulled out her phone. "How's pizza sound? We can take a break and talk about your next steps."

"Next steps?"

"Of course. What kind of dates you want to go on with Dante and Peter. Hawaiian or BBQ Chicken?" Angela asked.

"Half and half."

Angela nodded and ordered their pizza.

Half an hour later, they were sitting on a step in Therese's back garden, eating pizza, with big sunglasses and hats to protect them from the powerful afternoon sun.

"This place is really cute. You have enough room back here for a real garden, not to mention, some patio furniture. This would be a nice place to eat when it's warm enough. You could plant a vine to cover this trellis and get some extra shade," Angela said, pointing to the naked wood beams over their heads."

"Yeah, the landlord said I could plant whatever I wanted. That was part of why I took the place."

Angela wiped her hands on a napkin and put her plate down on the concrete. "Okay, Dante and Peter. Tell me what you thought."

Therese wiped her mouth. "Well, I liked how outdoorsy and positive Dante was. Of course, I was attracted to him, I mean, who wouldn't be. But it worries me that he doesn't have any kids of his own, I mean, I'm not going to have anymore."

Angela raised her eyebrows. "Perfect. You can get back in the saddle with him, but don't have to worry about it getting too serious."

"I love how you sum it up, Ange," Therese said, taking another bite of the bbq chicken pizza covered in wilted micro-cilantro.

"I just want to do what I can to get you eased into your new life while I'm here."

Therese sighed, appreciating her friend's help. Yesterday and today would have been so different without her. "You're a good friend. Thank you."

Angela flashed a huge smile. "I'm glad I get to repay you for the many times you helped me. So you should probably do something active with Dante. Go for a hike or something?"

"He mentioned sailing last night. I used to really enjoy that." Therese took another bite.

Angela's eyes lit up. "That's perfect. I wonder if he's free tomorrow."

"Tomorrow?" Therese gulped her half-chewed bite of pizza, and coughed.

Angela nodded seriously. "You have to get your first dates in this weekend because on Monday, the boys will be here for seven days. You don't want to wait two weeks before your first date, do you?"

Therese considered it. Two weeks wasn't *that* far away. She'd taken her first step, did she have to take her second step so soon? She shrugged. "I can wait."

Angela tutted. "Oh no you don't, Therese Marie Hartley. You are going on your first date this weekend if we have to spend all night at a bar tonight picking up men." The look on her face made it clear that she was serious.

Therese sighed and pulled out her phone.

"What are you doing?" Angela asked.

"I'm opening my email so I can ask Dante out on a date," Therese said, rolling her eyes when Angela gave her a satisfied smile.

When she opened her email, she saw that she had two emails from unfamiliar addresses. One was from dantesinferno@ and the other was from pmurtaza@. "I think they've already emailed me." She opened the first email, and felt Angela move the plates aside and read over her shoulder.

Hey Therese,

I'm so glad we matched. I thought we had a real connection last night and I look forward to seeing you again. Would you like to go out sometime this weekend? I have clients to train until mid-day, but I'm free after that. Let me know if you're available.

Dante.

She then read Peter's.

Dear Therese,

It was lovely to meet you. You were the only woman that I gave a "yes" to last night, and I was grateful to receive the email telling me we'd matched. I have my daughter this Saturday, but if you are free on Sunday, I'd love to take you out to brunch and then perhaps a visit to The Getty Center? They have an exhibit on pre-Columbian gold and jade of the Americas that sounds fantastic.

I look forward to hearing from you,

Peter.

"Perfect," Angela said. "You can go out with Dante on Saturday and Paul on Sunday."

"But I have so much to do to prepare for the boys," Therese protested, barely wrapping her mind around going on one date, let alone two.

"I'll get everything ready. You just tell me what to do. Groceries, laundry, whatever. I'll do it," Angela said with a smile.

Therese's heart swelled. "You're the best," she said, squeezing her friend's shoulder.

Just then, there was a knock at the door.

Angela raised a brow. "That must be IKEA. You reply to Dante and Peter and I'll let the delivery person in."

Therese groaned. "Ugh, assembling IKEA furniture. It really is like we're back in college."

The next day, Therese was standing on a pier next to Dante's sailboat, which was named *Paradiso*, the flowing calligraphy written in a steel gray on the side of the boat.

She inhaled deeply, and coughed, overwhelmed by the stagnant sea air, which smelled like a fishmonger's stall but wrapped in the pungent odors of sunbaked seaweed and seagull guano. It was stifling.

Dante laughed, as he moved around the deck of the boat, securing ropes and other items that Therese had a vague memory of from her sailing class days. "I don't smell it anymore, but I know the air here can be quite ripe if you aren't used to it." He gave her a reassuring smile, the skin around his eyes, crinkling behind the black lenses of his sunglasses. "Don't worry. Once we leave the pier, the air clears out. Just a few more minutes and then you can come aboard."

Therese watched, feeling empty-handed with only her car key tucked into a zippered pocket of her turquoise windbreaker, her long hair pulled back into a ponytail. She was so used to carrying around a giant mom-purse, it felt strange to need so little. However, Dante had insisted that she bring nothing in his email and again when he had confirmed that morning.

It was nice not to have to think about anything but herself for once.

Dante looked every bit the gentleman sailor, his dark brown curls almost grazing the top of his chiseled cheekbones, a loose, white linen shirt hanging open to his sternum, his powerful calves visible beneath khaki pants that where rolled up to his knees. He stalked gracefully around the deck barefoot, moving languidly like a jungle cat on a tree, as though sensing every potential tripping hazard without having to look.

He pulled on a pair of high-tech shoes that had the look of a canvas slip-on but with the telltale sheen of high-performance fabric; they were sleek but also functional and seemed to personify Dante perfectly: performance with style.

Therese had liked her nautical-striped boat-neck shirt and skinny jeans when she left the house, but now she felt rather dull next to Dante, who seemed to shimmer like an oasis. At least she knew her clothes fit well. Angela had said that the jeans did amazing things for her ass.

"Ready to come aboard?" he asked, flashing a brilliant smile.

Her heart thumped. She couldn't remember the last time it had done that in reaction to a man. A flush of heat washed over her. It was nice to have male attention again. To be seen as Therese and not just as an extension of her husband and children. It had been a long time. "I'm ready. Are my shoes okay?" she asked, looking down at the old Keds she'd found in the bottom of a cardboard box of shoes.

"Lift them up?"

She pivoted and lifted her foot.

He gave the soles a quick glance. "Yeah, the rubber still looks good."

He held his hand out to her and she took it, shivering slightly as his warm, calloused fingers closed, covering her hand completely. She stepped onto the deck.

"I've never sailed on anything this large," she said.

"She's thirty-eight feet, outfitted with a galley and sleeping quarters. She's big enough to spend a week on, but small enough that I can sail her by myself. We've sailed up and down the coast from Santa Barbara to San Diego and all through the Channel Islands. She's my best girl," he said with a wink.

"Should I be jealous?" she teased.

He smirked. "Ab. So. Lute. Ly," he said, his voice smokey.

She shivered again, despite the warm afternoon.

"Mind if I give you a quick review?" he asked. "I'll try not to get too technical, but I'm so used to the nautical terms, it will make it easier if you know them."

"Go ahead. Hopefully my muscle memory will kick in."

He gave her a quick tour of the boat, reminding her of port and starboard, aft and stern, while checking in to see what she felt comfortable handling on the boat. Before too long, they had loosed the lines holding them to the slip, and set their sails to carry them west, the sun about halfway to the horizon. They had three to four hours before sunset.

The *Paradiso* slipped through the water silently, the gentle ripple of the water like a soothing fountain.

Therese felt her shoulders and neck loosening, tension she hadn't even been aware of, leaking out of her as the minutes passed. For the first thirty minutes, Therese did nothing as Dante steered the boat through the marina's weekend traffic using the boat's motor. They headed past the breakwater—a large, concrete structure that marked the entrance of the marina—and were accosted by the barking of its resident sea lion population, whose throats produced a volume that seemed worthy of an animal many times their size. The marine mammals never took a break, their cacophonic song simply dying away with distance, but never actually stopping.

"That's quite a racket," Therese said, unable to look away from the huge sea lion colony, their serenade reminding her of childhood visits to Fisherman's Wharf in San Francisco and eating Ghirardelli chocolate.

The memory made her relax further, reminding her of how simple life could be. How much simpler life *would* be now that she no longer had to share space with her ex.

Dante nodded, tying off a line. "It's incredible how loud they are. I tried sleeping on the boat a couple of times. Forget about it. And it's nonstop during mating season, which, thankfully, was over a few months ago."

Once they'd hit the open water, and the boat traffic thinned out, Dante was able to sit next to Therese. They weren't so close that their legs touched, but they were close enough that Therese could smell the amber and orange scent she'd caught the night they met. It was warm and sensual, just like him.

Dante took off his sunglasses, stowing them in his shirt pocket, as he brushed a windswept lock of Therese's hair behind her ear. "You don't seem like the kind of woman who would need to go speed dating."

Therese colored at the compliment and told him about how Angela had dragged her there.

"So that explains why she was so excited to introduce us," he said, thoughtfully.

Therese suddenly wondered if Dante had marked a "yes" for Angela. Angela had deleted the email from the speed dating company without reading it, then again, since Angela hadn't marked any men as "yes" it would not say conclusively if Dante had chosen her.

As though reading her mind, Dante said, "I did mark Angela as 'yes', but that was because I met her before I met you. Once I realized you were friends, I crossed out her yes because I would never date two friends. That's just a recipe for disaster."

"Good thinking," Therese said, her admiration for Dante rising.

He tapped his temple with his index finger and smirked. "Are you hungry? I know you said you didn't have time for dinner after sailing, so I packed us food so we could dine on board."

"I could eat," Therese said, her stomach giving a Pavlovian growl.

Dante disappeared below deck and returned with a cutting board covered in crackers, cheese, and charcuterie, with dried fruits and nuts sprinkled about. He returned with a bottle of wine and two glasses, as well as some grapes.

It looked as beautiful as anything she'd seen in a restaurant.

"I prefer eating at sea, especially on a calm day like today. The smells of the marina aren't so nice for dining."

Therese wrinkled up her nose. "I can imagine." She took a bit of salami and enjoyed its fatty, peppery flavors as the clean sea air filled her lungs. She rolled her shoulders back, wincing, feeling the exertion of yesterday's furniture assembly in the tiny muscles of her arms and back.

"What's wrong?" Dante asked.

Therese circled her right arm and then her left. "Angela and I assembled IKEA furniture for over nine hours yesterday so that my boys can stay at my place this week. I'm a little sore from it."

He wiped his fingers on a napkin and pointed behind her. "May I?" he asked.

She nodded, and he slipped behind her, placing his strong fingers on her shoulder and then exploring nimbly along her upper back and arms. "Oh yeah, you have a knot in your trap," he said, holding her right arm by the wrist as his other hand kneaded into the underside of her back muscles.

"Oh, ow, oh," Therese said, alternating between pain and relief as he massaged the knot.

After a few minutes, he switched sides. "Does that feel better?" he asked, still massaging her on her left.

"Sooo much better. You must have magical hands," she said, an electric thrill shooting up her core at the accidental double entendre. Her cheeks flushed.

He chuckled, but didn't take advantage of her slip. "That's why I make the big bucks." He trailed his hand down her forearm as he returned to his seat, while a dull ache thudded in her belly.

Therese had a sudden image of Dante naked in her bed, and a rush of hot chills flooded her body, her nipples tightening.

She swallowed hard.

Dante met her gaze steadily as he put a grape in his mouth, chewed, and then swallowed, his Adam's apple bobbing.

Therese had never found an Adam's apple attractive before, but there was something seductive about Dante's

His eyes narrowed slightly and he cocked his head as though he was about to say something, but then straightened it again. "Why don't I remind you how to work the sails?"

Therese felt like he'd popped the moment with a pin, but nodded anyway.

The day continued to be mild, and Dante's refresher course on sailing gave him many opportunities to touch Therese as he adjusted the way she tied a knot, or pulled a line; repositioning her body to make sure the boom—the heavy bar of the mainsail that swung from side to side—didn't hit her as it moved.

The small touches seemed to be stoking a fire within her that she thought had been extinguished during the end of her passionless marriage, and she was grateful for the tender, affectionate handling. She felt safe, his thoughtfulness made her feel like her decision to start dating again had been a good one.

After a few hours, they headed back to the marina, the sun beginning to dip down into the ocean as they passed the breakwater.

Therese watched as Dante steered the boat, his eyes focused in confident concentration as he skillfully maneuvered between the other vessels. He licked his lips and her stomach clenched as she suddenly wondered if he would try to kiss her, unsure if she was ready for anything that intimate.

She imagined for a moment Dante pulling her close, his orange scent surrounding them, his dark eyes studying her face as he brought his warm, thick lips to rest on hers.

Tongue? Would there be tongue?

No.

Try as she might, she couldn't imagine more than a chaste kiss with Dante. There was something intimidating about the thought of crossing that threshold, and she just wasn't ready for it. This was, after all, the first date she'd been on in almost fifteen years and her yearning for intimacy had been satisfied by all of the touching that had happened throughout the day.

But she'd be open to a chaste goodbye kiss.

That would be nice.

Once the *Paradiso* was parked, the smells of the marina accosted Therese's senses once more, a bit milder without the heat of the afternoon sun intensifying them, but unpleasant none the less. She checked her watch, it was almost six-thirty and she wondered what progress Angela had made unpacking. The heat and exertion of the sail, combined with the lulling of the boat, caused her to stifle a yawn.

"Wow, I'm that exciting, huh?" Dante teased, arching a thick brow as he slipped a canvas cover over the wheel.

She stifled a laugh and shook her head. "I'm sorry. The sea is just so relaxing. I feel like I could curl up and go to bed right now."

He raised both brows this time. "Would you like that?" his voice, low and smoky.

Her hands tingled, his teasing jolting her awake.

She wasn't sure how to respond, but before she said anything, he smiled. "I'm just playing. This is a first date. What kind of guy do you think I am?" He jumped off the boat, tied it off to the dock, and offered his hand to Therese. "Let me walk you to your car."

She smiled as he laced his fingers through hers and pulled her towards the parking lot, the affectionate gesture warming her heart.

When was the last time someone held my hand?

They walked silently along the echoing wood of the pier, through the self-locking metal security gate, up to Therese's black sedan.

She unzipped the pocket of her windbreaker with her free hand and pulled out the key fob just as they came to a halt by the side of her car.

Clearing her throat, she felt the absorbed heat of the sun radiating off her car as they stood there.

This was the awkward part.

How to say goodbye?

Dante's eyes flicked to her lips and then to the door handle.

She knew it must look like she was trying to make a quick getaway, and maybe even part of her wanted that, but she had enjoyed the date, she didn't want to ruin it now. She wanted to see him again, but just didn't know how to communicate her discomfort.

She swallowed hard, forcing herself to stare into his dreamy brown eyes. "Thank you for a lovely time. Did I mention this was my first date since I met my ex?"

His lips curled in an amused smile. "You might have mentioned that, three or four times."

The tips of her ears burned. "Really?" She put her hand to her forehead. "How embarrassing."

He licked his lips and her nipples puckered.

Holy moly, this man is liquid sex.

"I had a really nice time too, Therese," he said lowly, smoothing a strand of hair behind her ear. "Would you like it if I kissed you?"

Her entire body felt like tiny sparks were shooting off everywhere. She was torn between appreciation for the honesty of the question, and embarrassment because…well, she didn't know why she was embarrassed, she just was.

"I like to ask before I do anything. Everything is so much sweeter when given rather than taken." His finger traced the shell of her ear.

Could her nipples get any tighter?

"Yes. I'd like that," she squeaked, the words felt like rocks in her mouth, but somehow took flight once she spoke them. It felt good to be asked permission, and the exchange made her want his kiss even more.

Maybe *not* a chaste kiss after all.

He leaned towards her and she felt her body tense involuntarily. She closed her eyes tightly in response, as though she was afraid she was going to be hit by a wayward foul ball, which would make Angela laugh uproariously when Therese recounted the story later.

Then she felt Dante place his hands on her upper arms, and pull her to him, the warmth of his chest and thighs lighting up her body.

She sighed and her face relaxed as Dante's full lips deposited a sweet, gentle kiss on her cheek, his calloused fingers cupping her chin.

And then…

Nothing.

Her eyes fluttered open. "That's all?"

The disappointment in her voice surprised her.

He chuckled, but his eyes looked serious as he searched her face. "I'd like to see you again."

She swallowed hard. "I'd like that too, but I have my boys for a week starting Monday."

He nodded. "I'll call you this week and we'll figure something out."

She nodded.

He took her hand, squeezed it, and then leaned forward to open her car door for her.

After Angela was done laughing—tears of mirth streaming down her cheeks—she turned to Therese, her lips still curled up in a smile. "So you yawned at him, kept telling him it was your first date in fifteen years, and then tensed up like a corpse when you said goodbye? Sounds like a fantastic first date, honey."

Therese took a sip of wine and rolled her eyes. "I was mortified. I felt like such an idiot. I'm surprised he wants to go out with me again at all."

"You're probably the first woman who hasn't jumped Dante on the first date since he hit puberty. I'm sure he finds it refreshing," Angela said, wiping at her eyes.

Therese ran her fingers through her still damp hair, needing to shower off the clammy feeling of an afternoon at sea as soon as she got home. She was sitting in her pajamas on the edge of her bed, Angela propped up against the headboard, also in her pajamas.

"I really need to get some more furniture so we have somewhere to sit besides the bed."

"If you want, I can go do some scouting for you tomorrow. I finished the kitchen today, and the fridge is fully stocked. I was going to work on your clothes tomorrow, but if you think furniture is more important, I can do that," Angela said, covering her mouth as she yawned.

"That would be great. You have amazing taste. A couch and four-person dining table with chairs would be great," Therese said, finishing off her wine. "Just text me pictures if you find something you think I'll like."

"Okay." Angela stood, pulling back the covers and getting into bed. "Well I'm glad you had such a good first date. Sailing with a hottie is a pretty great way to break your dating fast," she said raising a brow. "A sweet, thoughtful hottie, nonetheless. And I'm proud of you! You got back on the horse today, honey. That's a big step."

"I'm proud of myself too." Therese smiled as she turned back to the bathroom to get ready for bed.

Angela was right, it had been a big step, even if she hadn't conducted herself perfectly. Besides, Dante hadn't seemed to mind.

After brushing her teeth, she changed quickly and turned off the bathroom light, pulling back the covers of the bed and slipping between the sheets. "I'm looking forward to tomorrow. I haven't been to The Getty Center in a long time."

She waited for Angela to respond, but her friend only gave a half-asleep moan.

"Good night, Angela. I love you," she said quietly.

Her friend replied groggily, "Love you too."

The next morning, Therese woke up to an empty bed, her muscles tight and sore. She moaned as she stretched.

"Hey sleepyhead," Angela called, ducking her head out of the walk-in closet where she was busy hanging up clothes.

"Don't you ever sleep?" Therese rolled over and threw her pillow over her head, not able to remember the last time she'd been this sore.

"First of all, it's almost ten, and secondly, I have no idea what time zone I'm operating in, but I've been up since five. I'm so off schedule, I don't have a schedule. Why are you moaning and groaning?" she asked, coming to sit on the side of the bed. Before Therese could answer, she added, "You should wear this for your date."

Therese peeked out from under the pillow and saw a clingy, long-sleeve maxi dress in navy, and moaned, as she laid her neck back down. "I guess I overexerted myself sailing yesterday. I feel muscles I forgot I had."

"What time are you meeting Peter?" Angela asked.

Therese started, suddenly wide-awake, her muscle pain forgotten. "Crap. I'm going to be late." She threw the covers off—wincing a bit at the sudden movement—grabbed the dress out of Angela's hands, and scurried to the bathroom.

Fifty minutes later, she was running up the broad stone staircase of The Getty Center like Cinderella in reverse, or maybe she was the White Rabbit, as the words "I'm late, I'm late, for a very important date" seemed to be echoing through her mind.

The Getty Center was the newer of two museums with the surname of an infamous industrialist. A stark white monolith, it was perched on the point of a hill, overlooking the L.A. basin like a giant cubist bird about to pounce on its prey. Inconveniently located inside the mountain pass of one of the city's famously clogged freeway arteries, not only was it challenging to arrive at the location, but then one had to wait for a dedicated monorail to journey the final mile up to the top of the bird's nest.

Needless to say, it was not a stress-free trip, especially when one was running late.

Once Therese reached the plaza that lay before the museum's entrance, she stopped to catch her breath and briefly admire the view of the ocean that was arguably the ultra-modern building's best feature.

She wiped her brow and straightened the thin merino cardigan she had thrown over her dress. She had forgotten how clingy the fabric was and the fact that the dress had a mid-thigh slit; she tugged at it self-consciously. She'd paired the dress with thin, gold sandals and small, coordinating hoops. If it weren't for the fact that she felt like she'd just run a marathon, she'd have felt pretty, her blond hair pulled back in a neat ponytail.

She glanced at her watch, it was eleven-oh-six. She took a few more deep breaths, trying to bring her heart rate back to normal, and then walked the final thirty feet to the entrance of the restaurant, unoriginally named The Restaurant.

When she walked in and gave Peter's name, the host showed her to a seat alongside the ocean-facing wall. Peter stood expectantly as he saw her approach, breaking out into a broad smile as he clasped her hand.

She could sense that he wanted to pull her in for a hug, or a kiss on the cheek, but appreciated his restraint; however she was also a bit disappointed.

"I'm so sorry I'm late," she said, smoothing her dress as she sat.

He waved her apology away. "It's always such a process getting here: the freeway, the parking, the tram ride, the walk from the tram ride. It's like they are testing you to see how committed you are to coming up here."

She laughed, instantly put at ease. "I've never had brunch here, is it good?" Her eyes swept around the dining room, which was as blandly luxurious as the museum itself. The dining room was almost half-full, which seemed surprising since it had only been open a few minutes.

Peter nodded. "I brought my parents here for brunch when they visited from Toronto. They loved it."

"Are you Canadian?" she asked, suddenly intrigued. With his dark skin and West Coast-sounding English, she'd had him pegged as a local.

He nodded. "Born and raised. Everyone says I sound American. I guess we Canadians watch too much American television." He gave her his easy smile again, his teeth brilliantly white. "And you? Where are you from?"

She waved a hand upward. "The Bay Area. I grew up in San Jose before it was a cool place to be."

"Are your parents still there?" he asked, taking a tiny muffin out of a wire basket on the table, and slathering it with butter.

"No. My father passed a few years ago and mom moved down here to be closer to me and my boys." Therese's stomach grumbled.

He held the wire basket up to her. "You have to have one, they are still warm."

She took one of the two-bite blueberry muffins and tore it open, buttered it up, and slipped half into her mouth, the juice of the berries bursting in sweet and sour explosions perfectly contrasting with the salty creaminess of the butter. She moaned. "Wow, that's really good."

Peter nodded, an amused smile tugging at his lips. "I agree."

She felt like he wasn't referring to the muffins and blushed.

A waiter approached the table and Therese ordered the Dungeness crab toast and a lychee Bellini while Peter requested the eggs baked in shakshuka and sparkling water.

"The view is really the best thing about this place," Peter said, turning his gaze toward the wall of windows that framed a billion dollar view of the Pacific, literally.

"I agree. Although I read up a bit on this exhibit; it sounds like everyone thinks it's one of the best ever put on here."

"I read that too, which is why I wanted to come. And I do enjoy walking around the grounds. I thought we could do that after we eat, before going into the museum."

"That sounds great," Therese replied.

They fell into an easy conversation about their experience with law school and years working as lawyers. Peter spoke a bit about his current life, managing jazz musicians, but only when asked. There was a pleasant ebb and flow to their conversation; both of them asking questions, neither dominating the conversation.

After a lovely meal, Therese was full and happy, looking forward to the fact that they still had many hours to spend together. She hadn't enjoyed a stranger's company this much in a long time.

"Shall we?" Peter said, standing and walking around her chair; pulling it out for her.

He offered her his elbow, and she took it, slinging her small cross-body bag over her head as she wove her arm through his.

They exited back to the broad plaza where Therese had admired the ocean view earlier, the bright white of the stone—coupled with the white of the museum itself—causing both of them to reach for their sunglasses.

"If we head downstairs, there's that winding path along the brook," Peter suggested.

"Good idea. I usually do that last, but it's always one of my favorite things."

They headed down some stairs that were easily missed if one didn't know where they were, the building, floors, and stairs all made of the same Italian, ivory-colored travertine, allowing features like hallways and stairwells to blend into the background; hidden in plain sight.

The stairs emptied out into a small patio with a water feature that looked like a leak from the plaza above had been allowed to fester until it was dripping aggressively; like a modern, abstract take on a waterfall. The water then fed into a brook that zig-zagged down the sloping hillside along a planted border, edged in weathered steel, its patina arrested to the perfect shade of rust. The contrast of industrial and naturalistic made for a provocative garden composition that managed to maintain a tranquil feel, despite its highly designed nature.

"How old are your boys?" Peter asked, their footfalls on the decomposed granite, making a pleasant scratching sound.

"Twelve and ten. Just starting to make their first real push for independence."

Peter nodded as though he remembered those years. "My daughter is seventeen. She wants to go back east for college next year. She'll be getting college acceptance letters any day now."

Therese's heart clenched at the idea of her boys moving out of state.

Peter continued, "She's interested in environmental and chemical engineering. Wants to solve climate change or rid the Pacific of the giant plastic garbage patch. She can't decide which."

She looked up at him sideways, the trickle of the brook playing its watery music. "Sounds like a smart kid. Thank goodness, we need more scientists. She lives with you part-time?"

He shook his head, a shadow passing over his face. "No, full-time. She hasn't seen her mother since we split twelve years ago."

Therese could tell there was a painful story there, but didn't want to press.

The sounds of kids running on the lawns that bordered the path they were on, caught their attention, and she remembered her own sons, rolling down the same grassy hill not so long ago. "It's hard to believe they were that little not too long ago."

He sighed. "Yes, but I can't lie. As much as I'm going to miss her, it will be nice to only have myself to take care of. At least for a few weeks. I'm sure I'll be a zombie after that, walking around our empty house, wondering where all the life and energy she brings to it went."

Therese shivered, wondering how she'd feel once Angela left, and she had the house to herself every other week when the boys weren't with her. She didn't like that thought so she changed the topic. "How did you get into jazz music?"

Peter gave her a toothy grin, his eyes crinkling up. Clearly this was a topic he got excited about.

Just then, a family with a stroller approached from the opposite direction.

"Excuse us," Peter said, as he pulled Therese to the side to allow the stroller to pass on the narrow path.

The touch of his fingers on her forearm sent warm tendrils through her.

She was really enjoying her afternoon with Peter; he was thoughtful, smart, interesting. It was hard to tell under the blazer and button-down shirt he was wearing, but his chiseled face and strong hands made her think that he might be athletic. She'd have to probe later, having someone she could share her athletic interests with was important to her.

Once the family had passed, he guided them back down the path. "So, jazz. Where to begin? I guess it started in university. I lived in a residential college—a dormitory with faculty-in-residence—and the professor who lived in our building, Dr. Rothberg, was a jazz aficionado although his teaching expertise was on Chinese culture and politics."

He glanced up to see if Therese was listening, but she couldn't have paid attention anywhere else if she'd tried. There was something hypnotic about his voice, so strong and certain. Perhaps it was the fact that at this point in her life, she felt anything but strong and certain, and yet, there were three moments in her life when she could remember feeling both: when she decided to become a lawyer, when she decided to become a mother, and when she told her ex that she wanted a divorce. She yearned to have that feeling again, and here was someone who had it in spades.

"Dr. Rothberg loved sharing his passion for jazz with the students of our dorm, taking us to clubs to listen, so overcome by his own joy of the music that I was afraid he might rock out of his chair on many occasions." He paused and glanced towards her briefly. "You know, back then we just called him 'eccentric', but I think now Dr. Rothberg would be diagnosed as being 'on-the-spectrum.' He used to enjoying sharing how he washed his tee-shirts one at a time, in the washing machine, and he literally used his oven as a bookcase."

"That sounds like a fire hazard," Therese said, simultaneously amused and alarmed.

His eyes widened. "I had that same thought, but the college never burned down and he still lives there to this day. I saw him at my last reunion. He's just as brilliant as ever, with a zest for life that's admirable. I'll always be grateful to him for introducing me to jazz. It's like he set me up on a date with the love of my life."

They chuckled together, and Therese's heart panged, as though it was trying to escape her chest, urging her towards Peter. There was something compelling about him in a way she'd never experienced before.

Therese had never been particularly lucky in love, not like her friend Angela who had adored and been adored by three amazing men in the almost thirty years they had known each other. Of course, Angela's life had been filled with almost as much loss as love. However, Therese recognized that the pain of loss was only possible when preceded by joy.

Of course, romantic relationships were not something she had *actively* spent a lot of time thinking about; she'd been so busy achieving things she really wanted: lawyer, law partner, mother, but she realized now that she *wanted* to experience love and romance on a different scale than before. Angela had always been good at "putting herself out there" and Therese decided at that moment that she wanted to follow her lead.

She was ready to be adored.

"You look far away," Peter said, as the garden path ended, depositing them onto a plaza that overlooked a sunken garden and was shaded by enormous bougainvillea trellises composed of interwoven, vertical pieces of rebar that reached for the sky, continuing the industrially romantic look of the walkway.

"Sorry." She looked upward, suddenly becoming aware of their surroundings. "I love these trellises."

He hummed agreement. "What do you like about them?"

She pursed her lips, narrowing her eyes critically. She'd never really thought about *why* she liked them, instead just enjoying them, unexamined. "Well, I love the color of the flowers of course. That neon pink is almost unreal, it's so vibrant."

Peter nodded but remained silent, a raised brow directing her to continue.

She turned her gaze back up. "The shade they provide is quite nice of course. You can never have enough shade in Los Angeles."

The corners of his lips quirked upward, but she could tell he wanted more.

And she wanted to give him more.

She wasn't sure why, but she *wanted* to impress Peter, needed to in fact, just to prove to herself that she could. It had been a long time since she ached for anyone's approval.

She turned back to the trellises, determined not to open her mouth until she could say something interesting or profound, or, hopefully, both. "The way the landscape designer chose iron rebar as the material for the trellis is somehow elegant and in-your-face at the same time."

His eyes widened perceptibly.

She felt a thrill of accomplishment that reminded her of her years in a courtroom, waiting for the small visual cues from a judge or jury that would let her know that her words had hit home. Her brain felt like it was using areas that had been dormant for a while; as though gears and cogs that had been frozen with rust were starting to spin freely again. "It's usually a material that's hidden, prized only for its strength, not its beauty. But somehow the designer made it beautiful by showcasing its strength. I mean, I don't think you could build trellises this tall and self-supporting with anything but rebar, thereby elevating the material beyond strict functionality."

"Brava," Peter said, clapping quietly, putting an arm on her shoulder and giving her a light squeeze. "Very well put." His eyes sparkled with admiration.

Therese's heart seemed to be caught in her throat, having made progress in its journey away from its usual residence. She flushed, suddenly thinking of something else. "There's also something incredibly honest about the structure."

His brow quirked up. "Honest? How so?"

She pursed her lips and studied the design further. It was more of a feeling than a thought; she needed a moment to translate the emotion into words. After a few seconds, she said, "It doesn't feel like the rebar is trying to do anything it's not supposed to do. It's not putting on airs being a trellis. It's just doing its job: being supportive. The rebar is being true to its nature, which is honest."

He nodded. "I can see that." He turned to her and studied her face, lingering on her eyes. "I love that idea of being true to your nature."

She realized that she liked it to. *What's my nature? What's my job?* Although her kids were not out of the house, they also didn't need her for much beyond taxing them around and helping with homework, and now that responsibility had been cut in half.

She sighed heavily.

"This structure reminds me a lot of jazz music. Surprising and beautiful because it doesn't always stick to the expected rules. It's improvisational," he said, waving his hand towards the trellises.

She raised a brow. "I'm afraid I don't know jazz well enough to appreciate that comment."

They ambled over to the handrail that overlooked the dramatic sunken garden, the centerpiece of this area, with the ocean extending beyond.

"Like all musical genres, jazz is vast in its diversity. But I'd love to share with you some of what I like about it. Maybe our next date."

A warm thrill bloomed in her chest. "I'd like that."

He turned to her and reached for her hand, his palms warm and smooth, his touch sending a tingling lance of electricity up her arm. He caressed her cheek with the back of his hand and she felt herself being pulled forward, hoping that he was going to kiss her.

But he just stared at her, his chocolate eyes dancing. "I'm really glad we met. I feel like I've been waiting to meet you for years."

The poetry of his words left her speechless. Her verbal gymnastics had been limited to opening and closing arguments, however, she had mastered one valuable lesson: when in doubt, stay silent. So she said nothing.

He stuttered inhaled as though the spell had been broken, and she ached the loss of the kiss she had been hoping for.

Glancing at his watch, he said, "You said you needed to be home by five. It's almost three. We should go see the exhibit."

Almost three? She double-checked her watch. The four hours they'd spent together had felt like a moment. "Okay."

He smiled and held out his hand in offering. She didn't hesitate, lacing her fingers through his, enjoying the comfortable intimacy.

They walked through the exhibit, which was as fantastic as promised, but took second place to their animated conversation.

By the time he walked her to her car, it was already past five o'clock, but she wasn't complaining. In fact, she'd been so out of her own body that she didn't even notice when he asked her out for dinner that week and she'd accepted, completely forgetting that she had the boys.

When she got home, she plopped down on the couch and sat mutely; staring at some point in space only she could see.

Minutes later—or perhaps it was hours—Angela placed a glass of cold water in her hands, wrapping Therese's fingers around it.

"Earth to Therese," Angela said loudly.

"What?" Therese said, almost spilling the water, for she hadn't realized it was there.

"Wow. It was that good, huh?" Angela said.

Therese couldn't make sense of Angela's words. She placed the glass on the coffee table in front of her, and continued to stare into space, thinking about Peter, replaying their perfect date, wondering where he'd take her for dinner this week.

"Therese," Angela said sharply.

Angela's toned finally cut through Therese's reverie and she blinked rapidly.

"Are you okay?" Angela asked, her forehead wrinkled in concern. "You haven't said anything about the furniture you are sitting on."

"What?" Therese said, and then noticed that she was sitting on a couch that hadn't been there this morning before a coffee table that had likewise appeared during her time out. "Oh. Thanks. It looks great."

"You can take them back if you want. I paid a fifty-percent deposit, but the store will take them back this week if you change your mind."

"Ok," Therese said, still staring at the wall.

Angela narrowed her eyes. "What's going on? I've never seen you this spacey."

Therese blinked. "Spacey? Am I spacey?"

Therese had been called many things in her life: brilliant, tenacious, loyal, hard working, but never spacey.

Angela nodded. "Yes. Like outer space too, not even in this universe. What's going on?"

Therese leaned back into the soft throw pillow of the couch and smoothed out the jersey of her dress. "I just had the best date of my entire life."

Angela's eyes widened. "Therese Hartley, you're smitten!"

"Is that what this is?" she asked, not recognizing the feeling.

Angela smiled. "Yes! Tell me everything. I'll go get a bottle of wine."

They drank the wine, Therese enjoying the retelling of the date almost as much as the date itself. Angela pointed out details and analyzed every moment of it with her the way they used to do with Angela's dates, or with books they were both reading.

"So he didn't' kiss you?" Angela asked.

Therese frowned. "No, and I couldn't believe how much I wanted him to. My lips were tingling with anticipation when he said goodbye to me at my car, but no, no kiss. Just a nice hug."

"That's hot," Angela said. "I think it's sexy when a man shows restraint on the first date." She took a sip of her wine.

Therese could understand the logic of that sentiment, although her body would have been happy to defy it this afternoon. Suddenly, she remembered about the promised dinner. "He asked me to dinner this week and I accepted for some reason…" already dreading having to cancel.

"Go. I'll watch the boys. It's just dinner. You can make it a quick one if you feel the need to get back," Angela said.

"Really?" Therese asked, torn between motherly guilt and her personal desire to see if date two would be as good as date one.

"Of course. You deserve this."

Therese leaned forward and hugged her friend. "Thank you, thank you. You really are the best friend ever."

"Forget about it. It's part of my godmother duties to babysit them. I'm pretty sure it's somewhere in that contract you had me sign," Angela deadpanned.

Therese yawned, suddenly overcome by fatigue.

"What about Dante?" Angela asked.

Therese started. She had completely forgotten about Dante. "Oh. I don't know. I guess I shouldn't go out with him again."

Angela gave her a look that said Therese was crazy. "How can you be so brilliant and so innocent at the same time? You are going to date both of them. You haven't dated in forever; you aren't making any decisions now, especially after only one date. Just have fun and go out. In fact, you should date other men too, see what's out there. We're going to get your dating profile up."

A sense of dread thudded in Therese's gut. A profile on a dating site still felt like an adventure to an exotic land that she was ill prepared for, but Angela's argument was sound. However, part of her wasn't sure how to proceed; she'd always been more of a serial monogamist than a "dater".

"I know what you are thinking. You don't know how to date more than one man at a time, but think of it this way: if you like someone, keep dating them until you decide that he isn't for you or you decide to become exclusive with one of them. Easy."

"I can do that. So Dante's a 'yes' until he's a 'no', no matter what I feel for Peter."

Angela nodded. "Of course at some point your feelings for Peter might *make* Dante a 'no', but let's cross that bridge when we get to it. Your first date is *not* that time."

"This is going to be fun," Therese said, her new life as a divorced mother of two taking on an exciting sheen.

"That's the idea," Angela winked.

If you'd like me to write more about Therese, Dante, and Peter, cast your vote by visiting SmartURL.it/KNB1survey
Thanks!

Therese is a secondary character in the BECKONED series and appears in parts 3&4. To read it now, go to SmartURL.it/AmazonAviva

A Special Request: Please Review

Thanks for reading. If you enjoyed this book, it would mean the world to me if you would rate and/or review it at **Goodreads** and **Amazon.** Indie authors like me **need** your positive words to keep writing. It encourages other people to buy our books (cha ching) and keeps us motivated. Thanks! Aviva

And if you have an idea for improving it, email me at ReadingRocks@AvivaVaughn.com. Either way, I'd love to hear from you.

Other Titles from Aviva Vaughn

Novels

BECKONED (join the conversation at **Aviva Vaughn's Jetsetters on Facebook)**

-Part 1: From London with Love **AVAILABLE NOW** (link)

-Part 2: From Bath with Love **AVAILABLE NOW** (link)

-Part 3: From Los Angeles with Love **AVAILABLE NOW** (link)

-Part 4: From Barcelona with Love **AVAILABLE NOW** (link)

-Part 5: Adrift in Costa Rica **AVAILABLE NOW** (link)

-Part 6: Adrift in New Zealand **AVAILABLE NOW** (link)

BEYOND BECKONED

-Roaring in Rio (about Nacho Sol from BECKONED) **LATE 2019**

-Confused in California (about Erin Hung from BECKONED) **EARLY 2020**

Short Stories

Pressure (included in Beckoned, Part 4)

Knotty Naughty Bits Volume 1 **AVAILABLE NOW** (link)

Knotty Naughty Bits Volume 2 **MID 2020**

Links

Subscribe to Aviva's list to be notified of new releases and special offers—and get her favorite **FOOD | BOOK | TRAVEL tips** by clicking **SmartURL.it/BECKONEDfan**

Website: AvivaVaughn.com/

Facebook Group "Book Club" (where I do lots of "behind the scenes stuff") and share early material for feedback:

Facebook.com/groups/AvivaVaughnBookClub

Reader Survey: Like to give feedback? Want to help me decide what to write next? Fill out this survey SmartURL.it/ReaderSurvey

Corrections

For the grammar-philes, **please send any corrections to Corrections@AvivaVaughn.com.** To see if the correction you found has already been caught, **visit AvivaVaughn.com/corrections** . Thanks for your eagle eyes!

Love my writing? Consider becoming a patron at Patreon.com/Aviva Vaughn

Hi Reader!

It means so much to me that you are here! It means that you enjoy my unique "voice".

If you want more "behind-the-scenes", VIP access into my mind, then consider becoming a "patron" and help me bring more of my creative imaginings to life! There's even an opportunity to name a character in my book. To find out more, click Patreon.com/Aviva Vaughn

XOXO,

Thank you to my "Superfan" level patrons

1. Christiana Garcia	19.
2. Anonymous	20. –
3. J. Merriweather	21. –
4. YOUR NAME HERE	22. –
5. –	23. –
6. –	24. –
7. –	25. –
8. –	26. –
9. –	27. –
10. –	28. –
11. –	29. –
12. –	30. –
13. –	31. –
14. –	32. –
15. –	33. –
16. –	34. –
17. –	35. –
18. –	36. –

Simple Risotto Recipe

Risotto is SO EASY and delicious. The long cooking time—and minimal stirring—releases the starch of the rice more slowly, giving you a wonderfully creamy dish, even though there is actually very little dairy in it. Dress it up however you like. I like sautéed mushrooms, asparagus, and garlic over mine alongside a healthy piece of wild caught salmon. Add whatever veggie or meat you like! It's a blank slate. Enjoy!

Ingredients
- 32 ounces of water mixed with "Better than Bullion Roasted Chicken" to taste. Alternatively, you can use 32 ounces of whatever stock you like. I use BTB for everything. You can get it here: https://amzn.to/2Yzxqvz
- 2 tablespoons ghee (aka clarified butter oil. Try for grass-fed. Alternatively, you can use butter.)
- 1 cup Arborio rice (lots of options here https://amzn.to/2GHON3s)
- Freshly grated Parmigiano-Reggiano to flavor (but a minimum of about ¼ cup)
- Salt to flavor

Directions
Bring stock to a simmer in a separate pot.

Take a large pot—preferably a heavy pot such as enamel or cast iron Dutch oven, to keep the risotto from burning—and add ghee under medium flame. Once ghee has thinned/warmed a bit, add the rice and stir until all the grains are coated (about a minute.) Add ½-cup of stock and DON'T STIR, wait until absorbed (2-3 minutes) and then add another ½-cup of stock and stir entire pot one time and then leave it until absorbed, then repeat until only ½-cup of stock left (about 20 minutes will have passed.) Turn off flame, add the last bit of stock, cheese, and salt to flavor.

Thanks, Gracias, Do Jeh, Merci, Toda, Gratzie, Shukraan, Mahalo

My sincerest thanks and gratitude to anyone reading this sentence now. You are the reason this book exists. I appreciate you more than you'll ever know.

Thanks to the universe for allowing me to co-create this expression of its existence.

To my family: thank you for being with me on this journey called life. I love you and appreciate how you constantly challenge me to be my best. Especially to my mom who is always my First Reader and the person I think of pleasing when I write.

To my friends, colleagues and mentors in the indie publishing world: I'm eternally grateful to be a member of your tribe. It is your shoulders I stand on. I promise to pay it forward to the next generation.

To my dear, dear friends and first-draft readers who encourage me and root me on endlessly…you know who you are and I ADORE you. Especially to CSAK, my "sisters from another mother." Thank you to my "super readers", Amanda, Claire, Kim, and John, who make it all worthwhile by really "getting me" and always give me great feedback.

And to anyone who has ever wondered "what if?" You might have a book in you yet!

The point of life is to become the best version of yourself and to share that with the world.

Imagine what the world would look like if everyone lived that way!

Wishing you love and romance,

Made in the USA
Middletown, DE
02 August 2021

45218131R00177